Jean de Cartigny

The Wandering Knight

Jean de Cartigny

The Wandering Knight

ISBN/EAN: 9783741187452

Manufactured in Europe, USA, Canada, Australia, Japa

Cover: Foto ©Andreas Hilbeck / pixelio.de

Manufactured and distributed by brebook publishing software
(www.brebook.com)

Jean de Cartigny

The Wandering Knight

A

DEFENCE

OF

" THE ECLIPSE OF FAITH,"

BY ITS AUTHOR;

Y

BEING A REJOINDER TO PROFESSOR NEWMAN'S

" REPLY."

LONDON:
LONGMAN, BROWN, GREEN, AND LONGMANS.
1854.

LONDON :
SPOTTISWOODES and SHAW,
New-street-Square.

CONTENTS.

A

DEFENCE

OF

"THE ECLIPSE OF FAITH."

SECTION I.

INTRODUCTION.

PROFESSOR NEWMAN, in the recent edition of the "Phases," has published a brief "Reply" to "The Eclipse of Faith." This book, he tells us, he should have preferred "to pass by unnoticed, only that its popularity gives it a weight which it has not in itself."* He also says that his friends expected him to answer it. "Save me from my friends" is an excellent caution, which an author, above most men, will do well to bear in mind. It is almost as wise in such a case to listen to one's enemies.

My own reasons for noticing the "Reply" are widely different; and one of them imperative. Mr. Newman has charged me with "*stealthy* misrepresentation and gross garbling." No man should allow himself to be so charged unjustly, (and I will venture to say that no controvertist has a more sincere abhorrence of any

* Phases. Reply, p. 177.

B

such practices than myself,) without making the accu-
sation recoil on his calumniator; and this I pledge myself to do. Mr. Newman may rest assured that I will
reckon with him on all such points, to the uttermost
syllable.

But this would occupy only a few of the following
pages; and I have gone a little further. I have answered
every statement of the least moment which I can find
in Mr. Newman's strictures: nor have I contented
myself even with that. I have felt tempted to re-state
the argument of Harrington D——, from which Mr.
Newman so preposterously infers that I believe in an
" *unmoral* Deity "; — to make a few remarks on the in-
explicable explanations and obscure *éclaircissements* of
his former statements, respecting the relations of man's
religious nature to the external organon which deve-
lops it, —which last it still seems may, somehow, come
from man, but cannot come from God; — to offer some
observations on his new chapter on the " Moral Perfection of Christ " — strange mistitle, since it is to prove
his Moral Imperfection; —and to give my young Christian countrymen a few words of counsel in reference to
the Deism of the present day. Meantime in the present
section, I will give them an opportunity of judging
how far they prefer the charity of the new spiritualism
to that of the New Testament, and how far they can
trust the " free criticism " which asserts the moral de-
ficiencies of Christianity, and the moral defects of its
Founder.

Mr. Newman calls his little chapter a " Reply to ' The
Eclipse of Faith.' " One would think the whole book
professed to be formally and exclusively directed against
him! The slightest inspection of its very various contents will show that a multitude of topics are taken up
in which he has no concern in the world; and that his

opinions, like those of Parker, Strauss, and others, were introduced, only so far as they affected the particular topics under discussion. He is pleased even to say that one magical "sentence," which I have *not* allowed "Mr. Fellowes to press," would have sufficed "to crush the whole treatise of 450 pages!"* This sentence, so far from being neglected, Harrington makes (as I think), pretty good use of, only, of course, in a very different way: I mention it here merely to show the extravagance of Mr. Newman's assertions; since half at least of the volume is occupied with topics which have no reference to his peculiar speculations. But it is Mr. Newman's privilege to speak hastily, and to speak largely.

Again, Mr. Newman seems to suppose that there was some special animosity towards him, in selecting some of his opinions for comment in "The Eclipse"; if so, he is much mistaken. I felt none then: I may add, I feel none now. I had nothing in the world but his *opinions* in view; and I should not have commented upon them at all, had he not been a perfect stranger to me. Had he been either a friend, or an enemy, nay, had he been at all known to me, then, as in all cases in which I have been impelled by conscience or induced by importunity to enter into controversy, (which, whatever Mr. Newman may think, I thoroughly hate,) I should have refrained from noticing *his* writings at all; since I should have distrusted my own impartiality. It was easy to find others. I selected his writings, because I thought that from their half views and quarter views, and sometimes *tenth* of quarter views, they were likely to do mischief among the young. The "Phases," in particular, appeared likely to have this effect, by that volatile transition from subject to subject, and that summary and slashing treatment of all, which characterise that

* Reply, p. 199.

singular book. It seemed likely to leave as confused an impression on the mind as those exhibitions of " dissolving views," where we see mountains and lakes advancing upon us through receding cities; rocks and grottoes obtruding into the ruins of a cathedral; and a waterfall just tumbling out of a vanishing turret window.

Mr. Newman, having combined in his system the strangest eccentricities of opinion, seems resolved to try whether he cannot finish by one or two practical paradoxes quite equal to any of his theoretical; and certainly he promises to be perfectly consistent in inconsistency.

For example; he has said more in *one* chapter in this new edition of the " Phases " — to say nothing of his " Soul," and nothing of his " Hebrew Monarchy," — to wound and shock the religious feelings of his countrymen — to jar their inmost sense of all that is most sacred — than any other writer of his day. Yet no sooner does any one proceed to expose his own religious system, which seems so unreasonable to the world that probably not twenty people in it would profess adherence to it, than he looks grave, and protests against levity in the treatment of *sacred* things! I must answer, like Pascal when the Jesuits brought against him a similar charge, that " I am far enough from ridiculing *sacred* things, in ridiculing such notions." Mr. Newman warns me with much solemnity against thinking that " questions pertaining to God are advanced by boisterous glee." * I do not think " The Eclipse " is characterised by " *boisterous* glee;" and certainly I was not at all aware that the things which *alone* I have ridiculed — some of them advanced by him, and some by others, — deserved to be treated with solemnity. For example, that an authoritative external revelation, which most people have thought possible enough, is *im*possible, — that man is

* Reply, p. 200.

most likely born for a dog's life, and "there an end,"—
that there are great defects in the morality of the New
Testament, and much imperfection in the character of
its Founder,—that the miracles of Christ might be real,
because Christ was a *clairvoyant* and mesmerist, — that
God was not a Person, but Personality; — I say, I was
not at all aware that these things, and such as these,
which alone I have ridiculed, were questions "pertaining to God," in any other sense than the wildest hypotheses in some sense "pertain" to science, and the
grossest heresies to religion.

Again; in theory nothing can be more delightful
than Mr. Newman's charity; in practice nothing more
grotesque. He is full of fierce anathemas against
bigotry, and declaims most passionately on behalf of
charity and loving kindness. In "The Eclipse of
Faith" I, with my poor "Pagan" notions of morality—
so he is pleased to consider them, — carefully abstained
from questioning the *sincerity of his motives;* for I had
nothing to do with his motives — I had to do with his
arguments. These I exposed, and sometimes ridiculed;
I acknowledge it with becoming impenitence; I shall
repeat the offence, if offence it be; and I am prepared
presently to justify my conduct. What course does
Mr. Newman take? While enjoining charity, deprecating "personal antagonisms," and talking in a most
edifying strain about opening "the mind to truth, and
the heart to love," he indulges in the most acrimonious
imputations of "blasphemy," "dishonesty," "stealthy
misrepresentations," "gross garbling," "dealing unscru-
pulously," and I know not what.

He tells me in one place that unless I mean what he
says, I *must* mean — and which I certainly do *not* mean,
if *he* means what he seems to mean, for it is arrant
nonsense, — that my words are "palpably and inex-

cusably dishonest;" that unless I believe another equal
piece of nonsense, I am "grossly iniquitous;" that in
one place not only "spiritual insight, but *honesty*, seems
lacking;" and so forth.

But all such things are a mere bagatelle compared
with the invectives into which a threefold error — un-
paralleled, I believe, in the history of criticism—has betrayed him. Those errors are that Harrington D——
meant what he did not mean — that whatever Harrington D—— meant, *I* must mean; and, lastly, that Mr.
Fellowes was designed to be a *facsimile* of Mr. Newman; all which are pure illusions of Mr. Newman's
"free criticism." This I proceed to show.*

---

* There is one inadvertence, indeed, in Harrington's discussion,
which I sincerely regret, and I will take care to erase it in the next
edition ; for, however little designed to convey the meaning Mr. Newman attaches to it, I see it is fairly susceptible of it. Harrington says,
ironically, "This *most devout gentleman* somewhere quotes the words,
'for the spiritual man judgeth all things, but himself is judged of no
man.'" It is employed to express (what appears to me, I confess,) the
preposterous incongruity of using the words of Paul to sanction a system
which Paul would utterly have repudiated. I still adhere to that view,
and will justify it in a future section. But it was not my intention to
give pain, and the words *in italics* shall therefore willingly come out.
And so shall the "Professor of Spiritual Insight." Mr. Newman
says, indeed, that Harrington has so *nicknamed* him. Hardly ; it may
be taken so, but it was not intended ; for any *other name*, or none at all,
would have done just as well. The *question* (Shall we call, &c.?) in
which the phrase occurs, was obviously put in reference rather to Mr. Fellowes' *exigencies*, than to Mr. Newman's *qualifications*. Fellowes, in a *fix*,
hardly knows whether to say — denying, as he does, the possibility of all
external revelation, — that he got his religious notions from *nature* alone,
or in any way from without ; since he confesses his sentiments have been
practically elicited by his *spiritualist* writers. Harrington remarks, that
it is of little use for "nature to teach him, if somebody else is to teach
nature ;" and asks whether Mr. Newman shall be called Professor of
Spiritual Insight ? Mr. Parker's name, or that of any other writer to
whom Fellowes *professed obligations*, would have done just as well ; or
better still, — no name at all ; and no name there shall be.

As to the word *infidel*, I cannot humour Mr. Newman. It is a word

Hastily assuming that the *latter part* of Harrington D——'s argument is something more than a mere *reductiv ad absurdum from Mr. Newman's own premises;* that it was designed to embody not only the conclusions to which a sceptic might fairly drive any one who adopted those premises, not only the positive opinions of the sceptic himself; but the real opinions of the author of " The Eclipse of Faith,"—acting, I say, on this ludicrous misconception, Mr. Newman fires away with a vehemence which amazed me as I read it. What confidence, thought I, can be reposed in those powers of "free criticism," in virtue of which our author decides on an argument of such immense sweep and complexity as the " Truth of Christianity " — constructs the true " Hebrew Monarchy " out of the old Hebrew myths, and pronounces on the moral character of Jesus Christ?

In truth, I WAS NOT¯SORRY that he had fallen into these misconceptions; for people will be apt to argue that if he could thus err in his interpretation of so humble a book as " The Eclipse," he was not likely to be altogether infallible on the Word of God. A few specimens of the vehemence with which he pursues this phantom will illustrate at once the sagacity of his criticism, and the quality of his charity. It will be observed

---

he says, " which is the peculiar weapon of the proud and self-sufficient dogmatiser, who holds all to be *unfaithful* who do not adopt his opinions." " This epithet itself proves that, under the mask of the sceptic, the Christian (?) is venting his own pride and bitterness, which he unjustly attributes to another." Answer.—The reader will get used to Mr. Newman's style by and by. I content myself with remarking that if Mr. Newman will always interpret current words by their etymology he may take offence enough. I use the word as it is now, and has been long currently used among us, to indicate one who has utterly renounced all belief in the Divine authority of Christianity. Of course I think that a grievous error. How can I think otherwise? But from what cause proceeding in any individual case, I decline to speculate. I am no judge of the heart, and do not wish to judge it.

that I cite his invectives (such is their extravagance)
with precisely the same indifference as if I had been
charged with impaling somebody on the horns of the
moon. I shall here and there, indeed, interlace the
citations with a few words of my own; but of such a
different temperature from Mr. Newman's red hot diction, that I almost fear that the reader will imagine
himself plunged into a succession of hot and cold baths;
or the curious tesselation may remind him of the lower
regions of Hecla, where, through the fissures in the
snow and ice, ever and anon creeps into the cold, clear
air, the hot, sulphureous vapour from below. However,
I will take care he shall pass in safety over these *cre-
vasses* without being suffocated.

The ordinary reader of " The Eclipse " will no doubt
e surprised to find that its author, " speaking under a
mask, uses a bold license of blasphemy against Nature
and its God, which too clearly comes from the heart;" *
that " it is *impossible to doubt the intensity of my conviction*, that all nature testifies, with overpowering force,
to every impartial mind, that its Creator is reckless of
all moral considerations!" † — that " The Eclipse of
Faith " " abounds in *profane insults*, which Mr. Newman
does not see that any thing else than the author's own
heart can have suggested; " ‡ " that the author is *unaware*
" that an *unmoral God is the very essence of Paganism.*"
and " that this and nothing else is what he is urging on
us as Christianity." " Oh how clearly does he show,"
continues this master of " free " (and easy) " criticism,"
" that in him it is *hypocrisy* to cry Holy, holy, holy, to
the Lord of heaven, whose holiness he *professes* to be
totally unlike all that man calls either holy, or kind, or
just."§

* Reply, p. 194.   † Ib. p. 196.
‡ Ib. p. 180.   § Ib. p. 196, 197.

I say the reader must be surprised at all this, even prepared as he may be by acquaintance with Mr. Newman's writings, for any feats of logical legerdemain. I knew indeed, that it was possible for a man hastily to adopt and abandon any opinions, if he took but a half of a seventh of a tenth of a thirteenth of a survey of the evidence; but here I could not find that there was any survey of evidence at all.

Mr. Newman had defined the only guilty idolatry to be the worshipping, as "perfect and infinite," that which we *know* to be finite and imperfect; by which lax definition it may well be doubted whether there are ten idolaters in the world. He had also said that *Atheism* may be only a speculative error, which ought not to divide our "hearts from any man." For my smiling at all this singular liberality, he says, I have "caustically reproved" his spurious charity "towards honourable Pagans and Atheists, who fail of reaching his view of truth;" but adds, "I did not quite contemplate such a case as that before me. I must wait and learn what sort of charity — not bastard — I may cherish towards one who *wraps a Pagan heart in a Christian veil;* who scolds down and mocks at other men's piety; who constructs sophistical arguments to leave them no alternative between his own Paganism, which is to them detestable, and an Atheism which they deprecate, indeed, but feel far preferable to degrading, heart-deadening devil-worship."*

Mr. Newman mistakes vehemence of diction for energy of style. If I have constructed sophistical arguments, I presume they may be shown to be so. I did not know, and have yet to learn, that I have scolded down and mocked at any man's *piety*, by exposing the errors of those new revelations which begin by assuming

* Reply, p. 197.

that all external "revelations" are "impossible." However, in one point, Mr. Newman is quite right; he must "wait and learn," probably, many things; and certainly charity towards his critics. But I hope he will not hurry himself on my account — I can wait too; or, if he likes, he may bestow it, when it comes — my share of it I mean, it does not seem to be much — on the aforesaid honourable Pagans and Atheists, who have not yet reached our critic's views of truth. If that be true, they must surely stand in great need of it!

After speaking of the ridicule with which I have treated the notion that men are in some danger of undervaluing this world, he says, " But never, never did I address such an exhortation to one who *confesses* that he has no discernment whether the Author of Nature be just or unjust, kind or cruel; one who is inwardly so dark that he cannot possibly have any religion but what he receives blindly. Such a one naturally relishes a joke better than a psalm, a sceptical dialogue of Plato or Hume better than a treatise on Natural Theology, and will scarcely be so absurd as to sacrifice what is *substantial in this world* for a religion which cannot penetrate into his affections."* As to my uniform preference of a joke to a psalm, it is entirely a mistake; it depends on what the "joke" is, and whose the "psalm." A psalm of David, I hope I should prefer to the richest joke — say one of Mr. Newman's paradoxes. On the other hand, I should probably prefer even a dull joke to a psalm, if the "sacred ode" is to embody a theology which explodes the characteristic doctrines of the Bible, and whether expressed in "rhyme" or "unrhymed metre." However, I shall have an opportunity of judging if some worthy Deist will be kind enough to give us a specimen or two of his devotional

Reply, p. 197.

Muse. As to Hume and poor Plato, who by some strange association of contrast are here linked together, I suppose it is pretty clear from " The Eclipse," that the former is no great favourite with me, except for his genius; but I do frankly confess that I prefer the Phædo of Plato, with its twilight hopes of a Revelation, and its faint echoes of Immortality from the " everlasting hills," to a treatise on the " Soul " which, denying the possibility of the one, augments its " sorrows," and casting doubts on the other, quenches its " aspirations." As to the rest of this passage, I freely acknowledge to the world that I have many, many faults — as many as Mr. Newman, I have not the slightest doubt in the world; but those who know me, I think, will allow that there are not many persons who have less consulted what is " *substantial in this world*" in the maintenance or retention of their religious opinions, be they right or wrong. On the spirit of this passage I shall only add, that if I had been betrayed into saying any such thing of an utter stranger, merely because he had laughed at what he deemed a paradoxical opinion of mine, I should have thought it was rather too late in the day to lecture a controversial antagonist on the duty of " watching over his own heart, opening the mind to truth, and the heart to love, of casting away scorn and self-sufficiency,"* &c. &c. &c., &c., and should have feared lest the reader should ask, as he read, " Of whom speaks the prophet this? of himself or of some other man ?"

As one contrasts Mr. Newman's loving injunctions with his invectives, one seems to be transported into a world where the usual symbols of emotion are all inverted, where men frown in pure benevolence, and gnash their teeth in loving kindness and charity.

* Reply, p. 200.

One more sample of his style I must not withhold from the reader. "With Paul and Isaiah, with Æschylus and Cleanthes, with Socrates and Paley, with Philo and Swedenborg"—a curious collection—" I see that a good God reigns over all." Did I ever deny it? One would think so, for he goes on: " this author declares (!) all the evidence of facts to convict my sentiments as a gratuitous absurdity, yet he calls himself a Christian, and reviles me as an infidel." * It would be difficult, I rather think, to point out where I have *reviled* him at all, much less for holding any such sentiment. Whether Mr. Newman reviles me or not, I leave the reader to judge from what follows. "With the Hebrew psalmist my heart avows ' all thy works praise Thee, O God, and all Thy saints give thanks unto Thee!' My Christian monitor puts a new song into my mouth, ' All Thy works convict Thee, O God, and none but fools can praise Thee for them.'"† These last words are put in inverted commas; but of course Mr. Newman does not intend them as a *quotation;* so that I must beg to say that the " new song," which is equally " without rhyme and without reason," is of his own composing, and that instead of my putting it into his mouth, he has put it into mine. The theology I am quite willing to admit that Mr. Newman would think as execrable as I do.

Finally; Mr. Newman observes, " when the Bible has failed to develop in him spiritual insight, why should my words be more successful? Yes, it is hard to enlighten one who, after the outward washing of Christian baptism, has gone back into the mire of Pagan demonry."‡ To the former part of the sentence (one word altered) I subscribe; if the Bible has indeed failed

* Reply, p. 198.　　　† Ib.　　　‡ Ib. p. 200.

to develop spiritual insight, it is not likely that books which entirely disown its authority, its history, its miracles, its characteristic doctrines, will be more effectual. As to my supposed *relapse* into a belief of " Pagan demonry," it would be just as much to the purpose if I were to call Mr. Newman a transcendental curve, or the root of an impossible quantity.

I took up the new edition of " The Phases," in which a reply to " The Eclipse" was promised, with some curiosity.   Where, thought I, has " Faith " got by this time?   What is its " phase " at present?   Has it thinned off to a yet finer crescent than it had at the end of the " last period?" or has it returned to the first quarter? And oh! how rejoiced many would have been to see the faintest symptom that the cup of light was beginning to fill again — as I trust we yet may.   But when I read the preceding remarks, I could hardly help exclaiming, in nearly the words of one of the characters in Carleton's Tales, " Surely now, there is nothing to be *seen* at all, barring the *dark* side of the luminary, which is at present invisible by reason of the ' Eclipse.'"

As Mr. Newman seems to suppose that I *must* be of Harrington's opinions, and as he supposes that Harrington is unsettled as to whether there be a personal God*—though the contrary, I suppose, is manifest enough to every ordinary reader†—it may be doubted whether Mr. Newman thinks me an *Atheist in disguise*, or the *undisguised* " *Pagan*," he generally represents me.   But, at all events, he doubts my being a Christian; for when he speaks of his " Christian " opponent he has, in two places, after the word " Christian" placed an eloquent note of interrogation; a device by which thrifty wits, who feel they must economise

* Reply, p. 192.
† See his express avowal; Eclipse, p. 163.

sarcasm, may cheaply express it at the printer's expense.
At other times Mr. Newman is apparently pleased to
think it possible I may be a Christian, and to speak on
that hypothesis.   It is pretty clear that I cannot be
both.   As Sir Boyle Roche said, " No man can be in
two places at once, except he be a bird."   In like manner, I presume that either I am, or am not a Christian.
Many men in the present day have instructed us,
indeed, that the mutations of the human mind may be
very sudden, but still they require *some* interval; and
whatever the rapidity of the changes, a man would be
troubled, I imagine, to be absolutely two things at once.

So extraordinary is this misinterpretation of my sentiments, that some of my friends have said, " *Is* the
supposition that you are a believer in an ' *unmoral*
deity' *really* a misconception?   Is it not rather an
evasion to avoid the necessity of encountering Harrington D——'s argument?   Is it not obvious to every
impartial reader that the argument of Harrington
expressed nothing dogmatically, but was simply a de-
duction from Mr. Newman's own premises?   He merely
affirmed that if he adopted Mr. Newman's criterion
of what we are to believe of God, he must reject
many of the phenomena of the universe — not all, nor
the greater part — but *many* of the phenomena of the
universe, as God's work, just as Mr. Newman does
many of the statements of what God has done, as given
in his word, and thus become at last a *Manicheist*, or, if
he could not become that, an atheist, or else remain a
sceptic?   And further, that *supposing* Mr. Newman's
theory of the origin and destination of man true, it
increased the difficulty a thousand fold, and would
really involve the conception of what Mr. Newman calls
an *un*moral deity?   Is not all this plain?   *Can* it be a
misconception?"   For myself I have taken Mr. New-

man's part. I have said, "Let us in charity suppose it a misconception at all events; for if we suppose it a wilful perversion, will that make the case any better? It is not only the more charitable hypothesis, but Mr. Newman's precipitancy of logic is such as to render it as easy for him as for any man thus to turn things topsy turvy. I grant, indeed, that it is much more easy for Mr. Newman, instead of dissolving the connection between the premises and conclusion, and clearly showing that *his* premises do not lead to that conclusion, to represent Harrington as not reasoning on Mr. Newman's premises at all, and then to turn round and say, 'Well, if you believe in a God, reckless of all moral considerations, how can any Bible have any authority?'" Yet (I argued with my friends), the very extravagance of the supposition is sufficient to allow us to suppose it a misconception, however enormous. "For tell me," said I to one, "did you ever hear of any body who thought that the author of 'The Eclipse of Faith' proclaimed his own inability to see anything but blackness of darkness in the real known undeniable works of God?"* "Not a soul," said he; "I have indeed heard of one man in the country, who, happening to *plump down* in the middle of Harrington's disquisition, knew not what to make of it." "Well," said I, "that is not the case with Mr. Newman, for he has *not* 'plumped down' into the middle of Harrington's speech, but has evidently read the book all through. However, I will throw him in, though I protest it is unfair, since he had only read a portion. This old gentleman, then, shall be one; and Mr. Newman, that is two. But, at all events, besides these two, I never heard of any one who concluded that I was a believer in an *un*moral Deity." †

* Reply, p. 198.
† Since these passages were written, I find that a writer in the Pro-

But though on the principle on which I have acted in
" The Eclipse " and shall now, of not imputing ill
motives to Mr. Newman,—into which I shall not be
seduced by the example which he has set me, — I say,
though on that principle I shall call his gross misconception, a misconception, I think it is not too much to
say that it was aided by the unconscious instinct of self-
preservation;—for " Instinct," as Falstaff says, " is a
great matter."

But the reader will perhaps say; " Well, but suppose
Harrington did believe in an *unmoral* deity — which he
did not — what, in the name of common sense, has the
Author of ' The Eclipse of Faith' to do with it ?" It seems
quite sufficient for Mr. Newman to reason thus : " Harrington believed so and so, and *therefore*, the Author
believes so and so." If you look, you will see that he
argues it *must* be so from the vehemence of the argument! " The bold dogmatism of the sceptic *is endorsed
and confirmed by the Author.* Indeed, were it not so, the
elaborate and vehement argument would be obviously
ridiculous ; but he means it to be cogent, and avows that
it is."* Of course Harrington avowed and *I* avow it is
cogent against Mr. Newman and on Mr. Newman's principles. But did mortal man ever hear of such criticism ?
" It *must* be so from the vehemence of the argument !"
That is, if a character is naturally and dramatically
represented (and Harrington is expressly said to to
most impatient at the shallow theories which are offered
in lieu of his early faith), the biographer or the novelist

spective Review also expresses doubts. This completes the critical
triumvirate. I shall have a few words to say to him by and by. The
differences, however, are refined and exquisite. While Mr. Newman
seems rather inclined to think me a Pagan on the whole, this writer
seems rather to think me possibly an atheist ! " Risum teneatis, amici ?"
  * Reply, p. 193.

must resemble the subject of his memoir or the character he depicts. Shakspeare himself, then, I suppose, must have been of *all* men's characters and sentiments, for *he* could represent them all; and poor Walter Scott must have been "half Dutchman and half devil," because he describes Dirk Hatteraick as being so! Mr. James Martineau doubts (as he well may) Mr. Newman's aptitudes for that "higher moral criticism" necessary to judge rightly the character of Christ. Such curious preconceptions as those just mentioned, adopted without the slightest hesitation and vehemently acted on throughout his tirade, is enough to make one doubt whether criticism be his vocation at all. But I will say no more on Harrington's argument here; in the next section I will distinctly show in what sense I "endorse and confirm it," with a challenge to any worthy Deist to reply to it on Mr. Newman's behalf, since it is plain that he himself declines it.

A similar singularity of misconception is seen in Mr. Newman in another point. In the same style of reasoning in which he argues that I *must* think just as Harrington thinks, so he will have it that Mr. Fellowes *must* be intended as a full-length portrait of himself; and so determined is he that it shall be so, that he says if I deny it, it shall be to no purpose. His language is: " As to this Mr. Fellowes, who is he? his character is apparently intended to be a portrait of *mine*, as the Author conceives of me. Thus he insinuates a mean, degrading, and laughable opinion of me, if the reader will accept it: but if the reader cannot go quite so far, and says it is unfair, then the Author can back out and protest that Fellowes is not myself but only my admirer." * That is, he challenges an explanation and

* Reply, p. 181.

C

then has the civility to say, it shall be unsatisfactory.
" He will be drowned and nobody shall help him." He
may depend upon it that as I am very deliberate in
putting any thoughts of mine on paper, I am equally
slow in " backing out," as he calls it, of any thing I
have once written, except for the strongest reasons;
and shall leave him to appropriate to himself any portrait he thinks proper, among those with which the
very large gallery of biography or of fiction may supply
him.   Meantime I will say this; that I believe there are
two points, and only two, in which Mr. Fellowes bears
any resemblance to Mr. Newman; and I know, and the
world knows, by *experience*, that Mr. Newman is not
unique in those points.   I may add, that as I have never
expressed my belief of any resemblance even in those
two points, it is curious that Mr. Newman should thus
appropriate the portrait, while he, at the same time, de=
clares it to be most repulsive and unlike himself.   It is not
usual for men to affirm, without any warrant from the
painter, that a picture is intended for *them*, which at the
same time they feel themselves to be no way in love with;
and which they also declare to be unlike them.   Mr.
Newman even seems to imagine that the personal peculiarities of Mr. Fellowes* were designed to caricature *him.*
I beg to say that I knew no characteristics of Mr. Newman, except that he was a gentleman, a scholar, and a
very indifferent metaphysician; and if I had known any
personal traits, I should have been the last to bring
them into my book.   Meantime I will tell Mr. Newman
how he may henceforth distinguish himself from Mr.
Fellowes, and no longer unwisely assume, and still more
unwisely tell the world, that the character of Mr. Fellowes is intended to caricature his own.   First, Mr.
Fellowes is expressly said to be a youth of about *eight and*

---

* Reply, p. 181.

twenty years of age (in whom, therefore, some versatility of opinion and some rashness of judgment might be excusable); and I rather think Mr. Newman, like myself, is a little beyond those years. Secondly, Mr. Fellowes expressly *abjures* several of Mr. Newman's opinions, openly prefers those of Mr. Parker, and freely avows that he has *eclecticised* from the many delightful varieties of opinion which the distractions of our modern spiritualists so abundantly afforded him. This very circumstance, indeed, Mr. Newman strangely adduces to establish his preconception; and says Mr. Fellowes is employed to make "damaging concessions," when he dissents from Mr. Newman and prefers Mr. Parker! One would surely more reasonably infer (what is the truth), that he was *not* intended to be the counterpart of any author. I am astonished that those who choose to regard " The Eclipse " as " fundamentally fictitious," should fail to conjecture that the Author avails himself of this character to bring the sentiments of *different* men under discussion; which is naturally done by citations from their writings. Whether those citations are fair or not, is another thing: and the only real question between me and those authors is as to this point. I assert they *are ;* and, in Mr. Newman's case, I shall by and by show that they are.—Thirdly and lastly: the readers of " The Eclipse " will allow that Mr. Fellowes is uniformly gentle, affable, and patient in argument (whatever his infirmities); and though for aught I know (and I am sure I hope it), Mr. Newman is so *generally,* it must be acknowledged that the present tirade proves that he is not *uniformly* so.

I imagine, as people read the very acrimonious and vehement charges against the Author of " The Eclipse," that they will say, " We had better have the old-fashioned Christian charity than this new-coined liberality of the

' spiritual Deism.'" Or is it Mr. Newman's pleasure
to suppose that the principle of the " Division of
Labour" applies to moral science as well as to political
economy, and that while it is one man's province to
preach charity, it is another man's duty to practise it?
I wonder whether *that* is true of the " Faith, Hope, and
Charity" of " Spiritualism," which is true of the same
graces in Christianity. " And now abideth Faith,
Hope, Charity — but the *greatest* of these is Charity."
If so, surely the two former must be vanishing quantities.

I would also beseech Mr. Newman to consider how
unbecoming in the estimation of his " very insolent and
dictatorial critics," as he terms them, is that intense
positivity which characterises both his assertion of his
own opinions, and the imputation of evil motives to his
opponents. They will say that one who has experienced
so many changes of opinion himself should learn at
least caution and forbearance. Dogmatism, in conjunction with perpetual vacillation, should be left to him
of whom our great satirist said so bitterly : —

> " Stiff in opinions, — always in the wrong, —
> And everything by fits, and nothing long."

I think, also, people will be apt to say, " Here is a
gentleman who sees the imperfections of New Testament morality ; who is afraid lest the consciences of
men may be depressed to the ' Biblical Standard ;'
who points out the many and grievous imperfections
in the character of our Lord Jesus Christ ; who has
himself lighted on ' a fixed moral basis, which he
will not allow to be tampered with by authority or
miracle;' who inculcates the duty of ' opening the heart
to love, and the mind to truth :' having reached this
vantage ground, looking down with serene compassion
on us 'puir blinded mortals,' we naturally expect from

him great compassion, and magnanimity, and self-control, and must begin to doubt, from his acrimony and impatience, whether his system can be the complement of a defective Christianity!" They will think they had better have the New Testament, with all its claims to "authority," than a teacher who, professedly renouncing authority, is more impatient at his opinions being questioned than if he really had it. We are all in great trepidation, we can assure him, for the honour of the "fixed moral basis;" and, if he goes on so, predict that the obstinate world will resolutely shut its eyes against the new light that has visited it!

I cannot affect to be surprised at the misconceptions of "The Eclipse of Faith" into which Mr. Newman has fallen, when I turn to his chapter on the "Moral Perfection of Christ." If Mr. Newman can so construe fact and narrative as to charge our Lord with a "vain conceit of cleverness" and "blundering self-sufficiency" in his answer to the Pharisees concerning the tribute money; with "arrogance and error combined" in other cases; with "vacillation and pretension;" with "egregious vanity" and "moral unsoundness;" with guiltily provoking the Rulers, by virulent invectives, to slay him, *because* he had resolved on suicide in order to escape the alternative of *becoming* an impostor or renouncing his Messiahship, — I need not wonder at any vagaries into which such logic may wander, or at any invectives which that erroneous criticism may prompt. "The disciple is not above his master; it is sufficient"— O how much more than sufficient — "that he be as his master."

The reader will perhaps say, "Is it possible that Mr. Newman can have said all this? Will the world believe that you are not misrepresenting him, as he says you and so many more of his critics have done, by

not quoting enough to indicate his meaning?" This is
Mr. Newman's continual complaint.   On some points
it might be difficult to say how much was to be quoted
that would explain Mr. Newman's meaning; a good
deal more, I fancy, than Mr. Newman has ever written
or is ever likely to write.   But, in the present case,
the reader may rest content: Mr. Newman has expressed his meaning plainly enough; and in the section
in which I shall briefly examine this matter, I will make
extracts ample enough to enable the world to form a
complete notion of the powers of " free criticism" which
Mr. Newman brings to bear upon the Gospel narrative
and on the character of Christ!   If I could, I would
publish every syllable of that chapter in the present
little volume.   I am so far from being afraid of its
doing any injury to Christianity, that I am persuaded
there are few of its advocates who would do more for it
by their defence than such an assailant by his attacks;
and that if infidelity *could* be ruined, such imprudencies
would go far to ruin it.   Mr. Newman wonders at the
popularity of "The Eclipse," and asks, " What must be
the destitution of the Christian cause before it could
welcome such an ally?"*   I acknowledge, with profound conviction and undissembled sincerity, that the
book *is* infinitely unworthy of my theme.   But I cannot
retort this sarcasm; I acknowledge that Mr. Newman's
book, with its new chapter on the Perfection of Christ,
is *infinitely* worthy of Infidelity.

Still, I repeat, I am rejoiced to find Mr. Newman
falling into such flagrant errors respecting so simple a
book as " The Eclipse;" errors which resemble those of
certain disciples of Strauss, who, on the strength of their
infallible canons of criticism, pronounced the " Amber
Witch" no fiction, but veritable history.   I am rejoiced

* Phases, p. 200.

both on general and on special grounds; on general
grounds, for it shows us that this confident criticism,
which is so sagacious in dealing with ancient documents,
— which can tell us by internal evidence just where an
interpolation begins and ends, — how many chapters and
verses of the Acts are genuine and how many not, — that
so much is written by the *true* Isaiah and so much by
the *Pseudo*-Isaiah, — is no sooner compelled to deal with
a practical test than it falls into the most enormous mistakes. And I am rejoiced on special grounds; because
it shows me that, even in the strange chapter on the
" Personal Perfection" of Christ, it is not necessary to
form so painful an opinion of the critic as it would be
otherwise difficult to avoid forming.

It does astound me, I confess, beyond all measure,
that Mr. Newman can read the New Testament with
such eyes, and rest content with such criticism on that
" Bright Excellence," which has in general disarmed
hostility, even where the mind has been unfriendly to
Christianity itself; — on which so many millions of minds
have dwelt with unmingled love and veneration. If
only a picture, still it is a picture with which no history
nor fiction besides furnishes us; in which Power and
Wisdom — usually the exclusive gods of man's idolatry
— are *for once* subordinated to perfect Love. It is the
picture of one gentle towards the infirmities and follies
of man, patient with his waywardness, lovingly forgetful
of his wrongs; of one — and oh! how beautiful, if *only* a
fable! — who never broke " the bruised reed," who came
" to bind up the broken-hearted, to give deliverance
to the captive," to welcome penitence to his feet, and to
offer the " weary rest;" of one who sided unchangeably
with weakness and suffering against strong-handed
oppression, whose patience was proof against every
insult to himself, and whose indignation never gleamed

forth but twice, and was then only extorted by that comprehensive sympathy with humanity, which was the burden and the passion of his existence; once when, mingled with grief, it shot a momentary flash on the censorious hypocrites who grudged and murmured at his mercy to the wretched, and once when it gathered in thunderclouds, and launched its vivid bolts over the guilty abodes of those who had perverted every law, divine and human, to the purpose of oppressing and grinding their fellow-creatures, who "for a pretence made long prayers," " devoured widows' houses," "took away the key of knowledge," " sat in Moses' seat " and made it the Devil's throne. In a word, it is a picture of one whose whole life was one long yearning agony of sympathy with the guilt and sorrows of humanity, and whose death ——! ah! how strange! how passing strange it is, that any should have an ungentle word to say of *Him*, even though only a picture. Is it not a picture which, if the original never existed, we should long to *see* realised!—one from which we should turn away, after long and entranced contemplation, and sighing say,—

> " Oh, that those lips had language!"

And, in general, to do human nature justice,—yes, even unbelieving human nature,—it has not been insensible to the claims which that portrait has on human veneration. The "grim feature" of Infidelity has generally relaxed when it has looked at Him. Those whose foul breath has sullied every mirror which reflected any meaner excellence, has generally spared *that*. Once or twice in a century, indeed, some one or two have appeared, animated by such intense envy of greatness, or such pure hatred of goodness, that they have not spared even the character of Christ. They have been inspired by such a gratuitous malignity, that one almost feels that if they had lived in the time of Judas they would have done the traitor's office at a cheaper rate, and spared the too happy Pharisees their thirty pieces of silver.

I rejoice — unfeignedly rejoice — that it is *not* necessary to class Mr. Newman in this small category. I see in his " Hebrew Monarchy," in his chapter on the " Perfection of Christ," — *I know by my own experience* in his outrageous mistakes in relation to " The Eclipse of Faith," — that he can misread evidence which appears clear enough to the eyes of other men, and weigh it in analytic balances which set *their* notions of probability utterly at defiance.

And now for a word or two of defence of my *method* of controversy in " The Eclipse of Faith." I have said I have not imputed motives ; I did not before, and shall not do it now: nor will I enter into the question of moral dispositions at all. Each man must be judged in that matter by the only equitable Judge.* But beyond

---

* Mr. Newman, while so earnestly deprecating controversial indecorum and inculcating "charity," seems to be unaware of the character of many parts of his own publications. Does he think it can be pleasant to the "Irish Clergyman" to be *so* characterised that few who know anything of him can miss him, and yet be told that it was said he had been mistaken for a beggar in Dublin, and had been offered a halfpenny under that impression ? Does he think it can be pleasant to Dr. Henderson (Phases, p. 127., Sec. Ed. p. 78.) — one of the most venerable and conscientious men of our time, — to be told in print that Mr. Newman's friend, John Stirling, had flippantly said, — that " Mark was probably inspired, because he was an acquaintance of Peter, and *because Dr. Henderson would be reviled by other Dissenters if he doubted it?*" Does he know what that insult both to Dr. Henderson and to his religious contemporaries means? That it imputes to *both* the most unworthy motives, and the vilest conduct ? Does Mr. Newman think that, in similar style, he is to be allowed to ride over all his critics, as " very insolent and dictatorial ; " imputing "dishonesty" to some, wilful " misrepresentation" to others, and " gross garbling" to almost every-

that I will not go, for Mr. Newman or any man. Living in a free country, and with a free press, where all opinions are daily sifted, and if thought ridiculous, ridiculed, I will never surrender an iota of the privilege I freely concede to others. Least of all, will I surrender it to one who treats unceremoniously what his fellow men hold most sacred; who, by denying the very possibility of an external revelation, advertises me that his religious opinions are of private origination, who cannot get more than a very few to coincide with them, and who has surely passed through changes enough himself to make him indulgent towards others for freely canvassing his own opinions. On those opinions, expressed in his books, I have commented without hesitation. I freely confess it; and that I will ever do so in reference to any opinions expressed by mortal man, let his pretensions be what they may, let his resentment be what it will. Every one who publishes his opinions to the world in a free country must lay his account with that; and as it

body that touches him? I tell him plainly I know of no writer who so largely exacts the tributes of charity; none who repays them less.

He should remember, in charging his opponents with unworthy motives in defending any opinions he once held, how easy it would be for them to retort upon him. The opinions he now impugns, he once held and defended; and the fragments of the theories he has rejected strew the whole way through the "Phases," like the baggage of a flying army. Did he not once believe Mark inspired? Did he not once hold the Bible all true, which he says can only be defended by the "crooked" and immoral subterfuges which he charges on what he calls Bibliolatry? Did it never occur to him that his opponents might ask him, on his so lightly charging them with "dishonesty" for still holding what he once held, — "Pray, Mr. Newman, will you answer us this plain question? Were you 'honest' or 'dishonest' when you held the views which you now reject? If honest, is it impossible for you to imagine that those who still hold what you once held, may be honest too? If dishonest — which we are far from believing, — are you precisely the person to impute to us 'dishonesty?' Or, lastly, are you alone honest, no matter what you accept or what you reject?"

is a right which, as I have said, I yield to others, so
it is one I will never surrender for myself. Further,
if I believe those opinions, as I *do* many of those of
Mr. Newman, to be not only false but pernicious, I
will spare neither argument nor ridicule to make them
appear so to others. In a contest for truth—and I
believe that this controversy has to do with *vital* truth,
—truth in which the best interests of our children, of
our country, of our species, is involved,—it is unmanly
to flinch. I will use every weapon, whether of argument or ridicule, which God has given me, and I will
strike' home wherever my adversary leaves a rivet open
in his armour. It is a false charity to act otherwise.
Charity to each other as much as Mr. Newman will,
and, indeed, rather more than in his present mood
he seems disposed to exercise; but to opinions, if we
deem them false, none. In *argument*, as Socrates says,
it becomes neither party to ask for or to receive
quarter; and that quarter, which I disdain to ask, let
my opponent be assured I will never give.

But ridicule? it will be said. Yes; and ridicule too,
if motives be untouched.

It is a sword, I know, which cuts both ways; but
it is never so keen as when truth whets it. God is
my witness, that so far from calling down fire from
heaven to injure an opponent, I would not scorch one
hair of his head; but as for his opinions, if I believe them pernicious to mankind, I should be, in
my judgment, a traitor and renegade to truth and
conscience, if I did not tax every energy of my
nature to make them appear so to others. This cannot be done, as Mr. Newman himself says in his preface to the new edition of "The Hebrew Monarchy,"
without giving offence. But, as he truly says, it must
be done; and I accept and concede the equal terms.

No doubt it would be pleasant, if, in performing this friendly office for each other, men could find out some moral chloroform which might steep in painless slumber a too sensitive vanity, while some huge fungous growth was being dissected out. But this cannot be; and the scalpel must proceed. As for *my* opinions, if they be false, I yield them up freely to whoever will show them to be so. Let him, if he can, launch against them bolts compacted out of all the subtlest elements of mind, and pour out upon them argument, fancy, wit, sarcasm, passion, in a stream of living fire, "till they be consumed." Charity to men, I again say, as much as any man will; but as to that hateful indifferentism which is so rife in our day, and which threatens to be our plague, it is equally an insult to the claims of truth, and a mockery of the claims of charity. Charity is exercised in spite of differences, manfully stated and avowed.*

* Here is worthy Mr. Parker, for example, telling us, in a recent publication, "that many a philosopher has seemed without religion, even to a careful observer; sometimes has passed for an atheist. Some of them have to themselves seemed without any revelation, and have denied that there was any God; but all the while their nature was truer than their will . . . . They had the intellectual love of God, though they knew it not; though they denied it . . . . . These philosophers, with the mere love of truth, and yet a scorn of the name of God, understand many things, perhaps not known to common men; but this portion of their nature has yet escaped their eye, — they have not made an exact and exhaustive inventory of the facts of their own nature. Such men have unconsciously much of the intellectual part of piety."— *Ten Sermons on Religion*, p. 10.

No wonder that he finds all meaner differences swallowed up and absorbed in this "unconscious piety," and thinks that a Buddhist, or a Fetichist, or even a man whose "hands are smeared over with the blood of human sacrifices," may be all in a fair way enough. And this insipid broth, into which all conceivable opinions are shred, so as to become undistinguishable, is to be recommended as a concoction of true charity; that is, charity is to be exercised when there is no longer room for any!

The worst of it is, that this latitudinarian charity is apt to degenerate

" But will not the employment of ridicule *against* the opponents of Christianity lead them to use the same weapon?" I imagine some good timid Christian to say. I answer, and have they ever spared it, dear simple soul?   Will your *not using* it prevent their *abusing* it? Will your throwing away the arrow prevent their transfixing you with theirs? Is not the shield of Christianity stuck full of those shafts?   From Lucian to Voltaire, the whole literature of infidelity shows what sort of " reciprocity" forbearance is likely to meet with. Your enemies have tried the weapon, and it has been in vain; you may see that *somehow* it does not prevail. Nay, take heart, man; one of the most striking tests of the indomitable energy, the vital power of *your* religion, as striking as its resistance to persecution itself, is its invulnerability to ridicule. Though Shaftesbury was wrong in saying that ridicule was the test of truth, it is usually impossible for error long to stand against it; nor is there another historical religion on earth that could endure the ridicule poured upon Christianity, if poured upon it (as is the case with the ridicule the Gospel has encountered) by men growing up in the midst of it. If Christianity could have been laughed out of existence, she would have ceased to breathe long ago. We have but to look into the writings of the ancient philosophers and satirists to see how little the ancient mythologies would have stood against such weapons. Jupiter, with all his thunderbolts, could not have resisted the raillery of Plato and Cicero; and all the shafts of Apollo would be of no avail before those of Aristophanes and Lucian.

into a curious sort of bigotry. It is always vehement enough against any opinions that imply that opinions are of any importance, or indeed against any opinion *except* the opinion that no opinions are of any.

If you have, as you believe, Truth on your side, you will do well and wisely not wholly to cast aside a wea-pon, which has not been and will not be used the less against you for your rejecting it, and which Truth always, in the nature of things, can wield more power-fully than Error. As to the legitimacy of its occasional use against solemn " follies" and would-be sacred "im-pieties," read Pascal's immortal Eleventh Letter; if *that* does not convince you, I have nothing more to say.

But surely it is the drollest of all drolleries to hear our modern infidelity affecting a Puritan prudery in the treatment of religious subjects; to see its face glisten-ing with spiritual *onction;* its mystic eloquence gar-nished with terms of Scripture, taken in an esoteric sense, and poor Paul and Peter quoted to avouch what they never dreamed of. Assuredly this solemnity of visage and phraseology is both too recent and too inconsistent to render it particularly decorous to twit a Christian advocate with levity in the treatment of " sacred sub-jects." Has not the whole history of infidelity been marked by the freest employment of wit, satire, and ridicule in every form? Would to God it had stopped with refined ridicule ! Have not its writers been full of absolute mockery and scurrility against all that Christians deem most sacred ? are the names of Tindal, Bolingbroke, Voltaire, and Tom Paine, and a thousand more, forgotten ? Christianity may surely be pardoned, if it has now and then laughed a little in return at what are surely laughable enough — the theories infinitely various and discordant of those who would crush her. But no ; our opponents then immediately become grave, put on a long face, and begin to inculcate a seemly gravity in the treatment of such sacred subjects ! The enemies of Christianity are still a little like its earliest oppo-

nents, whom our Lord compares to "the children sitting
in the market-place." Christianity expostulates with
them often enough, and looks grave often enough, and
they have laughed at her; she ventures to laugh at
their follies in return, and they look suddenly grave;
" she mourns to them, and they do not lament — she
pipes unto them, and they will not dance." But it is
now as of old, " Wisdom is justified of her children."

But perhaps it is thought that this solemn warning
against levity may induce the readers of "The Eclipse of
Faith" to disown their ally. It is of no consequence to
the Author if they do, since his conscience justifies him,
whether they do or not; as his book was not written to
*dis*please Mr. Newman, so neither was it written to
please them. But let not my opponents think Christians
such simpletons as not to know *what* it is that the
Author of "The Eclipse" has laughed at; they will
answer as John Bunyan did, when in prison, to the
gentleman who sent him a Christmas pie, thinking
to add a petty "affliction to his bonds" by tantalising
him with the sight of a dainty which his scruples would
not let him touch. But John cried *Distinguo.* Few
could do it better. He munched up the pie with great
satisfaction, and told the messenger to say that John
Bunyan could tell the difference between Christmas
and a Christmas pie. In like manner will Christians
answer my opponents, when they warn them against
an unseemly "levity" in treating "spiritual" subjects.

It is obvious that the opponents of Christianity fear
lest reprisals should be made upon them by pointing out
the absurdities, incredibilities, and discordancies of the
systems they would substitute for it. I think Christians
have let them have their way long enough, in stating
and deriding the difficulties of Christianity; and I for

one shall take the liberty of reminding them that their own difficulties are greater still.

But if the creation of merriment on *any* subject in *any* way connected with religion be the error and the sin, I am by no means sure that many of our new spiritualists have not quite as much to answer for as myself. The great difference between us is that I have sometimes made my readers laugh at my illustrations, and they have as often made them laugh at their arguments; I have attacked error with irony, and they have assailed truth with paradox.

I confess, indeed, the sonorous solemnity with which they enforce their " Procul! oh procul! este profani;" but the words from such lips are not the less laughable for all that; often more so. If " wisdom " sometimes " wears motley," it is quite as often the case that folly puts on the garb of wisdom. The owl is the symbol of wisdom; but the owl herself is not wise.

But Mr. Newman complains also of the *plan* of " The Eclipse: " he says, " it is self-condemning as a medium of controversy." " The Socratic dialogue," it seems, " when used in *talk*, may possibly have a legitimate use to a teacher addressing uncultivated minds; "— but he objects to it in *print*. Very natural. " In writing, where one person works both the puppets, it really is too puerile." * But I divined Mr. Newman's answer, and guarded against it. It was easy to see, in his writings, on what mere splinters of evidence, a logic so buoyant as his could survive the wreck of an argument; and *therefore* I resolved that the greater part of the discussions in which his opinions were sifted, should be in the form of *disquisition*, and not dialogue. I made Harrington give, in this form, the sceptical

* Reply, p. 179.

results of accepting Mr. Newman's dogmas. In taking the *positive* argument on the other side ("On a Book-revelation") I used the same form; as also in the notes on the three questions of Marriage, Slavery, and the Early Progress of Christianity, given to Mr. Fellowes; and in the notes on a "Fundamental Fallacy!" The only Dialogue in which Mr. Newman's views of an external revelation are canvassed at any length (though I conceive abundantly sufficient as a *reductio ad absurdum*), concludes* with an express admission that the principles of his main doctrine have not been entered into, and that they are reserved for the subsequent *disquisition* on a "Book-revelation." I may remark in general that at least half the entire volume is free from this novel sin of— Dialogue !

Of course it would be pleasant to an adversary to dictate the form in which he shall sift our opinions; but he is not likely to grant it; nor shall I to mine. Nor do I allow that the Platonic dialogue need be the "screen of infinite sophistries." All depends on the fairness with which an adversary's opinions are cited; whether I have here done Mr. Newman injustice or not, will be seen in a future page : I contend that I have not. As to "working both the puppets," — it is in fact no more than is, to a great extent, necessarily done in every work of controversy, whatever its form, and rather more disguisedly in the ordinary form; in all alike, an opponent's arguments are stated by him who confutes them, and whether fairly stated and dealt with, or not, depends on the clearness of head and integrity of heart of him who states them.

Mr. Newman complains of having to fight with a "sham adversary" (the sceptic), and says, that he

* Eclipse, p. 96.

D

" shrinks with a most painful repugnance from one who,
by discarding his personality, thinks to get free from
moral responsibility."*   It is really hard to know what
to make of all this.   Does he refer to my having introduced Harrington — whether a real or imaginary character, matters not — to use the *argumentum ad hominem,*
or does he refer to my having published anonymously ?
I am quite in the dark.   If the former, I presume
Plato, Pascal, and Berkeley will be a sufficient apology ;
if the latter, I presume I require none.   I published
anonymously — partly and, indeed, principally — that
the book might sink or swim purely by its own merits
or demerits, without anything either to conciliate or
prejudice in a name.   I used it as a moral electrometer,
to ascertain the intensity of the " spiritual " currents in
our day ; or as a feather, to see which way the wind
blew, and whether my countrymen still took any considerable interest in that " historical Christianity," which
so many of our modern infidels have asserted is all but
exploded amongst us.   I am rejoiced to find that they do ;
and that I may apply, with a little alteration, to some of
our vaunting opponents, the passage in which Burke
characterises the noisy revolutionists of his day : —
" Because half a dozen grasshoppers under a fern make
the field ring with their importunate chink, whilst
thousands of great cattle repose in the shade, and are
silent, pray do not suppose that those who make the
noise are the only inhabitants of the field ; or that,
after all, they are other than the little, meagre, hopping,
though loud and troublesome insects of the hour."

But as to my being a " sham antagonist," — I should
have thought that the decision with which, when speaking in my own person, principles were laid down, and

* Phases.   Reply, p. 180.

the consequences of argument taken, might have left no
doubt that I was none. Though I rode into the field
with a plain shield and a barred vizor, I should have
thought there could be as little doubt about my being
no " sham antagonist," as Brian-de-Bois Guilbert could
have felt about Ivanhoe, when that knight touched his
shield with the sharp end of his lance.

In conclusion, the very worst thing I wish Mr. Newman, — and I am sure it is the very kindest, — is, that
he may re-trace his way to the faith he has abandoned,
and advocate the truths he now seeks to subvert. But
if this is not to be, and he will continue to write against
Christianity, then I hope it may be with the same force
of logic, the same taste, discrimination, and self-control,
which he has manifested in the chapter " on the Perfection of Christ," and his " Reply to ' The Eclipse of
Faith.'"

SECTION II.

HOW FAR I "ENDORSE" HARRINGTON D——'S ARGUMENT,
AND WHETHER I BELIEVE IN AN *UNMORAL* DEITY.

AND now I propose to re-state for Mr. Newman's
benefit, who seems inclined to evade it — or for the
benefit of any other Deist who is disposed to take up
the gauntlet for him — that argument of Harrington
D ——, from which my critic so preposterously infers
such strange things as these: — " It is impossible to
doubt the intensity of this Christian advocate's conviction that all nature testifies with overpowering force,
to every impartial mind, that its Creator is reckless of
all moral considerations" * . . . . . " With energetic
and dogmatic earnestness he enforces upon me, that
God, as revealed to him and me in Nature, has no con-
stent or trustworthy moral character." † I answer (as I
have already briefly done) that neither does Harrington
D —— profess any such " conviction," nor " enforce "
any such doctrine, nor if he did, do I. He argues
— and I so far quite " endorse " the reasoning — that the
rigid adoption of Mr. Newman's *own* criterion, by which
he rejects certain facts of Scripture, as morally unworthy of God, will necessitate a similar conclusion in
relation to *some* of the facts of the universe. I do not,
any more than Harrington, *assert* (he is a *sceptic* simply,
and *asserts* nothing, I am a Christian, I humbly hope,
and *assert* the contrary,) that the facts of the universe

---

* Phases, p. 196.   * Ib. p. 198.

prove an "*un*moral Deity," as Mr. Newman phrases it.
I believe that those facts of the Divine administration
which are to us utterly unaccountable (as I am free
to confess many of them are to me, and, as I imagine,
to every body else), are, like the analogous facts of the
Bible, to which Mr. Newman objects, — to be humbly
received by our faith as reconcilable, we know not how,
with perfect wisdom, justice, and goodness; on the
strength of that *general* evidence which establishes the
truths of Theism * *in spite* of these objections, just as the
general evidence for the Bible proves that to be divine
in spite of similar objections.

I believe firmly that the prevailing characteristics of
the universe indicate unlimited power and wisdom; and
in general, goodness; the last, however, so chequered
as to admit of being blessedly confirmed by an external
revelation, assuring the faltering reason of man, amidst
the conflicting phenomena around us, that the goodness
of the Deity *is* unlimited and perfect.

And, certainly, *facts* may sufficiently show that such
a revelation would be most useful, and should be most
welcome. Who can deeply reflect on the endless theories
which the unaided speculation of man has, in all ages
and countries, given birth to—the varieties of Atheism,
Manichæism, Polytheism — and doubt it ? Rarely, in-

---

* If I did not see that Mr. Newman was " reckless of all *logical* considerations," I should certainly think he must be "reckless of all *moral*
considerations," in representing me as believing what he imputes to me,
considering what is said of the *Christian's* point of view, by Harrington
himself, to say nothing of the whole tenor of the book :— " The Christian speaks on this wise : ' I find, in reference to Christianity, as in reference to Theism, what appears to me an immense preponderance of
evidence of various kinds in favour of its truth ; but both alike, I find
involved in many difficulties, which I acknowledge to be insurmountable, and in many mysteries which I cannot fathom. I believe the conclusions *in spite* of them.'"—P. 408.

deed, have we anything approaching an elevated and pure Monotheism, as the simple and undoubting conviction of human reason, except among that little knot of modern Deists, who, somehow, never appear except where the Bible has gone before them!

And now, with such a belief, which I suppose is far enough from enforcing the doctrine of a Deity "reckless of all moral considerations," how stands the argument in which Mr. Newman and I are at issue?

He believes that man's notion of God is the projected, indefinitely enlarged image of man's own intellectual and moral nature. In accordance with that, he declares that he rejects whatever facts of Scripture apparently attribute to God what *we* should call harsh, cruel, or unjust *in man*. I ask him, then, how he disposes of certain "facts" of the universe, which would be certainly called harsh, cruel, or unjust in man? Instead of answering, and discriminating the *facts,* he forgets that the argument is founded *entirely* on his own premises, and represents me as believing in a God "reckless of all moral considerations!"

Mr. Newman says that he does not look at the universe with "my gloomy eyes." I reply that I do not, as I have just shown, look at it with "gloomy eyes;" and that the facts in question appear gloomy only as seen through his spectacles; in other words, that the argument is purely founded on his own premises. My complaint is, that he will not look on certain facts of the universe by the light of his own hypothesis at all. His argument, again re-stated in this professed reply, *requires* that he should give no account of those facts, and he accordingly gives none. As he says I have not permitted the reader to know what his sentiments are, I give them at length.

His words are, " If we had no intelligence, we

should have no idea of an Intelligent God any more than have the beasts. But, conscious of my own intelligence, I cannot imagine that the great Unknown Power from which it sprang is not far *more* intelligent. So, too, if we had no Moral Affections, it could never occur to us to impute Moral Affections to God. But, being conscious that I have personally a little love, and a little goodness, I ask concerning it, as concerning intelligence, ' where did I pick it up?' and I feel an invincible persuasion, that if I have some moral goodness, the great Author of my being has infinitely more. He did not merely make rocks, and seas, and stars, and brutes, but the human soul also; and *therefore* I am assured He possesses all the powers and excellences of that soul in an infinitely higher degree. Hence it is from *within* that we know the morality of God. To the author of ' The Eclipse' this seems such a piece of cant, that I deserve to be chained to a stake, and torn to pieces by a profane dog !"* On the latter part of this passage I shall make no other remark than to express my hope and belief that Mr. Newman usually finds in himself a little *more* "intelligence," "goodness," and "love" than appears there, or else I am afraid the inference to the infinite perfection of the Deity would be rather precarious; nor would it much matter where Mr. Newman "picked them up." Of the "stake," the "chain," and the "profane dog," I know nothing; and if Mr. Newman will suggest to his readers ideas as little complimentary to himself as to me, it is his fault, not mine.

But to look at his argument: Whether "God has all the perfections of the human soul in an infinite degree," I shall not dispute; though I suppose, if Mr.

* Reply, p. 199.

D 4

Newman carefully reflects, he will see that there are several (and those among the noblest), which, if God be perfect, he cannot have at all; and among them gratitude, veneration, and all which constitutes adoration of Him. But at all events, though man unquestionably has an intellectual and moral nature, yet, *somehow or other*, both are very variously developed — are susceptible, as facts abundantly show, of all sorts of deflections from the *true* and the *right*, and lead to correspondent "projections" of the Deity. The representation is, in fact, just one of the *half* views with which Mr. Newman's books abound. It is *one* thing to say that man's nature *truly* developed by appropriate external training, and especially by that which I believe is essential, but which he declares *impossible*, — an external revelation, sees in the then polished mirror a faint image of *some* of the Infinite Perfections of God; and quite *another* to say, that each man, looking exclusively *within*, can at once rise to the conception of those infinite perfections. The fallacy is at once seen when we appeal to facts. Numberless questions may be asked, to which the theory gives no answer. As, for example, whether Mr. Newman alone, or a few like him, are in a condition thus to "project" the Deity, or whether all mankind have the same privilege? or if all mankind have not, who has? Whether all the different gods which, acting on that very principle, they *have* projected, are truly gods, and to be worshipped? Whether, in that case, we shall not have " Gods many and Lords many,"—most of them *unmoral* and even *immoral* enough? Whether these variable deities, the product of the variable condition of human nature in different ages and nations, nay, even in the same individual at different periods, does not prove that man at least *needs* a light more pure than that of nature, and a

'guide more safe than reason, whether he can get them
or not?   Whether, if the greater part of "these Gods
many and Lords many" are to be rejected, there is any
criterion whereby to judge whose projection is the true
one?   Whether Mr. Newman has anything to show
that his "projection" of the Deity is, amidst so many
differences, the only true projection?   But I stay to ask
none of these questions here, though only to ask them
is to show the precariousness of his hypothesis.   I am
willing, for the argument's sake, to take his hypothesis;
for whether God has *all* the perfections of the human
soul or not, I fully agree with Mr. Newman, that at
least His power, wisdom, and goodness are *infinite;*
but then it is precisely *because* I think so that I hesitate
to allow that the "little wisdom," and "little goodness,"
and "little love," which give us the inkling of such
attributes, are competent to say in *all* cases what God
certainly will and can do with rectitude and goodness,
and what he will not and cannot.   Now Mr. Newman
assumes the contrary; for he expressly tells us, that in
virtue of his "little wisdom" and "little goodness," man
is "competent to sit in moral and spiritual judgment on
a professed revelation, and to decide if the case seem to
require it in the following tone : — ' This doctrine
attributes to God what we should call harsh, cruel, or
unjust *in Man*; it is therefore intrinsically inadmissible;
for if God may be (what we should call) cruel, he may
equally well be (what we should call) a liar; and if so,
of what use is his word to us?'"*   Very well; then
the Universe of God is a revelation of him; that is the
next step; and if this criterion (purely internal be it
remembered, and what is still worse, necessarily varying with the moral condition of him who applies it,) be

* Phases, p. 189.

absolutely true, then I say, with Harrington (and so far I fully " endorse" his reasoning), that the " little wisdom" and " little goodness" will justify man in saying the same of *all such* phenomena in the works and ways of God as are, to all appearance, no less opposed to our moral intuitions, — to our conceptions of equity and goodness, — than the objected difficulties of Scripture.   Mr. Newman, for example, will have it that God *could* not have commanded Abraham to sacrifice his son, as an exercise of his obedience, even though He did not permit the sacrifice, because it is inconsistent with man's " little wisdom" and " little love and goodness" to suppose it.   I ask, then, how he makes it consistent with those same infinitesimals, that God, every day and all day long, and in all parts of .the world, does things and allows things to be done equally baffling to the conceptions of those same infinitesimals; involving innocence and guilt in indiscriminate suffering, and permitting the infliction of all-unutterable wrongs, without an attempt to prevent, or, in this world, to redress them ?

He sends His pestilence, and produces horrors on which imagination dares not dwell; horrors not only physical, but indirectly moral; often transforming man into something like the fiend so many say he can never become.   He sends his famine, and thousands perish, — men and women, and " the child that knows not its right hand from its left,"—in prolonged and frightful agonies.   He opens the mouth of volcanoes, and bakes, boils, and fries the population of a whole city in torrents of burning lava.   He opens the yawning earth, and crushes and mangles men, women, and children, with as little ceremony as a lion would crunch a kid between his jaws.   I am speaking of *facts*, very dreadful, no doubt, but they cannot be

denied, can hardly be exaggerated, and are not likely
to be diminished by our shutting our eyes to them.
Diseases, again, in infinite forms, in endless variety of
anguish, are racking and torturing, crushing and grinding, myriads of human beings in all ages and countries,
and in every moment of the world's history, apparently
without any reference whatever to the moral worth or
turpitude of those who suffer. "The discipline," as
Harrington truly says, in as far as *our* little wisdom
and little love can see, is "often most agonising in those
who seem least to need it, or in those who are past
learning from it, or in the innocents who *cannot* learn
from it!"*

* I know it may be said, in the presumptuous jargon of a certain school
in our day, that "famine and pestilence" may be altogether prevented,
—in time; in short, that it is through *wise* man's *ignorance*, and by
his fault that they ever come at all! If it were so, the time for banish-
ing them has been long in coming, and I rather think is still remotely
future; though I thankfully acknowledge that it is in man's power,
and becomes his most solemn duty, to diminish the probability of their
occurrence, and to mitigate them when they come. Still, as long as he
does not know how to anticipate the next week's weather,—and all the
illuminati of Europe are so long puzzling their heads over cholera and
the potatoe disease alone, with so little power to solve their mystery, I
am afraid we are still a considerable distance from the sanitary millen-
nium. And when men have found out (if they ever *do* find out) these
riddles, it is to be feared from the analogies of the past that new "de-
velopments" of nature, which now present us with diseases our fathers
never dreamt of, will furnish man with new nuts to crack. The
"subtlety of nature," as Bacon terms it, will be found too hard for his
little godship. However, as respects the *present* argument, if it were
ever so true that, towards the end of some millions of years, man could
prevent these evils, it would not remove one *iota* of the difficulties which
attach to a constitution of things, by which millions of millions of the
race had suffered such an infinity of sorrows, because men had lacked
a little "sanitary" science; or show why he was doomed to such a
long curriculum to attain it.

"Atheist" or "Pagan," as Mr. Newman thinks me, I acknowledge I
am often equally astonished and scandalised at the "vain boastings" of
science; which, after all, with all its vaunted attainments, gives us but
the alphabet of the universe. I suppose, as "pestilence" and "famine"

The evils God permits are as incomprehensible as those He inflicts.   He smites a man with madness, and the maniac cuts the throats of his innocent wife and children.   He gives a man an idiot for his son, and the idiot with a laugh burns down his father's dwelling. He assigns a poor innocent a vicious intemperate father, and he bears about him for threescore years the miserable heritage of his father's vices.   He lets some savage tyrant — nay, a succession of them, — fill a whole country with groans, and tears, and broken hearts, and curses. He lets the infamous slave-dealer buy his living cargoes, and consign them to all the agonies of the middle passage; and His patient Omnipotence stands silently by while, in a living death of weeks or months, they long for " the death which comes not," and would bless that tornado which should send them : to the bottom, — a tornado which, perchance, falls on some slumbering city, or sinks the avenging cruiser instead.   Is not God good then, even in these things?   Yes, I say; yes, with an unfaltering faith; but I *believe* it, and cannot *see* it; these things are what *we* should call " harsh, cruel, and unjust in man," and are utterly incomprehensible to our " little wisdom," and " little goodness," and "little love ; " just as His command to exterminate the Canaanites, though not *so* perplexing, nor a tenth part so perplexing, is also incomprehensible.   But I believe that God is good *in spite* of these facts.   Mr. Newman, on the other hand, says in effect, " I believe the *last*-mentioned fact incredible, because it contradicts my moral and spiritual convictions of what God would do.   It attributes to God what would ' be harsh, cruel, and unjust in man;' and *therefore* I must reject it; the *other* facts I can see are

are to vanish, some philosophic quacks will next promise us — like him of whom Horace Walpole tells us, — an excellent " pill" against earthquakes, or a patent for an engine to " put out " volcanoes !

quite consistent with all the said convictions." Try your
hand on them, then, I say, and show it. Show that they
would not be " harsh, cruel, and unjust in man," equally
at war with man's " little wisdom," " little goodness,"
and all the other little things.   What! God's command
to Abraham more incomprehensible than many of the
things He does and permits?   It can only be because
the objector does not give himself time to dwell adequately on the things that *are* done and suffered to be
done by the Universal Ruler in all parts of the earth in
all ages.   I have heard one of the most benevolent phy-
sicians declare, as he has seen a patient wear out long
years of agony in cancer, — agony which it was agony
only to witness, — agony which was all remediless and
all fruitless (as far as man could conceive), that he would
have accepted with rapture a permission to put an end to
the scene of sorrow ; which it was infinitely more mysterious to him, that God should suffer, than that he
should have given the command to Abraham.   But, at
any rate, Mr. Newman must *show* the difference between
the cases.   If he says, It is true God may do such
things himself, but He could not command Abraham to
do them, because Abraham had a moral nature, so and
so constituted, let Mr. Newman take heed; this would
be a queer proof that God's *moral* nature was *like that*
of Abraham (from which resemblance alone Abraham
inferred *what* God was), that He could and might do the
things which for that reason He could *not* command
Abraham to do. — The reasons, then, which make certain
facts of the universe conformable to Mr. Newman's intuitions, and certain facts of Scripture *not* conformable,
must be given.   That is all I ask.   Instead of com-
plying, Mr. Newman turns round and says, " He per-
ceives that I believe in an *unmoral* Deity !"   Let us
see whether I do; but whether, at the same time, I

am not rather more consistent than he in the uniform
exercise of faith.

When the young bride walks to her home with sun-
shine in her heart and on her path, and all life is full of
promise and of hope before her,—what is God then?
Good, we say. And what is He, when we see the same
bride smitten down, and carried to the sepulchre almost
before the bridal chaplet has withered in her hair, and
her widowed husband returns to his desolate hearth with
a broken heart? What is God then? Good, I say;
oh! doubtless good; but in strong faith I say it, not
because I can comprehend it; for man's "little wisdom"
and "little goodness" would never have thus clouded
the young dawn of hope and love. And when the
young mother, in ecstacy of maternal joy, clasps her
blooming child to her bosom, and blesses God for the
life He has given, what is God then? Good, I say.
And what is He when the same mother watches, in
agony and tears, through weeks of wasting sickness,
the same young face from which the bloom has all departed, and begs, but begs in vain, as she gazes on suf-
ferings which, after all, but faintly reflect her own—
that God would be pleased in mercy to resume the life
He had given? What is God then? Good, good I
say still; though thus to have searched and wrung the
fibres of a mother's heart would have been harsh and
cruel in man, with "his little wisdom" and "his little
love." "I find no difficulty," Mr. Newman must say,
"in allowing that God can do all this in harmony with
my 'intuitions' of equity, justice, and goodness; but I
cannot believe that, *for any purpose in the universe*, even
for the instruction of all ages, he would *half as much*
have tried the heart of the faithful patriarch." I say,
why? I beseech you, why? Instead of answering, Mr.

Newman says, " I perceive, sir, you believe in an *un-*
moral Deity."

And when the " gentle west wind ungirds the bosom
of the earth," and flowers and blossoms spring forth at
its bidding, and all nature laughs in the sun, and in the
prophecy of plenty, — what is God then? Good, all
nature says, rejoicingly. But when the " heavens are
brass," and the " earth iron; " or the " winds of death "
cover the ocean with wrecks, suffocate the caravan in
the desert, or fill the city with sickness and pestilence; or locusts strip in an hour the fruits of God's
bounty and man's industry, and leave his creatures to
die, — what is He then? Good, still I say; I doubt it
not — good and just, and holy still. But, " O God!
clouds and darkness are round about thee," and man's
"little wisdom " and "little goodness " cannot penetrate
Thee; I *believe*, but cannot *see*, that " justice and
judgment are the habitation of thy throne." Shrouded
in tempests, thy path tracked with earthquake, and
pestilence, and famine, " how unsearchable are thy judgments, and thy ways past finding out!" I do not see,
virtually replies Mr. Newman, — I do not see that these
" *natural* events," comprehensive, and as far as we can
see, undiscriminating as are the ruin and the agony they
bring, are any thing but what may be quite made to
harmonise with man's notions of what is just, and good,
and kind; but I cannot believe that the God who can
blamelessly do all these things, irrespective of degrees
of guilt — nay, to millions who could have none, —
would have ever enjoined the destruction of the Canaanites, let " their iniquity have been ever so full."
Why so? I ask; how do you *discriminate* the two
classes of facts, so as to show that *though* the one would
be harsh and cruel in the light of our moral and spiritual
judgments, the other would not be? — " I perceive," is

still Mr. Newman's only answer, — " I perceive, sir, that you believe in an *unmoral* Deity."

Why, so laughable is the misrepresentation of the argument, that, as I have said, it is not even true that Harrington does so. He sees and admits that the only solution may be true; but then he consistently applies its possible relief to *both* classes of phenomena, or to neither: he says, " If it be said that there *may be reasons* for such apparent violations of rectitude, which we cannot fathom, I deny it not; but *that* is to acknowledge that the supposed maxims derived from the analogies of our own being are most deceptive as applied to the Supreme. It is to remit us to an act of absolute faith, by which with no greater effort, nor so great, we may be reconciled to similar mysteries of the Bible."*

Mr. Newman says that I " admit the difficulties of the Scripture facts to be insoluble; " I answer, that I admit that *some* of them are, except by that which makes both them and the *parallel* difficulties of the universe soluble; by a reference to a power, wisdom, and goodness infinitely greater than our own, and which requires that we can be allowed only *partially* to judge of God's character, rights, and jurisdiction. Harrington admits them also to be insoluble, but only for the sake of argument, as he expressly says : — " Now, whether the Bible represents God, or not, in all these cases as *sanctioning* the things in question, I shall not be at the pains to inquire, because I am willing to *take it for granted* that Mr. Newman's representation is perfectly correct; "† but he also expresses his conviction that the difficulties in question are neither so great nor so numerous as many of the parallel difficulties in nature; and here I fully " endorse and confirm " his argument. But I do

---

* Eclipse, p. 158.   † Ib. pp. 148, 149.

not admit that either the one class of difficulties or the other invalidates the conclusion, from a vast preponderance of proof, external and internal, that God is holy, just, and good.

Such is my defence — I venture to say a consistent one — against Mr. Newman's misrepresentation, which I do not wonder that many should think a *ruse* to escape from an inconvenient dilemma. This passionate iteration of my belief in an *unmoral* Deity, is the only answer that Harrington gets to his argument, and I rather think the only answer Mr. Newman is likely to give. If not, there it is; let him try his hand upon it.

If Mr. Newman attempt an answer to these stupendous difficulties by saying that God must act according to " general laws," which necessarily involve an infinitude of misery in their application, he carries the argument only one step further back; for then, of course, he is requested to tell us why God *must* act according to *such* general laws; and whether he can demonstrate that Infinite Power, Wisdom, and Love could not construct a world without an infinity of sorrow in it, or even a world without any sorrow at all? He tells us in " The Soul," " that when the flesh of a martyr is agonised by the flames, God gives the fire power to burn him, *not because* He wishes it on that particular occasion to burn, *but because* it is better to adhere to a fixed system, so that the element which burns at one time should burn also at another."* But can he demonstrate the necessity of a " fixed system," in which there should be martyrs to burn, and cities to be swallowed up alive by earthquakes, and baked in volcanic lava? Let him not say again that *I* doubt any more than he that " a good God reigns over all: " I

* Soul, p. 37.

E

doubt it as little as he can do; and I am only anxious to show that the difficulties against which we must all contend are of the same nature and of equal insolubility — only a thousand times more numerous — with the parallel difficulties of Scripture. If he attempt to remove them by his theories respecting the origin of evil, I laugh — just as Harrington does, and as every body else must do — at the complacent flourish of his little metaphysical conjuring wand. Mr. Newman's petty theories throw no light on this great mystery; as little as if he brought a farthing candle to illumine the dread abyss out of whose yawning archway the icy waters of an Alpine glacier sullenly rushes into day.

He says, indeed, with the same instinct for keeping at a safe distance from the argument, " What hinders me from saying that I know all these facts, and I do not see that they prove *Paganism ?* What hinders me? — is it only the intense dogmatism of a fictitious person, who blusteringly rules that (whatever I pretend to the contrary) the FACTS of the universe ARE Pagan?"* Who said that they prove Paganism? — who said they proved an " immoral Deity?" What Mr. Newman has to show is, that these facts are (not merely *believed* to be reconcilable with equity and goodness; *I* believe it as much as he can, though I see it not); but to prove that these facts *are* reconcilable with equity and goodness, and that the parallel difficulties of the Scripture are *not.* When he has shown that, he will have said something to the purpose.

Now if he ask what shall " hinder him " from simply affirming, without proving, *that,* I reply, I know not what *will* hinder him from so acting, because it is easy to see that very few things can hinder so wayward a

* Phases. Reply, p. 193.

logic as his from coming to any conclusion whatever;
but I know what *ought* to hinder him, and that is,
Reason and Modesty. But, at all events, till he can
show that the appalling facts which the history of Providence presents are more reconcilable with man's " little
wisdom, goodness, and love" than the facts he objects
to in the Bible, it will be as well (as he does at present)
to keep silence on the matter; for if he *says* he can re-
solve the problem and does not, there is not one out of
a million that will not believe him egregiously mistaken.
If he can solve the problem, the sooner he sets about it
the better. But it will not be enough simply to call
these " natural " events.*

To call the " events " in question " natural," (such as
the earthquake at Lisbon, the destruction of Catania,
and so on,) is to slur over the difficulty. They *occur*—
we know that too well, if that is what is meant by
" natural." But the perplexity is to reconcile them with
our moral notions of the equitable and the kind. If it
be said the general tendency of such events may be
beneficial, though attended with exquisite misery and
destruction to thousands; the question returns, how it
can be reconciled with our notions of equity, to make
thousands " exquisitely miserable " to secure a benefit
to some other thousands, or some multiple of them.
Lastly, if it be said, " it is doubtless very unfortunate,
but even Infinite Power, Wisdom, and Goodness could
not do any better," that is to beg the question, and to
remit us to a Faith, which will not be apt to stumble at
the few *parallel* difficulties of the Bible. The only
other escapes are by Atheism (or Pantheism) and
Manichæism. Of these I have said little in " The
Eclipse of Faith; " but not because I have nothing to

---

* Phases, p. 192.

E 2

say, as I may perhaps show hereafter. The "Chaos of Faith" might furnish as ample and as instructive a theme.

Mr. Newman tells us, that "his faith in the moral qualities of the Infinite Deity does not rest" on the "sterner facts" of the universe.* I should think not. Did ever any body's faith rest on the very difficulties which oppose and try it? Once more; what he has to show is, that those facts are *consistent* with that faith, while those of Scripture are not.

Mr. Newman, indeed, *hints* at an answer which he seems half afraid to resort to; and wisely; for, doubtless, he felt the frail ice cracking under him. He tells me that "I demand, as a reasonable preliminary, that we will approach the Book with the very same reverence as we approach the Universe, and will *assume* that the Book is the 'Word' of God as surely as the Universe is his 'Work.'"† I do not want him to *assume* either; but if he means that I think it reasonable to apply his *internal criterion* of what is to be rejected as unworthy of God (a test derived exclusively from our moral intuitions) equally to the alleged Works and alleged Word of God,—I answer, to be sure I do, if I am to apply his own criterion at all, and that criterion is worth a button, —namely, that what we should feel to be in man harsh, cruel, or unjust, we reject as at once unworthy of God. If this be true, there is no help for it. If this criterion is to be *absolutely* trusted, then it *will* be equally applicable to the big "world" and to the little "book,"—to the works and to the words of God. It is, in fact, strictly applicable to neither, and for these very sufficient reasons; first, that men themselves are not agreed that any such criterion will apply (as these very controversies sufficiently show) to *all* that God can rightfully

do; and secondly, that men do not agree as to what are
the " moral and spiritual" intuitions by which they can
measure God; but all " nations, kindreds, and people,"
making gods after their own " corrupt minds," have
manufactured for themselves a variety of deities, most
of them *un*moral and *im*moral enough.

Mr. Newman has a curious comment on Harrington's
brusque dismissal of his little theories for getting rid of
the difficulties connected with the permission of such an
infinitude of Physical and Moral evil; — " those awful
forms," as the sceptic calls them, which Mr. Newman,
with his accustomed candour and felicity, translates to
mean " the horrible phenomena of Nature which suggest
the immorality of God."* Harrington says: " I certainly
know of no other man who has stood so unabashed in
front of these awful forms.   One almost envies him the
truly childlike faith with which he waves his hand to
these Alps, and says, ' Be ye removed and cast into the
sea;' but the feeling is exchanged for another, when
he seems to rub his eyes, and exclaim, ' Presto! they
are gone sure enough!' while you still feel that you
stand far within the circumference of their awful
shadows."†

* Phases, p.198.

† Mr. Newman says, — " The author of ' The Eclipse' admits that the
charges of immorality which he so vehemently urges against the God
of Nature (!) press with equal weight against the God of Christianity."
I need not say that I urge no such charges against either the God of
Nature or the God of Christianity. The reader, I dare say, understands
by this time — though it is convenient for Mr. Newman to forget it, —
that the argument is purely hypothetical, and on the assumption of Mr.
Newman's premises; that *if*, as he says, the God of the Bible is chargeable with *im*moralities, the charge must be extended to the God of Nature, for he does the same things.   " If I tell him," says my critic, " that
the intended sacrifice of a first-born son did not deserve eulogy: he has
no reply whatever, except that the God of Nature is equally *atrocious*."
. . . I need not say that the word "atrocious" is Mr. Newman's, not

Mr. Newman, for reasons best known to himself, printed the last words in *italics,* and the personal pronoun "YOU" in capitals; and then asks "On which then of *us two* has an Eclipse of Faith fallen?" What wonderful power of refutation is to consist in the *capitals* I know not, the meaning of the passage being plain enough without any such emphasis,—that in spite of Mr. Newman's curt formulæ of conjuration, you, gentle reader! I, and every one, are encompassed in those shadows which the dread mystery of the "origin of evil" has cast on every spirit that has ever profoundly meditated it, and which Faith, and nothing but Faith, relieves.

mine. I may here take notice of a convenient abridgment of Mr. Newman's. In lieu of quoting Harrington's illustration of the difficulties which are "found" in the administration of the universe, Mr. Newman says, " *What* are found? I cannot quote such diffuse writing at full; but it is, 'things which shock the moral sense as flagrantly immoral, and which Mr. Newman must reject as not sanctioned by God.' He presently (p. 151.) gives, as examples, the earthquake of Lisbon and the plague of London, which are thus laid down to be flagrant immoralities, which not only will make Mr. Harrington an atheist or pagan, but (he adds) ought to make *me* such, if I am consistent." (Reply, p. 192.) Here Mr. Newman, who complains that people do not quote enough of him, cannot quote such *diffuse* writing as "The Eclipse of Faith." However, short as is the passage in single inverted commas, it is rather too *much;* and though given *as* Harrington's statement, it is not his, nor do I accept it: as before and all along, Mr. Newman quite forgets that the argument is founded on Mr. Newman's own principles; that if the things he objects to in the Bible be "immoral," the things cited by Harrington are so. One as hasty as himself might ask here, Who is guilty of "stealthy misrepresentation," and "gross garbling?" But I do not: the eccentricity of Mr. Newman's logic shall still entitle him to charity.

SECTION III.

WHETHER MR. NEWMAN'S THEORY, THOUGH HE MEANS IT NOT, DOES NOT INVOLVE THE CONCEPTION OF AN IMMORAL DEITY.

HAVING defended myself from the grotesque charge of having pleaded for an *unmoral* or *immoral* Deity, let not Mr. Newman imagine that I am content to let it end with defence. With more reason I make reprisals. Though I will not imitate Mr. Newman's injustice, by representing him as consciously pleading for an "immoral Deity," I *do contend* that it is his theory, not mine, (notwithstanding all his moral and spiritual intuitions,) which directly involves the notion.

I believe in the God of the Bible; I believe in a God who created man holy, innocent, and happy, reflecting his image, and participating in his felicity; and that *when* God created him he said of him, as of all else that came immediately from his hand, that his creature was "very good!" I believe in that God, if *that* is to believe in an *immoral* Deity; but what sort of God is it which Mr. Newman's theory requires? Why, one who is supposed to have launched man into the world, not only with a *nature* no better than he possesses now, but in a *condition* worse than that of the worst idolater, as the starting point for that long *curriculum* of "Progress," in which "the old barbarism" and "methodised Egyptian idolatry" are to be supposed hopeful epochs and notable stages of improvement from

his original condition! " The law of God's moral universe," says Mr. Newman, " as known to us, is that of
Progress. We trace it from old barbarism to the
methodised Egyptian idolatry, — to the more flexible
polytheism of Syria and Greece," — (is the worship of
Baal and Astarte, of Venus and Bacchus, the most
hateful and fearful exhibitions of the corruptions of man,
veiled under this polite periphrasis?) — " to the poetical
pantheism of philosophers, and the moral monotheism of
a few sages;" * — the last term not being of the nature
of a *return* in the right direction after deflection from
it, but a gradual ascent from the depths of something
worse than Plato's Cave — a gradual advance from the
" old barbarism" and " Fetichism" to which the Theory
of Progress remits us. In such a condition is man supposed to have made his *début,* on this most hopeful of
all theories of God and the universe! It is certainly
not my idea of a moral Deity — for it is not, thanks be
to God! that of the Bible, — that the Deity chucked
his human offspring into the world, such in his original
nature as he is now, with all its infirmities, and such in
his *condition* that an Egyptian idolater adoring his
Apes, his Cats, and his Onions, might regard him with
compassion, as not having yet reached his own happy
religious improvements on the primeval " barbarism!"
Deliberately doomed, *ab initio,* to grope his way through
unnumbered ages, from the starting-point of Fetichism
through all the horrors and cruelties of the darkest
superstition, each stage is an *improvement,* it seems, on
the original felicity in which a God of unlimited benevolence had fixed his lot! — the result being, that after
ten thousand years or so — it may be much more (for
aught Mr. Newman professes to be able to tell us),

* Phases, p. 169.

some score or two of philosophers—I fear I am ex-
aggerating the number, or, rather, I hope it,—may
luxuriate in the delightful prospect thus unfolded of the
beneficence and *morality* of the Deity! It is true,
indeed, that Mr. Newman does not, so far as I can
find, expressly sanction the old theory of man's original
savageism; but, as Harrington says, it is the necessary
complement of the correspondent religious theory.
For would it not be an absurdity to imagine a developed intellect and the lowest Fetichism,—a mind
in full possession of its powers and a soul brutish
enough to flatter itself that it was making "progress"
as it passed through the preliminary stages of such
Fetichism to the remote *refinements* of the Syrian or
Egyptian idolatry? We must therefore fancy man
feeling his way at once to the lowest elements of civilisation and the most elementary conceptions of religion.
And as savages make no rapid progress (*some* philosophers say they cannot, and all history shows they
do not,) without instruction from *without,* and as by
the supposition primeval man could not have any, it
is hard to say how many ages he crawled before he
walked, lived on berries and acorns before his first incipient attempts at cookery, yelled his uncouth gibberish
before he made (if he could ever make) the refined discovery of an articulate language, and lighted on his first
deity in the shape of a bright pebble or an old fishbone,
and was in raptures at the discovery! Or, rather, it is
hard to say how the poor wretch ever survived the experiment of any such introduction to the world at all.

Some philosophers have defined man as a laughing
animal. I am afraid that on this theory it was some
ages before he found any thing to laugh at. It must
have been very long before his "differentia" appeared.

I have said that I do not know whether Mr. Newman

would formally accept the hypothesis of the originally
savage condition of man; but it is obviously the only
logical complement of the religious theory in question,
and the mention of the "old barbarism" would also
imply it.   I am sure it will be admitted by any one
admitting the religious theory, unless he is prepared to
rush into the most outrageous incongruities.   But,
whether Mr. Newman accepts it or not, I lay no stress
upon it; that man began in the "old barbarism," and in
the condition of the lowest Fetish worshipper, is quite
sufficient for me; the nature of the progress of the
unhappy creature, from such a hopeful beginning, may
be easily anticipated, and forms a melancholy comment
on the moral character of the Deity who is thus supposed to have sent man into the world, so strangely
equipped for his destinies.   The advocates of this
"progress" often speak of it as if it were like the
"progress" of a happy child under the guidance of
a wise and beneficent father, or our "progress" in
science, where each step is an advance, and unat-
tended with regrets; whereas *this* progress is tracked
all the way through with tears and slaughter, groans
and curses, ignorance and impurity, the most hateful
cruelties, the most degrading superstition.   If perfectly
innocent man was *ab initio* doomed to such a curriculum as this (and what its remaining term, if Christianity
indeed be false, and not destined to abridge it, no
mortal can tell), can any one say with a safe conscience
that he thinks this theory *relieves* the difficulties of the
Bible?   On this hypothesis, the fearful condition of our
world is not a *calamity,* not a thing to be deplored,
not the shadow of sin thrown across it, but the natural
evolution, the spontaneous product of creative energy
and unlimited love.   I say, and say it fearlessly, that
this Juggernaut which a fantastical Theory of Progress

presents us with, is what men will not believe in, and that they would sooner become Atheists than do so.

No; if this be the idea of a *moral* Deity,—of infinite Power, Wisdom, and Goodness manifesting their creative energies,—I thankfully acknowledge it receives no countenance from the Bible. It is not *there* that I find that man entered the universe as a " barbarian " and Fetish-worshipper, who might envy the beasts themselves. Let but the imagination duly dwell on the picture of innocent man making his appearance, under the benediction of an infinitely beneficent Creator, in the condition of one of the aborigines of Australia, — with similar tatters of an understanding and conscience, little better than Lord Monboddo's first monkey-man, only without the tail;—and I defy any man to lay his hand on his heart and say that this is an improvement on the Bible theory of the " Morality of God."

And as such notions of the *origin* of man certainly give one a very queer idea of a *moral* Deity, not less strange is that given by Mr. Newman's views of his *destiny;* for, according to *his* theology, it is most *probable* that the successive generations of men, with perfect indifference to their relative moral conditions, their crimes or wrongs, are all knocked on the head together, and that future adjustment and retribution is a dream. I believe, as the Bible tells me, that our God is a perfectly righteous Governor; that He will " awake to judgment," though He be silent long; that He is an exact observer of the moral character of men, and will treat them accordingly ; not willing to punish any, and when He does finally punish (*that* at least is the declaration of the Bible, however we may dispute about some texts), punishing only according to demerit in this life. According to Mr. Newman's theory, a *moral* Deity is *formally* and precisely what man, even with his " little

wisdom and goodness," considers as the very type and
essence of an *immoral* Governor; — one to whom the
despot and his victim — the oppressor and the oppressed
— the Neros and the Howards, — the Hayleys and the
Uncle Toms, are alike indifferent; or, rather, by whom
the former are often better treated than the latter, being
allowed to flourish " like the green bay-tree," and
swept away at last, along with their victims, by the
" besom of destruction " into one common oblivion!
And all for what, once more?   For little more, so far
as can be discovered, than this, — that a few philosophers
may, after a million of years or so, arise to establish this
delightful idea of a *moral* Deity; they, in like manner,
after enjoying this satisfactory glimpse, being destined
to pass away for ever!*   One thing I am perfectly certain of, that this theory of the future is so utterly untenable with the notions of a moral Deity possessed of a
moral nature at all like our own, — that any one who
has got as far as Mr. Newman's " fixed moral basis,"
and is capable of pursuing a principle to its consequences, will say, " Either I must give up the idea of a
moral Deity altogether*, or I must reject Mr. Newman's
views of man's immortality."

It is vain to say that the Bible *also* has its difficulties
on the subject of the *permission* of evil, and the *destinies*
of man.   It is true.   What theory has not?   But I
feel, as Harrington urges, that the theory we have just
considered indefinitely aggravates them all.   The Bible
theory does, at all events, represent man as created innocent, and holy, and happy, and does *not* shut the door

---

* If Mr. Newman says, that he has left the question of immortality
doubtful, it does not affect *this* argument; for, as he admits the probability of there being no Future Life, he must be prepared to vindicate
the administration of his *moral* Deity on that supposition.   The cord
cannot be stronger than its weakest part.

against the possibility of God's proving himself a moral
Governor;—on the contrary, assures us that He will
prove himself an exact one. Now, since the above
curious theory is devised to supplant the biblical theory,
and for the benefit of those who are invited to abandon
the latter, it is of no use to plead the biblical difficulties, while its own are greater.

Every syllable, therefore, of Harrington's argument on
the God of Mr. Newman's theory (I believe Mr. N.'s conception happily does *not* correspond to his theory), I *do*
" endorse and confirm." I say with the sceptic—" It
is not even true that the difficulties in question are left
where they were by the adoption of any such theory as
that of either Mr. Parker or Mr. Newman . . . . According to this theory, I must believe that God cast
man forth, so constituted by the unhappy mal-admixture
of the elements of his nature; with such an inevitable
subjection of the ' idea' to the ' conception,' of the ' spiritual faculty' to the ' degraded types,' that for unnumbered ages — for ought we know, myriads of ages,
—man has been gradually crawling up, a very sloth in
' progress' (poor beast!) from the lowest Fetichism to
Polytheism; from Polytheism, in all its infinitude of
degrading forms, to imperfect forms of Monotheism;
and how small a portion of the race have even imperfectly reached this last term, let the spectacle of the
world's religions at the present moment proclaim.* . . . .
For this gradual transformation from the veriest religious grub into the spiritual Psyche, man was expressly equipped by the constitution of his nature;—he
was created this grub! For all this truly geological
spiritualism, and for all the infinitude of hideous superstitions and cruel wrongs involved in the course of this

* Eclipse, pp. 160—1.

precious development, Mr. Parker tells us there was a
necessity,— nothing less!* . . . . . For this, then,
man was *created;* such a thing he was — through this
'ordeal' he passes, — by original destination. If *this*
be the picture of the Father of all, He is less kind to
His offspring than the most intimate 'intuitions' teach
them to be to their's . . . . . If I am to abjure the
Bible, because it gives me unworthy conceptions of the
Deity, I must, with more reason abjure, on similar
grounds, such a detestable theory of man's creation,
destination, and history."†

When Mr. Newman therefore says, " I pollute and
defile his God," I deny it.   I hope and believe that he
does not realise his own theory ; but I say that, regarded
as a *moral* Deity — the Deity of his theory — the Moloch
of Progress, — *cannot* be defiled or polluted.   It is not
the God of the Bible ; it is not the God of Nature, which
is silent as to any such intimations either of the *origin*
of man, or the *administration* of the universe; and the
general convictions of men in all ages, when framed in
obedience to those moral intuitions, to which Mr. Newman so confidently appeals, prove that such a God is
not the God of human consciousness !

Such, however, are the difficulties into which our
deistical philosophers are perforce led, and of which they
will never get rid.   Discarding the revelations of the
Bible with contempt, they yet are compelled to give us
a book of " Genesis" of their own, and a book of " Revelation;" and in doing so present us with theories of
the origin, primeval condition, and destiny of our race,
not only purely conjectural and abundantly contra-
dictory, but unspeakably more difficult to believe than

* Page 160.   † Page 161.

that of the Bible itself; and such, let Mr. Newman be assured, that men will sooner become atheists than adopt.

It is in vain for Mr. Newman to say, that we Christians endeavour to destroy every " *third*" possibility between the Bible and Atheism. *This* third possibility— such a god as he describes, —is felt by the best instincts of man to be none at all, but an absolute *incredibility*. They *cannot* worship the Deity which this theory of Progress presents them with, and would sooner become stark atheists at once. Mr. Newman says that Mr. Holyoake has lectured on his book, and " behaved with courtesy and generosity." No doubt Mr. Holyoake will regard his books with leniency. He well knows whither Mr. Newman's theory will lead, and what sort of converts it will ultimately make. The sportsman does not shoot his own pointer.

Mr. Newman himself instructs us whither his " fixed moral basis" is likely to carry him. He says,—" A serious atheist like Mr. G. J. Holyoake holds *morality*, as I do, to be a fixed certainty, but doubts whether there is any personal God. But Mr. Harrington is unsettled on *both* points." I should have thought, by the way, that any reader of " The Eclipse " must have been certain that he was *not*.[*] Mr. Newman goes on,—" With him morality has no fixedness; indeed, he is insolent with me because I treat it as an immovable foundation which I will not allow to be tampered with by any pretence of miracle; and he is equally uncertain whether there is any good God. Thus, of my *two* principles, the real atheist, Mr. Holyoake, holds one, *and the more fundamental one*; but Mr. Harrington holds neither."[†] I shall be heartily glad to hear that the words in Italics are an inadvertence; for amidst the variety of human

[*] See his express disavowal of Atheism, Eclipse, pp. 163—4.

[†] Phases, pp. 191—2.

judgments, a *fixed basis of morality* may easily be shown to be a quicksand without any personal God.

In fine, in reference to the whole subject of these two sections, people will more and more say,— "If the *positive* evidences for Theism, and the *positive* evidences for Christianity, be found of force, we cannot allow the parallel *moral* difficulties still besetting *both*, to be treated on totally different principles. Reason for both, if you will, or Faith for both, if you will; but not Reason to object to the latter, and then Faith to digest the former. We will not be told that our reason is to bow to the one, and then to rebel against the other, because *some* man tells us that God cannot do this or that, when not only do we see that He *does* similar things, (which you tell us are to be received by faith alone,) but the *generality* of men themselves tell us that they can as soon apply faith to the one class of difficulties as the other." This is the cage which Butler provides for those who reject the Bible *on account* of a certain class of difficulties; and a fair way of escape must be found.

SECTION IV.

THE EXIGENCIES OF DEISM.

AND now, because I insist that there are facts in the universe of God, as difficult to be accounted for, and as baffling to man's reason, as the facts for which the infidel so often rejects the Scripture; and because I insist that the image of the God they often "project"— though they intend it not — aggravates all those difficulties a thousand fold, — let Mr. Newman, if he will, reiterate his charge, that I am uttering "profane scoffs against the God of Nature, which too clearly come from the heart:"— to that I condescend to make no reply. My appeal is to Him who knows the heart, who knows mine, with all its infirmities, faults, and follies, and how much, how infinitely, it needs His compassion and forgiveness; but He knows this also, that it desires to harbour not one disloyal thought to Him as " the King of Kings, and the Lord of Lords;" as "the King eternal, immortal, invisible, the Blessed and only Potentate;" not a thought that would impugn His infinite Justice, Wisdom, and Goodness. These I believe perfect and infinite, on *preponderating* evidence, though I confess I cannot reconcile all the acts of His infinite government with the little measure of man's infinitesimal wisdom and goodness. These are my sentiments, in harmony, as I believe, with that Book which has reinforced what at best would have been, *but* for that, the faltering conclusions of my reason : as such conclusions have ever been but faltering among all the nations that have been without it. I have said what I have said,

F

only to prove the precarious grounds on which many
infidels would *chiefly* persuade us to reject that Book,
without even considering the positive evidence for it;
and to prevent some of my young countrymen from in-
dulging presumptuous hopes, under the notion that
" God is *altogether* such a one as" themselves, or rather
the variable thing *several* men would make him; sometimes with analogous moral qualities and sometimes not;
sometimes exercising a general providence only, sometimes a special one; sometimes this and sometimes that:
I have spoken to prevent their resting in vain theories,
which tell us, though professedly without authority and
infinitely discordant, that God cannot do this or that
which He is reported to have done in the Scriptures,
when we have but to open our eyes and see that He
can do, and does, *like* things equally strange; and to prevent their rashly casting away that light which wise
heathen longed to see, and which would have been so
welcome;—light which we must have as the (shifting
course of human speculation shows), if we would confront the mysteries in which the Divine government
and our ignorance of the origin and destinies of man
involve us.   The face of God to guilty man resembles
that of the sun — that type and image of His glory;—
in *himself* too bright for the dazzled eye to bear, he now
bathes rejoicing nature in the glowing tints of morning
or the golden pomp of sunset, now piles the thunderclouds about him and casts a lurid light upon the world
from behind that stormy pavilion;—and anon hides
himself for days together within an impenetrable cur-
tain of wintry cloud and tempest. — Thrice welcome
surely, under the changing aspects of the Infinite One,
should be the message of Him who came to make known
to us the Father in disclosures equally "full of grace
and truth;" and to assure us, amidst the variable pheno-

mena of the universe, that " He is without variableness or the shadow of a turning."

That the Atheist should sullenly acquiesce in his ignorance, I can understand. Not that he is not the victim of an infinite fallacy, if he supposes (as he is so apt to suppose) that Atheism gives him any hostages against futurity ; for if his stray consciousness has somehow wandered into this world,—we cannot say why, for none can know that on his hypothesis,—it *may* find its way into another world, not quite so eligible as this. His next move, for aught he can tell, may be for eight thousand years into Saturn, with a hump on his back and a cancer in his stomach. But at all events he cannot help himself; he must take the " goods," not " which the Gods provide " him, but the goods, or perchance the evils which necessity may supply. He can only say, as to the one, " I need exercise no gratitude" —pleasant thought !—and, as to the other, " I must exercise my fortitude."

The acquiescence of the Deist, considering the hopeless discordance of his theories and his utter darkness in relation to the origin and the destinies of man, I do not so easily understand. But one thing is clear, clear as the day, that human nature in general perfectly understands his pretensions, and has plainly shown throughout Europe for the last two hundred and fifty years (where the Deist has often spoken under every advantage), that it will have nothing to do with *him;* that it will not accept his guidance. Man asks, as I have before said, for a book of Genesis and a book of Revelations, and these the Deist cannot give. Rejecting all authority, he can, by the very terms of his theory, give only his own conjectures, and these are infinitely discordant; and to one and all of them man asks, who told you all this? It is in vain for him to say that

nothing better than conjecture *can* be offered, because
man feels this is the very thing he must escape. Thus
the Deist's inability to give any solution of questions to
which all history shows that man intensely craves, and
will have an answer true or false,—together with the
discordances and vacillations of the systems of Deism in
reference to the true theory of religion and morals, even
within the little sphere of its ordinary speculations,
prevents it from exercising any considerable influence.
All facts show that whomsoever man takes as his religious guide, he will not take the Deist.   Hence the
slow progress, or rather the no progress, which Deism
has made since Lord Herbert's time to this.   Deism is
always carting away what it calls rubbish, and always
digging foundations; but the promised building never
peeps above the surface of the earth, or if it does rise
a few inches above it, the thing " of hay, wood, and
stubble " is swept away again in the next tempest of
controversy.   If " Christ speaks with authority and not
as the Scribes," the Deists in this, as in other respects,
are diametrically opposed to him; for they speak as
Scribes, and *not* with authority.   To demonstrate simply
the existence of a Being of infinite attributes, — man
feels is not sufficient for him.   He wants to know his
relations to that Being, and that Being's aspects towards
him ; for a profound consciousness on his own part, the
deepest philosophy and a million facts, assure him that
there is something wrong in the world — something
" out of course."   He turns to the Deist, who gives him
a variety of conjectures; and that is all.

Whether the Deist frames so peculiar a notion of a
" moral Deity," as to suppose that God created the first
man as a grotesque savage, doomed to ignorance, misery,
vice, and superstition by the *original* constitution of his
nature; and that his *almost* equally luckless children,

after their "few and evil days," are (oppressors and
oppressed alike) consigned to indiscriminate annihilation;
whether he pleads, as many have done, that there is a
future state, or, as many others have done, that there
is none; whether he says, as some have said, that there
is a happy immortality for a few, and a convenient
annihilation for the many, or that all are at last to be
brought, somehow or other, and sometime or other, to
a stable felicity; whether he contends that God has
moral qualities analogous to ours, or, with Bolingbroke,
that He has *not*; whether he believes, with Bolingbroke,
that there is no special providence at all, but only a
general one; or, with others, that a general providence
without a special one is an absurdity and contradiction;
— still, in these and numberless other cases, the question is asked, "And which of these men am I to believe? and why?"

Mr. Parker, for example, in the course of *his* "development," *seems* at length to be in a little dubiety
whether the phenomena of external nature will justify
us in referring the entire universe to one only absolutely
beneficent Deity. But it little matters; for he conde-
scends to assure us, in a recent publication, that it will
all come right at last. The tremors which may fill the
heart when we commit the Atheist to the grave, and
the tranquil hope with which we lay the sincere
Christian there, are alike illusive; if the Atheist is not
converted in this world, he will be in Jupiter or
Sirius, or somewhere or other; and if not now, a thousand, or ten thousand, or a million of years hence!
Mr. Parker is *such* a man! He can tell us *such* things!
Is this Universalism now a real communication from
" our own correspondent" in the future world? Is it
some deep echo from the eternal abyss that salutes our
ears, or is it the tinkle of the little bell which summons

us to consult Mr. Parker's private oracle ? Alas ! he does
not tell us, *why* an Atheist, who has been so for eighty
years amidst the proofs of a God here, may not be one
for a million of years, or for ever, supposing only proofs
of the same moral kind to be given ; or why he, who
has persisted in spite of present laws to violate the
conditions of his existence, may not continue to do so in
perpetuity ; or why, if he cannot be amended, he should
not, as some say, be annihilated at death ; or why, as
others say, he should not be punished for a time, and
then annihilated, but *not* "restored ;" or why, as yet
others say, both good and bad should not be annihilated together at death ; or why,—— in short, there is
no end to conjecture, and this is all, avowedly, that Mr.
Parker can give ; for he rejects all external revelation.
Why, then, should men believe Mr. Parker any more
than anybody else ? They may say, with Socrates,
" Hear a dream for a dream." If the Deist replies, and
why should the Christian expect his fellowmen to bow
down to *his* dream ? he answers, that he is not fool
enough to expect or wish anything of the kind. He
says, " It is not like your theory, one of many guesses ; it
is nothing of *mine*. Christianity professes to be founded
on sufficient evidence, of various kinds, addressed to
men in general ; examine that evidence, and reject it, if
you *really* find it insufficient ; but do not impute to the
Christian the absurdity which you Deists are all prac-
tising ; that is, of giving us your divers guesses as if
they were anything more than guesses, with as much
dogmatism and confidence as if you could appeal to
some external evidence ; while, in the very midst of
reciprocally discordant theories, which, to us and to
your fellow-deists who differ from you, can only rest on
external evidence, you exclaim, that no such external
evidence is accessible or (as some of you say) even possible !"

I faithfully promise to recant these taunts, when I find the faintest symptoms of Deism being a thing of influence, measured by any of the criteria by which we judge a thing to be so; when I find any the slightest appearance of *internal* cohesion or *outward* activity; when I find as many of its votaries as make the smallest sect amongst Christians, professing approximate agreement in their own religious theory, or so far in love with it, as to make the minutest sacrifices of wealth or ease, to render it triumphant*; when I find them taking the smallest islet of the Pacific, or the smallest tribe of barbarian idolaters, under their religious teaching, and endeavouring to establish at least one little model farm of the true Deistico-spiritual culture! But no; it is easier to stay at home, and talk,—and talk,—and talk, and say that " faith is departed," and " Christianity obsolete." I feel very much at my ease when Mr. Newman rebukes *me* for rebuking Mr. Parker for his excessive latitudinarianism; towards whom Mr. Newman says, " I am so scornful," because Mr. Parker has a "brother's heart" towards the pagans whose happy " absolute religion " he celebrates.

No; I shall not go to Mr. Parker to learn " charity," but to a very different class of men; men who do not regard gross idolatry and superstition as very good things in their way, and all in their turn of signal

* It is easy, of course, to conceive of a combination, (I am told there is one) not exactly for "the propagation of " Deism " in foreign parts," nor, indeed, at home, but for the promotion of *anything* called " Free thought," between systems of Atheism and Pantheism, and that thrice-distilled Spiritualism, which nothing but the language of the Scriptures can satisfy! Of course such combination would be simply *destructive*; it would just set every thing afloat, not fix any thing. Many of our new theologians seem to think it is of little consequence what is believed, provided historical Christianity is *not.* I almost fancy that if some were asked, " What is Truth?" they would reply, " Truth consists — in the falsehood of historical Christianity."

service to the world! Nor is it because Mr. Parker has "a brother's heart," that I smile at his easy charity; God forbid; but because the theories he patronises have never stretched out yet a " brother's *hands*." That charity is but a cheap sort of charity which consists in talking and doing nothing; which sits at home by the blazing hearth, and in the happy homes of civilisation, and will not even pay emissaries to do its work, if itself cannot; which calumniates the Christian, who is endeavouring to do for the world what the Deist never attempts to do, though he tells us he knows how it could be done much better than by preaching " an historical Christianity ;"—who says to the perishing heathen, " Be ye warmed, and be ye filled," but neither warms nor fills them; or rather, perhaps gives them the cold comfort, " My good savage friends, you look very wretched; but you do not want warming, and you do not want filling ; — have you not the absolute religion? Take it amongst you, and my blessing go with you."

And, indeed, though infinitely different, why should any of these accommodating theories of Deism exact a more expensive charity ? are they not all arguments for that same practical indolence which, account for it how we will, has ever characterised Deism, and characterises it still ? What would a disciple of Mr. Parker, under the last Parkerian development, be prone to say, as he saw a band of idolaters at their dismal rites on some savage shore ? I think he would be apt to say, "Well, these savages are in a miserable plight, to be sure, in spite of the absolute religion; but why should I trouble myself about the matter? it will all come right, some day or other, I have no doubt, in another planet, or in one of the fixed stars." On the other hand, the Deist who thinks, with Mr. Newman, that immortality is most probably a delusion, would be tempted perhaps to

say, " Why yes; it will all come right some day, no
doubt, but not for the reason Mr. Parker supposes :
but because all these poor wretches will be knocked on
the head together." Nevertheless, he might add perhaps, " I may as well give them a word of exhortation
too, on Mr. Newman's theory as to what makes idolatry
a crime. I hope," he might say, " my dear savage
friends, that you take care not to worship *idolatrously*
that curious monster — I don't know his name, but we
should call him in England three Guys rolled into
one, — with the delightfully open mouth, and the great
goggle eyes; I hope you take care that it does not fall
below your ideal of Divinity; I beseech you not to
worship it as perfect and infinite, if you do not feel it
to be so. Always take care, my friends, that your
worship does not fall *below* your ideal ! Bearing that in
mind, I will lay no further burden upon you; so fare
you well."

. But this subject is worth pursuing a little further;
and if I live I will endeavour to show the Deist what
are the conditions of his success, and what he must *do*,
as well as *say*, before he can expect to make much impression on the world.

As to the dreaded alternative of Atheism, I have no
fear of it. If the history of the world and of man
teaches any thing, it is that men will not be Atheists;
and that, even if ATHEISM be the TRUTH, there is no
chance of its being established. Nor, on its own principles, need it wonder at that; for if blind necessity or
pure chance has framed the world, it has merely, as one
would have expected, egregiously blundered; has so
pleasantly constituted the universe and man, that man
cannot but believe there is a God, even though there be
none !

SECTION V.

CHARGES OF A "MISREPRESENTATION" AND "GARBLING."

AND now for the paraded charges of "gross garbling" and "stealthy misrepresentation."

There are two subjects on which Mr. Newman more particularly insists that I have done injustice to his sentiments. First, as respects his theory of the relations of Faith to Intellect—between which I have supposed him to wish to effect a "divorce;" and secondly, as respects the relation of the religious faculties in man to the transmission, or external presentation to the mind, of religious truth. On the latter subject he gives an *éclaircissement*, not before it was needed, and still, I venture to say, requiring a further *éclaircissement*, as we shall presently see. But before proceeding to that, I will consider the charges of "garbling" and "misrepresentation," and distinctly show that I have been guilty of nothing of the kind. *If* I have misunderstood him, it is only just as others—even many who are supposed more or less to sympathise with him—have done; if we have *all* misunderstood him, it may be modestly conjectured that it was only because our author never understood himself.

First then, Mr. Newman says; "This writer instils into his readers the belief that I make a fanatical separation between the intellectual and the spiritual, a 'divorce' between them, and concludes that I hold that Faith need not rest upon Truth; and, I ought to be indifferent as to the worship of Jehovah or of the image

which fell down from Jupiter. He never quotes enough
from me to let his reader understand what is meant by
the words which he does quote."* I say with an unfaltering conscience, that no controvertist ever more
honestly and sincerely sought to give his opponent's
views, than I did Mr. Newman's, after the most diligent
study of his rather obscure books; and that whether I
succeeded or not in giving what he *thought*, I have certainly given what he *expressed*. It is quite true that I
supposed Mr. Newman intended to "divorce" Faith and
Intellect; and what else on earth could I suppose, in
common even with those who were most leniently disposed towards him, from such sentiments as these?
"ALL THE GROUNDS OF BELIEF PROPOSED TO THE
MERE UNDERSTANDING, HAVE NOTHING TO DO WITH
FAITH AT ALL."† "THE PROCESSES OF THOUGHT
HAVE NOTHING TO QUICKEN THE CONSCIENCE OR
AFFECT THE SOUL."‡ "*How then can the state of the soul
be tested by the conclusion to which the intellect is led?*"§
I was *compelled*, I say, to take these passages as every
body else took them — to *mean* what they obviously *express*. Again; was I not compelled to regard Mr.
Newman's notions on the claims of Religious Truth —
as opposed to what he calls Sentiment — very lax, when
I find him saying that though "he knew not how to
avoid calling Atheism 'a moral error,' yet we must
not forget that it might be still a merely speculative
error, which ought not to separate our hearts from any
man."‖ Was I not driven to the same inferences from
his definition of idolatry, which he frames in such a
way that it may be doubted whether there are any
idolators in the world? that is, that only those are

* Phases, p. 186.　　　　　† Soul, p. 223., 2d ed.
‡ Soul, p. 245., 2d ed.　　　§ Soul, p. 30.
‖ Ibid.

chargeable with it, in any "bad" sense, who knowingly degrade their "ideal" of the Divinity by consciously worshipping as infinite and perfect what is *known* to be imperfect and finite. Once more; how else was I to interpret that communion of the Faithful for which he contends in the "Phases," in which "sentiment," not "opinion" (the utmost varieties of which, as his reasoning shows, are all to be worked up into this new amalgam), is to be the "bond of union?" * Charity towards those who differ, every one can understand; but this new "family of love," which is to be maintained, maugre all sorts of opinions, in virtue of identical "*sentiment*," — a sort of Noah's Ark, only with the proportions of clean and unclean beasts reversed, seven of the latter to two of the former — is an impossibility *per se.* — Once more, Mr. Newman *approvingly* says of what he conceives the spirit of the New Testament, (I have nothing to do with his criticism;) "By every writer of the New Testament it is manifestly presumed, that the historical and logical faculties have *nothing to do* with *that* faith which is distinctive of God's people. Everywhere it is either stated or implied, that the soul or spirit of man is alone concerned in receiving God's revelation. Unless we can recover this position, we have lost the essential *spirit* of apostolic doctrine; and then, by holding to the *form*, we do but tie ourselves to a dead carcase, which may poison us, and disgust mankind." †

But Mr. Newman says there were passages (and he cites one or two) scattered up and down his writings which are, more or less, inconsistent with such an hypothesis. I answer that I have *expressly admitted* as much; for Mr. Newman is the last man in the world to whom I would deny the benefit of having contradicted himself.

* Pages 72, 73., 2d ed.   † Soul, p. 248.

I have said, speaking to Mr. Fellowes*, " The divorce between the ' spiritual faculties' and the intellect, which your favourite, Mr. Newman, has attempted to effect, is impossible. It is an attempt to sever phenomena, which co-exist in the unity of our own consciousness. I am bound in justice to admit that there are others of our ' modern spiritualists' who condemn this preposterous attempt to separate what God hath joined so inseparably. Even Mr. Newman does *practically contradict his own assertions ;* and outraged reason and intellect have avenged his wrongs upon them by deserting him when he has invoked them, and left him to express his paradoxes in endless perplexity and confusion."† . . . A similar assertion, that it is impossible for even the most " fanatical spiritualist" to avoid using expressions at variance with the theory, may be seen at a subsequent page.‡

But whatever inconsistencies any such passages might present, is it any fault of mine that the above-cited clear categorical assertions were taken to mean what they seemed to mean? and that, however incapable of being harmonised with less absolute or obscure assertions in other places, here, if any where, was to be found Mr. Newman's true theory of the relations of Intellect and Faith?

Mr. Newman says, that I do not quote enough to let the reader know his sentiments. I answer that I know nothing more precise than the statements I have quoted, and I admitted that they were abundantly inconsistent with other passages. I ask, as I have already done, how *much* of so peculiar a writer must I quote before the reader can be made acquainted with his sentiments?

* Eclipse, p. 304.   † Ib.   ‡ Ib. p. 307 – 8.

Similar observations apply to the related case of alleged
" gross garbling," of which Mr. Newman accuses the
author of " The Eclipse." It occurs in Harrington's
disquisition, who ascribes to Mr. Newman, (I think
naturally enough,) a belief in a spiritual faculty of
internal illumination in man, which " supersedes, by
anticipating, all external revelation, and renders it
superfluous ; " or, as he elsewhere expresses it, " antici-
pates all essential spiritual verities." This Mr. Newman
declares to be " the direct and most intense reverse of
all that he has most carefully and elaborately written ! " *

Let us see. Harrington took what seemed the most
precise statements imaginable. They are as follows : —
" *What* God reveals to us he reveals *within,* through the
medium of our moral and spiritual senses."† " Christianity has practically confessed what is theoretically
clear," (Harrington adds, ' you must take his word for
both,') " that an authoritative *external* revelation of
moral and spiritual truth is essentially impossible to
man."‡ " No book revelation can (without sapping its
own pedestal) authoritatively dictate laws of human
virtue, or alter our *à priori* view of the Divine character."§ These are the passages which involve the
imputed garbling. Of that anon.

Mr. Newman also says, in a passage Harrington did
not quote (but which he might well have done, only that
his object evidently was to give the briefest expression
of the dogma to be confuted), what is yet stronger.
In speaking of the apologies for the destruction of the
Canaanites as a judicial act, he observes, " But next,
the analogy *assumes* most falsely, that God, like man,
speaks from without ; that what we call Reason and

---

* Reply, p. 182.   † Soul, p. 59.
‡ Ibid. p. 59.   § Ibid. p. 58.

Conscience is *not* his mode of commanding and revealing his will, but that words to strike the ear, or symbols displayed before the senses, are emphatically and exclusively ' Revelation.' ON THE CONTRARY, OF OUR MORAL AND SPIRITUAL GOD WE KNOW NOTHING WITHOUT, EVERY THING WITHIN. IT IS IN THE SPIRIT THAT WE MEET HIM, NOT IN THE COMMUNICATIONS OF SENSE."*

Mr. Newman complains bitterly of a most elaborate contrivance to conceal his reasoning, of all which the Author of " The Eclipse " had not the slightest conception. He says that Harrington in the citations on the preceding page omitted an adverb of inference, — " Christianity has *thus* confessed," — for the purpose of concealing traces of the preceding arguments ; — that Harrington has said, " you must take his word for both " the facts asserted in the second sentence, when Mr. Newman had " *carefully proved them ;* " — and that he has dislocated the *order* for the same reasons as he

---

* Phases, p. 152. The two sentences in small capitals are not found in the new edition of the " Phases." *They are struck out.* It is no doubt the right of an author to erase in a new edition any expressions he pleases ; but when he is about to charge another with having " grossly garbled," and " stealthily misrepresented him," it is as well to let the world know *what* he has erased, and *why?* He says that my representation of his sentiments is the most direct and intense reverse of all that he has most elaborately and carefully written." It certainly is not the " intense reverse of all that he has most elaborately and carefully" *scratched out.* The above extract, I find, now begins in the new edition thus : — " But next, the analogy *assumes* (what none of my very dictatorial and insolent critics make even the faintest effort to prove to be a fact), that God, like man, speaks from without . . . . " (Pp. 92, 93.)

I do not know what it was intended by his " very insolent and dictatorial critics" (if he has any) to prove ; but it was sufficient for me that my object was to disprove the dogma that any such external revelation was *à priori* impossible. Whether God has spoken *in fact* depends on the appropriate evidence.

omitted the particle. Let us hear Mr. Newman in full.

" The reader will observe that the Author inserts a clause of his own, 'you must take Mr. Newman's word for both; *i. e.* both for the fact that Christianity has confessed it, and for the fact that theory makes it clear. He thus informs his reader that I have dog-matised without giving reasons. And to deceive the reader into easy credence, he dislocates my sentences, alters their order, omits an adverb of inference, and isolates these three sentences out of a paragraph of forty-six closely printed lines, which carefully reason out the whole question."*

I answer, and will distinctly prove, that however plausible this statement, not one of the facts is susceptible of the interpretation Mr. Newman has put upon it. First, the omission of the adverb of inference was *not* for the reason assigned by Mr. Newman; it was simply because, as the whole context in Har-rington's speech shows, he wished to give at the outset, in the briefest form, the *conclusions* against which he was about to contend by a distinct class of argu-ments of his own; no matter whether it was "thus," or *otherwise,* or in no way at all (as I believe it *was*), that Mr. Newman arrived at them. That this was the *object* is clear from the omission of the last, longest, and strongest quotation now supplied. It was of no more consequence, in the mere stating of the question to be discussed, that Harrington should make reference to the supposed arguments by which Mr. Newman came to the contested conclusion, than that in enunciating any other proposition, which we are about to confute by totally different arguments, we should encumber it with the

* Reply, p. 189.

reasons alleged for it. All that is necessary at that stage, is to give a precise statement of the disputed thesis in the words of the author; and this, Harrington gave in three of the clearest and most explicit statements that could be found.

. . But Mr. Newman further complains, that Harrington says the reader must take Mr. Newman's word for both the alleged facts in the citation,—"whereas he had carefully proved and reasoned out the whole question." I answer, that Harrington's statement expressed his real conviction,—though another form of expression might have been more precise—that what Mr. Newman calls his "careful proofs," were in his estimate, and are still in mine, *words, words,* and *nothing but words.* What he dignifies by the name of arguments are assertions, and nothing more. I *now* say, "you must take his word" for the above conclusions, and I proceed immediately to prove it. I will engage to make good every word I utter. In order to do so, it will be necessary to cite the professed *reasonings.* After saying, what I will not dispute, that "No heaven-sent Bible can guarantee the *veracity* of God to a man who doubts that veracity;" and also, which, for argument's sake, I as little dispute, that "unless we have independent means of knowing that *God knows the truth, and is disposed to tell it to us,* his Word (if we be ever so certain that it is really his Word) might as well not have been spoken," he proceeds with prodigious strides, thus; "But if we know, independently of the
" Bible, that God knows the truth, and is disposed to
" tell it to us, obviously we know a great deal more
" also : we know, not only the existence of God, but
" much concerning his character. *For,* only by discern-
" ing that he has virtues similar in kind to human vir-
" tues, do we know of his truthfulness and goodness.

G

" Without this à priori belief, a book revelation is a
" useless impertinence ; hence no book revelation can,
" without sapping its own pedestal, authoritatively dic-
" tate laws of human virtue, or alter our à priori views
" of the divine character.   The nature of the case im-
" plies, that the human mind is competent to sit in
" moral and spiritual judgment on a professed revelation,
" and to decide (if the case seem to require it) in the
" following tone:—This doctrine attributes to God what
" we should call harsh, cruel, and unjust in man ; it is,
" therefore, intrinsically inadmissible ; for if God may
" be (what we should call) cruel, he may equally well
" be (what we should call) a liar ; and if so, of what use
" is his Word to us !   And in fact, all Christian apostles
" and missionaries, like the Hebrew prophets, have al-
" ways refuted Paganism by direct attacks on its immoral
" and unspiritual doctrines; and have appealed to the
" consciences of heathens, as competent to decide in the
" controversy.   Christianity itself has thus practically
" confessed what is theoretically clear, that an authori-
" tative external revelation of moral and spiritual truth
" is essentially impossible to man.   What God reveals to
" us, he reveals within, through the medium of our
" moral and spiritual senses.   External teaching may
" be a training of those senses, but affords no foundation
" for certitude."*

He then proceeds in the "Reply" thus:—

" Of this passage, the first six sentences carefully
" prove that a book guaranteed by God is worthless to a
" man who has no convictions concerning the heart of
" God, and in consequence, that it is necessarily inca-
" pable of overturning and reversing moral judgments.
" After thus proving it to be ' theoretically clear,' I add,

* Soul, pp. 58, 59.

" ' and in fact,' &c., and go on to show how Christians
" have actually proceeded. Then I sum up : ' Christi-
" anity itself has THUS practically confessed what is
" theoretically clear,' &c.   The omission of the word
" THUS by this author, shows his deliberate intention to
" destroy the reader's clue to the fact, that I had given
" proof where he suppresses it, and says that I have
" given none."*

Now, before saying a word further, may it not be
asked, in relation to the above assertions, what evidence
would satisfy any body in the world that the Apostles
confessed that an authoritative revelation of moral and
spiritual truth was impossible to man, when they, at the
very moment, professed to be giving it, — claiming men's
obedience to it and receiving their homage?—making
known, as they said, "what eye had not seen, nor ear
heard, nor had entered into the heart of man to conceive?"   But, not to content myself with such an appeal
to the reader's common sense, let us test it by experience.
There is some savage cannibal, I suppose, who is ready
to gobble up his fellow-man, — or a worthy creature
who puts his children out of the way with as little
remorse as you would drown a kitten; devoutly worshipping at the same time a wooden thing, which certainly is *not* the "likeness of anything in heaven above,
nor the earth beneath," and so far does not infringe upon
the second commandment.   Well, you naturally think
his "moral and spiritual" perceptions somewhat out of
sorts.   The missionaries, worthy souls, succeed in
convincing him of his abominable errors and in amend-
ing his practice.   "Ah!" then cries the savage, "I see
a thing or two.   It is true that you found me dining
upon my neighbour, and quite ready to dine upon you;

* Reply, p. 190.
G 2

murdering my children, and living in all sorts of licen-
tiousness and beastliness without compunction. Yet,
let me tell you, Mr. Missionary, you could not have
given me a 'revelation' of all this error unless I had had
faculties which could be educated to the perception of
it; and I therefore conclude that an authoritative revelation of moral and spiritual truth is impossible!" What,
think you, would the missionary reply? I apprehend
something like this:—"My good Mr. Savage that *was*,
I perceive you have a little of the savage about you
still; or at least I should say so, only I perceive that it
is possible for highly civilised folks to be of the same
way of thinking.   Just as it is because you are a *reasonable* creature and not an *idiot*, that I can instruct you in
anything, so it is because you had a spiritual faculty,
—though, as your sentiments and practices too
plainly showed, in a very dormant state,—that a revelation was *possible ;* not *im*possible, my good friend.
It was because your faculties were asleep, not dead, that
I could awaken them; had you *not* had those faculties
which, you so strangely say, render a revelation *impos*-
sible, it would have been impossible : it was possible
only because you had them." Thus, I imagine, the
missionary would answer; and thus Apostles would
have answered, instead of befooling themselves by saying, that that very authoritative revelation, which they
declared they came to make known — to which they
claimed obedience, and to which men actually sub-
mitted, — was impossible! Thus, Mr. Newman's "careful
proof" is a mere texture of cobweb, which cannot be
touched without falling to pieces.

If men had no eyes, the perception of light would be
impossible; but, if they had eyes, it were equally impossible to have that perception except the light shone
upon them.   Hence the apparent paradox remains true,

that man has capacities which enable him to apprehend a revelation when propounded, and nevertheless that the capacities do not and cannot render the revelation impossible. And hence, too, Harrington's *argumentum ad hominem* remains: — "I do not see how we can doubt, on the principles on which Mr. Newman *acts* and yet denies, that a Book revelation of moral and spiritual truth is very possible; and, if given, would be signally useful to mankind in general. If Mr. Newman, as you *admit*, has written a book which has put you in possession of moral and spiritual truth, surely it may be modestly contended that God might dictate a better. Either you were in possession of the truths in question, before he announced them, or you were not; if not, Mr. Newman is your benefactor, and God may be at least as great a one: if you were, then Mr. Newman, like Job's comforters, 'has plentifully declared the thing as it is.' If you say, that you were in possession of them, but only by implication,—that you did not see them clearly or vividly till they were propounded; that is, that you saw them, only practically you were blind, and knew them, only you were virtually ignorant; still, whatever Mr. Newman does (and it amounts, in *fact*, to revelation), that may the Bible also do. If even that be not possible — and man naturally possesses these truths explicitly as well as implicitly,—then, indeed, the Bible is an impertinence, and so is Mr. Newman."* Let Mr. Newman fairly answer the dilemma.

But the strangest thing is to see the way in which, after parading this supposed "artful dodge"—which I assure you, gentle reader, was all a perfect novelty to my consciousness,—Mr. Newman goes on to say, that the author of "The Eclipse" has altered the order of his

* Eclipse, pp. 86, 87.

a 3

sentences to suit a purpose. He says, " The sentences quoted as 1, 2, 3, by him, with *me* have the order 3, 2, 1." I answer, as before, that Harrington was simply anxious to set forth at the head of his argument, in the clearest and briefest form, the *conclusions* he believed Mr. Newman to hold, and which he was going to confute. He had no idea of any relation of subordination or dependence in the above sophisms, as I have just proved them to be, whether arranged as 3, 2, 1, or 1, 2, 3, or 2, 3, 1, or in any other order in which the possible permutations of three things, taken three and three together, can exhibit them; *ex nihilo, nihil fit:* and three nonentities can yield just as little. Jangle as many changes as you will on these three cracked bells, no logical harmony can ever issue out of them. But they may do very well perhaps for the tumble-down steeple and cracking walls of the Church in which one of our spiritual reformers may dispense the new doctrine.

And now for Mr. Newman's four inferences from the whole, which he introduces with so much solemnity. 1. " That I feel so *painfully* the *pressure* of his reasoning, that I dare not bring it forward."

Answer. I was and am as unconscious of any *pressure*, as was the ox in the fable, of the fly who sat on his horn, and who politely hoped that he gave him no inconvenience. " I should not have known you were there," said the ox, " if you had not told me of your presence."

2. Mr. Newman says, that " since I have not impugned his arguments, but have suppressed them, and told my readers that he has given none, a sufficient reply on his part is to reprint them, and to warn people that merriment may be founded on fiction."

Answer. That since I have now certainly not suppressed his *soi-disant* " *careful proof*," but confuted it,—

a sufficient reply on my part is to remind people that there are other reasons for not noticing arguments besides their being incontrovertible.

3. Mr. Newman says, "it will be seen that he should need to write folios to expose tricks of this kind."

Answer. Very likely; if, as in the present case, he is to *imagine* the tricks before exposing them.

4. Mr. Newman says, that it is in "the long paragraph just quoted, that, according to the discerning author of 'The Eclipse of Faith,' he makes himself merry with the subject of a book-revelation."

Answer. The "discerning author of 'The Phases'" is mistaken in supposing that he is represented as making himself merry with a Book revelation *in that paragraph,* nor does the author of "The Eclipse" say that it is *there* that Mr. Newman does so. On the other hand, it would be easy to cite many passages in which Mr. Newman speaks most contemptuously of what he calls "Bibliolatry," and this would be called, in ordinary *parlance,* making merry with the subject.

Mr. Newman loudly denies, by the way, the truth of this charge brought against him in conjunction with Mr. Parker, and says, that "I wish my readers to suppose him as flippant as myself." I really have no wishes on the subject, and willingly leave the reader to form any opinion on the point he thinks proper.* Perhaps, however, it would have been more accurate to say, that Mr. Newman, instead of making himself merry with the idea of a book-revelation, had made other people very merry by his arguments against its possibility.

* See "Soul," pp. 57.; Ibid. pp. 240—248.; Phases, pp. 117, 118, 132. Sec. ed.; or the chapters entitled "The Religion of the Letter Renounced," and "Faith at Second-hand found to be Vain"—*passim.*

SECTION VI.

WHETHER MR. NEWMAN'S DISTINCTION OF MORALLY AND
SPIRITUALLY "AUTHORITATIVE" AND MORALLY AND SPI-
RITUALLY "INSTRUCTIVE" WILL STAND.   ?

IT would appear, then, from all this, that Mr. Newman
still maintains that an authoritative book-revelation is
impossible to man; and as for his complaint, that I had
omitted to notice the "arguments" by which he proved
his assertion, I have now, I should hope, sufficiently
shown their futility.   But how then does he attempt
to obviate the reasoning by which Harrington shows
that if it be impossible to God, it is at all events
possible to man, since Mr. Newman has furnished *that*
to Mr. Fellowes which it seems God himself could not
have given to Mr. Newman?*   "Surely," says Mr.
Newman, "the author means merely that Mr. Fellowes found my book *instructive*.   If so, with what
sort of honesty can he pretend that I do not admit
the Bible to be instructive?"   *Answer :* I do not deny
that he admits the Bible to be instructive, *as he immediately proceeds to allow ;* but I admit that he is

* "The latter," says Mr. Newman, "is the cardinal fact adduced by
the historical genius of our author, who here, as elsewhere, desires to
found the spiritual upon the legendary, and abhors the basis of moral
truth." (Reply, p. 191.) I answer, that " here" as "elsewhere," Mr.
Newman finds it necessary to misrepresent my sentiments.   Read, instead of the above clauses, that "I do not deem man competent, and
Mr. Newman singularly *in*competent, to determine all necessary spiritual
truth apart from the 'historical,' *not* the legendary, revelation of God's
Book, and that I distrust the ever-variable theories of truth which
unaided reason has so plentifully supplied," and you will be near the
mark.

inconsistent in doing so, if his theory be true that
"we know nothing of God from without, everything
from within." "But," he goes on to say, "if I ever
so much despised the Bible, have I ever inculcated
that all books, as such, are worthless, so as to be
confuted by the bare fact of writing a book at all?" *
Let us look at the principle involved.

It appears that there is a convenient distinction
to be made between what is morally and spiritually
instructive, and what is morally and spiritually *authoritative*. I answer, in sound only; not in meaning.
For to convince any one, who believes in a God and
moral and spiritual truth at all, of any moral and
spiritual truth — no matter how the man who imparts
it, came by it — whether he got it direct from heaven,
or it has percolated through a hundred minds before it
reached his, — is *ipso facto* to make it authoritative in the
sense that it is felt it *ought* to have authority; though
whether it will *have* it, will depend marvellously upon
whether it be believed to come certainly and immediately
from God or not. He who knows what he means when
he talks of *God* and his *claims* — *man* and his *duty* — will
smile at the paradox of any moral or spiritual truth being
proved to him — no matter how or by whom — while
yet it is considered optional with him, whether he shall
regard it as merely instructive and *not* authoritative!
The *experimentum crucis*, therefore, which Harrington
proposes to Mr. Fellowes, remains just as it was.
Fellowes acknowledges that he once thought, as did
Mr. Newman, that various current doctrines of Christianity were true; but confesses, as does Mr. Newman,
that he sees them to be wholly false, and (like that of
a Mediator) morally "mischievous." If so, the new

* Reply, p. 191.

light must be *authoritative* with him. Well then, if
Mr. Newman can thus communicate truth, which is
not only *instructive*, but being " spiritual and moral,"
must in the nature of things be felt to be authoritative
(whether obeyed or not), much more is it possible, one
would imagine, for God to do the like,— to do it infinitely
better, and to do it with infinitely greater probability of
its *being*, as well as *being acknowledged* to be, authoritative ;—as Christians believe he has done. But Mr.
Newman says, it is impossible that such a revelation
can be given. *Therefore*, the reasoning remains, that
Mr. Newman has given *that* to Mr. Fellowes, which it
seems God himself could not give to Mr. Newman.

Take a simple example, and the whole fallacy appears
in a moment. You find a Tahitian, or a New Zealander, quite as a matter of course, and thinking no
harm in the world, ready, the one to bury his new-born
child or a dozen of them, and the other to bake and
eat his enemy taken in war, or perhaps a worthy gentleman just shipwrecked on his coast; both the one and
the other evincing, in all sorts of ways, that their
" moral basis " is a very queer one. And so it goes on
for ages : you convince them—no matter how you got
your truth, though I suspect that if you got your
truth in two ways, you will not get the requisite zeal
to go and proclaim it but in one — that all this is
wrong ; and you *instruct* them, but it is on subjects
which, being moral and spiritual, involves the " *ought ;*"
and every truth they admit necessarily becomes authoritative in the sense that it is felt it *ought* to have
authority. It may be error that is so taught,—as when
superstition teaches, and, as I believe, when Mr. Newman often teaches ; but such is the nature of the things
taught, and their relation to the conscience, that it is
no longer simply information, in the sense in which

it is *instructive*, to tell them how to make shoes, or that
the earth goes round the sun, and not the sun round
the earth. If, therefore, man, by convincing his fellows even of error *as* truth on such subjects, not only
makes it, as his pupil supposes, instructive, but authoritative — as we see, in fact, he too often does, — *à
fortiori*, he can do it when he teaches his fellows
truth — as we also see he can ; much more, therefore,
may one humbly imagine that God can externally
communicate truths which will be both *instructive* and
authoritative. The argument, therefore, remains as
Harrington puts it : — " Why," said Harrington, " while
you were without the truth, as you say you *were*,
it was not likely to be authoritative : if, when you have
it, it is recognised as authoritative — which you say is
the case with the truth you have got from Mr. Newman — if you acknowledge that it *ought* to have authority as soon as known, that is all (so far as I know)
that is contended for in the case of the Bible."

But Mr. Newman comments most oddly on the con-
cluding paragraph of the work, in which I express
a hope that the discussions may convince the " youth-
ful reader of the precarious nature of those modern
book revelations which are somewhat inconsistently
given us in books, which tell us that all book revelations of religious truth are superfluous, or even impossible." Here Mr. Newman pleasantly infers that
I intend to set the Bible as an authoritative revelation
and such books as his own on a level ; and that I
am " palpably and inexcusably dishonest !" if I do not.
" Here then," says he " we have the author without a
mask. Let us consider what he avows ; 1. That he is
satisfied to have the Bible regarded as a " book-revelation " *in that sense*, and in that *only*, in which my
writings are " book-revelations " to those whom they

happen to convince.   If he does not mean this, the
words are palpably and inexcusably dishonest."*   I
cannot even imagine how my thinking, as I well may,
book-revelations " precarious " which declare all book-
revelations " impossible," are yet book-revelations in
that sense, and in that only, in which I believe the
Bible (which talks no such nonsense) is one.   On the
contrary, instead of being palpably and inexcusably
dishonest if I did *not* mean what Mr. Newman says
I must mean, I should be so, if I did.   No: there is
a sense, as I have just now shown, in which Mr. Newman's writings, being on " spiritual " and "moral " subjects, will be authoritative with the persons — I rather
think they will be a small flock—whom they "may
happen to convince."   If his proselytes know what they
are talking about, the " moral and spiritual " truths (or
errors) of which he *convinces* them will be recognised as
what ought to have authority ; just as those who think
the Bible comes from God will acknowledge the same of
what they find in that ; but as to the Bible being in that
sense, and in that *only*, a book revelation in which Mr.
Newman's volumes are to those " whom he may happen
to convince," Mr. Newman must pardon me.   There is
a vast interval between truth and error; what only
seems moral and spiritual truth (while it seems so) is
authoritative, though it may be most perniciously misleading; it is authoritative on the well-known principle
that " even an erroneous conscience obliges."

In admitting that books on spiritual and religious
subjects may be instructive, Mr. Newman admits all
that is essential to the argument.   *Instructive!*   Yes :
but if books be *so* instructive as to teach men who
have no scruple in banquetting on their fellow creatures
—in strangling their new-born infants—in exposing

* Reply, p. 193.

their parents — that all these things are "abominations"
— then in such *instruction* is shown plainly the possibility of an external revelation;—it is to teach men to
recognise doctrines which were before unrecognised —
to realise truth of which they were before unconscious
—and to practise duties they had never suspected to
be duties before. If this be so, then the argument
returns, that what man can do, God can surely do, and do
much more effectually, both as regards the things taught,
and the manner of teaching them. Will it be any gain
to Mr. Newman's argument to say, that a book of
Divine "*revelation*" of moral and spiritual truth is impossible to man, but that he never meant to deny that a
book of Divine "instruction" in moral and spiritual
truth was possible?

The concession of the *principle*, that from *without*
there may come a light which may develope into act
the latent moral and spiritual capacities of our nature,
is sufficient for the overthrow of his dogma, "that an
authoritative revelation of moral and spiritual truth is
essentially impossible to man."

SECTION VII.

MR. NEWMAN'S ÉCLAIRCISSEMENT.

ONE more remark, and I proceed to consider the value
of that *éclaircissement* which Mr. Newman gives of his
doctrine, and whether it really makes any difference to
the argument.

The reader must remember, that in reality Mr. Newman adheres to the statement in the previous quotations
from the "Soul." He still asserts, it seems, that no
external revelation can alter our *à priori* notions of the
Deity or dictate laws of virtue. If there be then *à priori*
notions, did I do his views injustice? Must not these *à*
priori notions already exist before the revelation is given;
and since they cannot be altered by it, must they not
"anticipate, and supersede by anticipating, that revelation?" The fallacy consists in confounding *notions*
with *capacities* for arriving at them — in supposing, in
contradiction to fact (as I have endeavoured to show
in the discussion on the possibility of an external
revelation*), that the original *capacities* of man, which
may be dormant or active, well or ill-developed, according to the nature and the efficacy of the external
instrument of their extrication, are not mere capacities, but definite *à priori notions*, which every where
enable man at once to pronounce on the truth or
falsehood of whatever professes to be an external
revelation. Any such *notions* do not in strictness
exist till an external influence elicits them, and though
the capacities be in the soul, yet, whether they be nor-

---

* Eclipse, "On a Book-Revelation," p. 281.

mally developed or not, depends, as we see *in fact,* on
the character of the educating instrument; and all sorts
and almost all degrees of abnormal development are too
plainly very possible according to the imperfection of
that instrument. To say that the external revelation
does not modify the action of these latent capacities,
would of course be notoriously false; and the substitu-
tion of *capacities* for *notions* at once discloses the fallacy
lurking under the imposing dogma we have been considering.

With these remarks let us consider Mr. Newman's
further explication of his theory. He affirms that my
representations of his views on this subject are "the
direct and most intense reverse of all that he has
most elaborately and carefully written!" He still
says, "*what* God reveals, he reveals within and not
without;" and he *did* say (though, it seems, he says
no longer) that, "of God we know every thing from
within, nothing from without;" yet he says I have
grossly misrepresented him, for that in the "Soul"
he has "dwelt largely on the historical progress of
Religion, and has shown how each age *depends ordinarily on the preceding.*"* Well, if Mr. Newman
will engage to prove contradictions, and that God
reveals himself exclusively from within, though each
age notwithstanding *depends* for its views of religion
on the preceding, I think it is no wonder that his
readers do not understand him. I took what seemed
the plainest of his declarations, and dealt with them. I
allowed, as I have said, that Mr. Newman's views were
inconsistently expressed. This, Mr. Newman himself
not only admits, but, it seems, complains of.† However,

---

* Reply, p. 183.

† Reply, p. 183. My assertions of his *inconsistency* are strangely
enough adduced by our author as a *proof* that I knew he did *not* mean

he has endeavoured to clear his paradox by re-stating his views, — with what success we shall now see.

Let us take Mr. Newman's explication of his doctrine, and see what it is worth. It will not make any difference: the whole ground is bog, and it does not matter in what particular spot he chooses that his argument shall sink and be suffocated. His words are: "For the sake of any one who is really and *honestly stupid* as to my meaning, I will here reiterate that when I deny that history can *be* Religion or *a part of* Religion, I mean it exactly in the same sense in which we all say that history is not mathematics. ' Newton wrote the Principia;' true: but to make that proposition a part of mathematics would be an egregious blunder as to the very nature of the science. A man might be quite as good a mathematician, though he had never heard of Newton's name. In the above, change Newton and Principia into Moses and Pentateuch, or David and Psalms, or Paul and Epistles, and change mathematics into religion — and (I say) all remains true. I may be right or I may be wrong; but I speak most distinctly. Religion and mathematics alike come to us by historical transmission; but where the sciences flourish we judge of them for ourselves, make them our own, become independent of our teachers, add to their wisdom, and bequeath an improved store to our successors; but these sciences have never flourished, and cannot flourish, where received on authority. They come to us *by* external transmission, but are not believed be-

what the declaration, that *no* external revelation can alter our *à priori* notions of the Deity, made me suppose he *did* mean. "Why this writer," he says, "perfectly knows the contrary. In this very discussion he argues against my doctrine of 'progress' in religion." Yes; but he should have said, that I admit he has a doctrine of "progress," only that it is incomprehensible in conjunction with his notions of the impossibility of all external revelation, — as I still think it.

cause of that transmission; and no historical facts concerning that transmission are any part of the science at all.　Mathematics is concerned with Relations of Quantities, Religion with the normal Relations between Divine and Human Nature.　*That is all.*"

Now, first, I remark that, even if we were to suppose *for argument's sake,* the case of religion and mathematics (!) to be exactly parallel — and that the former, like the latter, was purely dependent on demonstrative evidence — still what could be more misleading than to say, in *that* case, what Mr. Newman *did* say of a revelation of God — "we know every thing from within, nothing from without; " when, apart from the proposal from without addressed to latent but not active capacities, the man who has mastered " Newton and Euler and Descartes," might have been without a knowledge of a single mathematical theorem; as, in fact, there are very few who do attain even the thousandth part of the possibilities of knowledge which are latent within them.

But, in fact, few but Mr. Newman would have chosen to forget what most men will find it impossible not to remember, that the difference of the evidence on which we receive mathematical and religious truth respectively, is vital.

Religious truth is received not on demonstrative but on moral evidence, and therefore, the notions of religion vary not only in degree but in kind, in different ages and nations, and in the same individuals at different times; and of that evidence — often of various kinds — authority, as usual, is an element that cannot be left out.　Mr. Newman cannot find, I suppose, any one who knows at all that the three angles of a triangle are equal to two right angles, who has ever believed that they are *not*: nor any one who knows any half-dozen mathematical truths who differ about them.　But let

H

him tell me whether he does not think there have been
men who believe there is no God at all? who believe in
an idol? who believe in fifty? who think revenge
a duty? who offer human sacrifices, and think they
honour their gods by it? who burn widows on the
funeral pile of their husbands, and think it highly
proper? who kill their children? who expose their
parents, and do with an unmurmuring conscience a
thousand other things at war with what *he* deems moral
and spiritual truths? Mathematics merely differ by
the *more and the less.* He who does not get beyond the
first book of Euclid, believes nothing *contrary* to or *inconsistent* with the knowledge of him who has mastered
Newton's "Principia." Hence the extreme, the fantastical absurdity of this false parallel.

If Mr. Newman says that the variety of judgment is
the result of external authority, *that* admits that his
criterion is false, since the external authority will not,
I presume, do the like in mathematics.

If he says, it is because man mistakes historical for
moral truth (which again has no parallel in the mathematics), it does not matter; he *does* mistake them, and
on external authority.

Let us look at the matter in another light, and the
preposterous character of the analogy will appear still
more evident. In the closing pages of a little mathematical book published by Mr. Newman some years
ago, there is a confession that he was mistaken in a
demonstration that he flattered himself he had once
given respecting the Theory of Parallels. It is no dis-
grace to Mr. Newman to have failed in a matter which
has ever been the *crux mathematicorum ;* but now let us
suppose that he and others had disputed just as much
about a thousand *other* mathematical points; in short, just
as they do about those of religion ;—that some thought

that two intersecting right lines would meet again, and
some the contrary;—that some thought that the three
angles of a triangle were equal to two right angles, and
some to four;—some, that similar triangles were in the
duplicate ratio of their homologous sides, and some not;
—some, that the diameters and circumferences of circles
were commensurable, while some doubted. What then?
would not the questions which now find place in religion immediately intrude into mathematics? Would
not the authority of him who spoke enter as one of the
elements of decision? Would not men then begin to
ask, whether Professor De Morgan or Professor Newman was the most reliable source of mathematical
truth?—a question, I apprehend, which they would
not, even as it is, be very long in deciding; for *mathematics*, too, have their *metaphysics*.

Hobbes truly declared, that if mathematics had to do
with the will and passions of men, they would dispute
about them just as much as about any thing else; and
assuredly the obstinate old fellow proved it; for he was
engaged in a bitter contest, which lasted to his death,
with one of the first mathematicians of his day, and
died unconvinced of his own absurdities.

Now, if it were affirmed that an omniscient intellect
had decided questions that had been everlastingly de-
bated, would it make no difference whether or not that
" historical" fact were true or otherwise? Every one
can see, I suppose, that this at once alters Mr. Newman's strange parallel about Newton and Paul. Let
us try his propositions, which he declares to be logically
equipollent, by just introducing a similar element into
each pair.

" Newton wrote the Principia;—true: but to make
that proposition a part of mathematics would be an
egregious blunder as to the nature of the science;" nor

would it make any difference, even if God secretly inspired them; for we receive the theorems on their own evidence.

"Paul wrote the Epistles; — true: but to make that proposition a part of religion would be an egregious blunder as to the nature of the science;" nor would it make any difference even if God inspired them, *though* men have been everlastingly disputing on the matters to which they relate!

Is there no difference in the last case, even *though* God inspired Paul to write the Epistles? the conclusions being, not like those of Newton, on matters which are seen by their own light, but such as men have perpetually differed about?

The close of the paragraph is exquisite: —" Mathematics is concerned with relations of quantities; religion with the *normal* relations between divine and human nature. *That is all.*" All, indeed! and enough too. This is just the way in which Mr. Newman slurs over a difficulty with vague language. The moment we ask, " what are the relations of quantity," all mankind are *agreed*. No one supposes that two and two make five. But when we ask, what are " the *normal* relations of divine and human nature," I suppose the hubbub that will arise, will distinctly show that the case is very different. Or are we to take Mr. Newman's theory of the said normal relations as infallibly true? Mr. Newman's demonstration in relation to the Theory of Parallels was unfortunate, but not half so unfortunate as his demonstration of the *parallelism* between mathematics and religion. And yet this is the view which a man is very " stupid" if he does not clearly comprehend! and which I am not stupid enough, it appears, *not* to comprehend, but only " dishonestly " affect to be " stupid!"

The real parallels for Mr. Newman to select would

have been the practical sciences,—ethics, politics, physical and historical science,—in a word, any that depend, as religion does, on moral evidence, and vary with it. But this would not have been convenient, because it would have been seen at once that the analogy was false.

But the argument is palpably refuted by appeal to FACT. "Religion is historically transmitted to us," argues Mr. Newman, "but we do not receive it *because* it is historically transmitted to us." Mr. Newman takes it for granted that the historical transmission of religious truth, its external presentation to the mind, merely presents it with the materials of forming a judgment, and that the moral and spiritual faculties will effectually make the separation. We see, in fact, they do *not;* and Mr. Newman's statement,—however true it may be for aught I know with respect to him, that he does not receive religious truth because historically transmitted,—yet is palpably false in relation to the mass of mankind. Men of all religions say, we believe and practise this and that *because* it has been historically transmitted to us. Mr. Newman may say, this is no part, and can be no part, of *true* religion; but that is the very question. If the *facts,* "though historical," are given by God, the belief of them may be a part of religion; and that men think so in fact is seen in their universal subjection to a historical religion. If, Mr. Newman says, that "will not be where the sciences flourish," then religious science in that sense has never flourished, nor is very likely to flourish, if we may judge by experience.

SECTION VIII.

SHOWING THAT FACTS ARE AS INTRACTABLE TO THE À
PRIORI SPIRITUAL PHILOSOPHER AS TO EVERY OTHER
À PRIORI PHILOSOPHER.

IN short, these favourite *dicta* of Mr. Newman's: that
" an authoritative *moral* and spiritual revelation is impossible; that it cannot alter our *à priori* notions of the
divine character; that man is capable of universally
' criticising the contents' of every presumed external
revelation; and that not even a miracle can authorise
any departure from some presumed ' fixed moral basis '
' reconcilable with the heart-morality, and common conscience of human nature'"—these dicta, I say, taken
how you will, if supposed absolutely true, immediately
involve us in manifold absurdities. Admit that man has
a moral nature and moral capacities (as I for one fully
admit), but capable of being warped in all sorts of ways
from the true and the right, and needing apt instruments
of education and culture; still more, admit that those
capacities are originally corrupt; and then there is no
difficulty about the matter; the various facts are harmonised: but in that case any one can see that there is
ample scope for an external authoritative revelation.
Otherwise there is immense difficulty.

Let us assume, for example, the dogma about the " *à
priori* notions of the Deity, which no revelation, it seems,
can alter ;" and I ask, " Are they the same in all men
or only in some men ?" In all men, I suppose it must
be said, for we are inquiring about what is a characteristic

of Man, not the idiosyncratic felicity of this or that man. "Well, then, I should say, are these "*à priori* notions," which *nothing* can alter, the same as their subsequent notions?" What a simpleton you must be to ask the question, would be the reply. Do you not see that men believe in gods of all sorts and sizes? In one—in fifty—in none? Do they not offer to them all sorts of sacrifices — even including *human*? "Of course," I should say; "*something* then must have altered the invariable *à priori* into the variable *à posteriori* notions." To be sure, must be the answer; historical religions, false miracles, pretended revelations—any thing can do it—a thousand things have done it. "It appears then," I think I should say;—"it appears then, my friend, that these *à priori* notions, which nothing it seems can alter, any thing can, except an authoritative revelation from God: it seems that though a true revelation is impotent, any false one is omnipotent! You are very complimentary both to human nature and the Deity."

Take, again, the "principles of moral judgment" in *man*, (not in some Mr. Newman, but in man,) which are supposed to be such as to authorise and capacitate him to pronounce on any thing and every thing in a presumed revelation.—Is it meant that these principles exist in all men or only in some?—In all, it will be said, of course; for we are talking still about what is characteristic of humanity, not the peculiar privilege of some critico-moral Pope; and indeed who would consent to abide by such a decision, which itself would affirm the external authority, which the theory itself denies?—Do all *exercise* then these critical faculties? and if those faculties do not "supersede," as Mr. Newman admits, external *instruction*, do they eliminate successfully the true only, and instinctively reject the false?—How can you ask the question, will be again answered? All the facts in the world's history proclaim the contrary. Are not the vast majority of men at this moment — have they not been in all ages — bowing down to stocks and stones; worshipping all sorts of false deities, and honouring them with rites well worthy of them? Has there not been among vast communities for unknown ages, the easiest reception of the most hideous superstition, the most unshrinking, unquestioning perpetration of the most horrible cruelties and pollutions in obedience to even the falsest pretensions of priestcraft? Is it not the rarest thing to find men evincing any capacity for criticising the religious and moral systems by which their faculties have been swathed and bound from infancy? It is plain they *do* not.—It must be admitted, the objector will say. But then, is it because they would if they could, but cannot; or could if they would, but will not? If the former, or in the degree in which it may be true, they are to be pitied and excused; and it was in such pity that Christianity professed to come to their rescue; indeed the supposition affords ample scope for the offices of that external revelation which is so derided. If the latter, and men might universally and promptly exercise these faculties, but *will* not, Oh! what a blessed theory is this! "Truly," as Harrington says, "I think it makes man the most detestable beast that ever crawled under the cope of heaven." It is no longer, I grant, of much consequence to discuss the "moral and spiritual" prerogatives of *such* a creature. In *his* regeneration he will want an *authoritative* revelation, and miracles too, with a witness.

If it be said, "Well, practically, all men have not their powers of moral and spiritual criticism sufficiently active to eliminate what is false in the systems presented to them from their childhood, but (as the produce of the silkworm is dyed by the food it lives on,) their religious system will be morally and spiritually what that of their immediate parents has been;" then this is to admit that, *practically*, in the vast majority of cases, their moral and spiritual faculties are put *hors de combat*.

If it be further said; " Nay, but from time to time, *individuals* will arise in the course of 'progress,' who will indefinitely improve the moral and religious systems of man and extricate the world from its errors — men like Mr. Newman, for example;"—then this is to admit the incompetence of the spiritual and moral faculties of man *in general*, and at the same time the possibility and utility of what is so stoutly denied— an external divine revelation; unless it be pretended that though man *can* perform this task, God *cannot*, which needs, I suppose, no refutation; or that though God can, man can do it better, which, I think, requires as little; or lastly, that man can and God has not performed it and will not, — which requires proof. Whether any such revelation has been given depends of course on the appropriate evidence; but that it *could* be given, and with singular advantage, the preceding reasoning shows clearly enough.

Take, again, "the fixed basis of morality," "the common conscience and heart-morality;" is it, as before, an absolutely invariable standard, or a variable one that is spoken of? or is it a measure of India rubber that will hold three bushels or one? *Whose* " fixed moral basis?" That of the New Zealander, or of a Hottentot, or of an ancient Greek, a Roman, a Jew, or of a Hindoo, or of a Chinese, or of an Englishman? For all these have had very discordant notions on many points of morals, and *therefore* (as well as for other reasons) about God. Or is every body in general meant, and nobody in particular? Will Mr. Newman allow that the moral judgment of the *generality* of his countrymen will determine what they ought or ought not to believe (say) respecting the moral character of the Deity as determined by *their* "fixed moral basis:" and in spite of the *depressing* effects of the "Bible standard" on conscience, I do not think he will find, on the whole, any community more enlightened. Well, if so, the great bulk of them have had *no* difficulty in believing that God's command to Abraham, to sacrifice his son as a test of faith (which Mr. Newman compares to a sacrifice to Moloch), was *not* incompatible with what God might rightfully do. Will Mr. Newman say these are to be set aside as incapable of judging? What sort of test is this which appeals to the constitution of human nature, and first sets the bulk aside, and then the most enlightened of them? Will he say that he will take the spiritual *élites* of the race, the most devout of them? Still the same thing is evident; *they* do not see the incompatibility with the divine holiness which makes him so indignant. The ancient Jews, and modern Christians — those of them whom our critic himself admits to have given the world the *best* examples of spiritual religion — men like Paul and James, who, one would imagine, were not deficient in moral sensibility, both praise, *as the most heroic virtue*, that conduct of Abraham which Mr. Newman would denounce as a crime worthy only of a worshipper of Moloch to commit, in obedience to a command which only a Deity like Moloch could give; a singular scrupulosity, I should say, in Mr. Newman, if we reflect what strange things he *does* suppose his moral Deity to be capable of performing, as seen in a previous section! However, I think it may be said, not only that Paul and James could see no moral discrepancy in the supposed command, but that multitudes of men now, fully the equals of Mr. Newman in moral culture, in spiritual worth, in

mental power — have no difficulty in the world in sub-
scribing to the three following propositions ; — first,
that they do not see and dare not say that morally it was
impossible that the Divine Being could thus try the faith
of his ancient servant ; secondly, that if it were *not*
incompatible with his attributes, it *was very* possible
for him to convey his will to Abraham in a way
which could leave no doubt on the patriarch's mind that
the command was no illusion of the imagination ; and
thirdly, that in *that* case, it would be Abraham's duty
implicitly to obey ; — the first principle of *morals* with
such men being the implicit submission of a creature to
the Creator, the absolute surrender of the finite to the
Infinite, whose declared will is of itself all-sufficient authority. It is an element which Mr. Newman continually
leaves out of the question, for he will not permit even God
to command him to do anything which does not square
with his previously "fixed moral basis ;" while other men
would rather imagine in such a case that they had been
a little mistaken in their " fixed moral basis ; " a supposition of no difficulty, considering how *variable* that
" fixed" basis has been. Though far from comparing
myself, either for power of mind or moral excellence,
with the ten thousand times ten thousand the excellent of the earth who have held the truth of the above
three propositions, I acknowledge, without hesitation,
that I devoutly believe in the absolute truth of all of
them. Will Mr. Newman say, that all these " excellent
of the earth " were mistaken, and that the true moral
test is to be found elsewhere ; and, in fact, is to be
found with him alone, or the few who think with him?
I thought we must come to that at last ; that is, in the
variety of moral judgments we find the insufficiency of
the criterion, unless we will all accept the criterion of
Mr. Newman and the few who think with him.

Well, it may be said, this does not prove that *he* may not be right; I grant it; but it conclusively proves *this*, which was what I brought it forward for,—that the criterion in question, the moral test from the "common conscience and heart-morality of human nature," as to what we shall deem fitting in the Deity, breaks down with us, since the most cultivated and excellent of the earth utterly dissent from Mr. Newman's own application of it.

And here I may, by the way, observe, that, all contravention of moral notion aside, Mr. Newman *seems* to assume that God can never issue any such commands as rest simply on *authority.* He says, speaking of what he calls "blind external obedience," "God cannot speak thus to man;" * and blames Christ, as well as "unscrupulous churches for so doing." A Christian, on the other hand, will feel no inconsistency in believing that God might issue commands, for some of which the reasons are well known, for others partially known, and, in some cases, not known at all; and that in the last case his law is just as stringent, if it be made known, as in the first: yes, if only given as a test of obedience to the creature he has made. Nor would Christians feel that they wanted abundant analogy for the faith they exercised. If they can lay commands on their children, and expect obedience when the children cannot understand their reasons, even if they were explained, and when the parents will not always explain the reasons, even where they can be understood, is it impossible that the same may occur between the "Father of our spirits," (in comparison with whom we shrink to nothing,) and *his* offspring? We all know very well how it would fare

---

* Phases, Sec. Ed. pp. 88, 89.

with any obstinate child of man if he were to refuse obedience, except where he could, à priori, see the reasons of parental authority. He would soon be favoured, I suppose, with a demonstration, not à priori, of the reasonableness of *obedience*, if not of *authority*. Will man claim an authority which he denies to God?

To resume.

Take, again, the dogma that no miracle could authorise any act which would without such authority be deemed morally wrong. " I farther inquired," says Mr. Newman, " what sort of miracle I could conceive that would alter my opinion on a moral question? . . . . No outward impressions on the eye or ear *can* be so valid an assurance to me of God's will as my inward judgment."* I will not here repeat the question, Is there the *same* "inward judgment" in all, and if not, *whose* is the moral test? but, Is the above the feeling of man in general? Is it true to the principles of our nature? Let us take again the practical test. Have not men in all countries and races, and of almost all religions—some of them practised, and nearly all of them approved, (Jews and Christians amongst them,) some acts *because* they believed them miraculously authorised by God, though they would have disapproved them without such supposed authority? Yes, it will be said; but they were *reports* of miracles merely. Very good; if mere reports are sufficient to do it, would not the miracles themselves be likely, à fortiori, to be still more efficacious? And if *false* reports of *false miracles* can thus modify the moral conceptions of men, and shake the " fixed moral basis," would *true* reports of *true* miracles be likely to be less efficacious? Nay, let us hear Mr. Newman himself; let us hear him confessing,

* Phases, p. 91.

that after twenty years' study, he has only just eman-
cipated himself from the errors and burdens which had
oppressed his "critical faculties." He says, "As to
moral criticism, my mind was practically prostrate before
the Bible. By the end of this period I had persuaded.
myself that morality so changes with the commands of
God that we can scarcely attach any idea of immuta-
bility to it. . . . . As for miracles, scarcely anything
staggered me."* Ever in extremes, "In medio tutissi-.
mus," does not seem a favourite maxim with Mr. Newman. But at all events, this does not look as if it
would be very easy to establish the exact limits of the
"fixed moral basis"—that curious *variable constant!*

And again: "Moral criticism is precisely that which
I was slowest to use against authoritative claims. To
me the system broke down *first* precisely on that side
which alone this author (of 'The Eclipse') counts de-
fensible—the *external* evidences."† He is quite mistaken, as I shall show in the next section, in attributing
to me the above sentiment; but his confession shows
distinctly enough that mankind are not very likely to see
that *no* miracle can *in any way* modify their convictions
of the moral quality of actions, supposing them enjoined by Divine authority.

For many years it appears that he was all the while
looking, (as Socrates would say,) for that which, by the
hypothesis, he had in his hand. If he was twenty years,
it is likely that the generality of men will be forty; for
no sooner does he declare that he has the "fixed moral
basis" in his hands, and assures them that they have it
also in theirs, than they exclaim that they have it not,
and distrust the criterion which he says he has in his!
The world will make but slow "progress" at this rate.
But, in point of fact, though man unquestionably has

* Phases, p. 40, 41.   † Reply, p. 196, *note.*

a moral nature, and there are actions which all mankind would call virtuous and vicious, that nature is so
far from being invariably developed, that even a plausible pretence of divine authority miraculously enforced,
is too often sufficient to overbear it. Mr. Newman may
perhaps say that this is a thing he complains of; I
reply, that I think it *is* often a thing to be complained
of; but nothing can be more clear than that this
universal disregard of his criterion makes that criterion
no criterion at all, and shows that, somehow or other,
man cannot trust, and will not acknowledge, any *such*
"fixed moral basis," as not even the voice of God
himself can in any degree alter. Take the most cultivated and enlightened consciences, you still cannot
get one in a million to affirm, (as we have seen in
the case of Abraham,) that there are *no* actions ordinarily called unlawful, that would be made lawful by
the command of God authentically made known by
miraculous intervention. They shudder at the thought
of affirming the contrary; and that for a reason which
Mr. Newman entirely ignores, and denies utterly the
force of,—namely, that the authority of God is itself,
even if no reasons were given, and none were imaginable
but his will, the sufficient and all-sufficient authority.

SECTION IX.

WHETHER THE CHRISTIAN THROWS AWAY HIS "MORAL JUDGMENT" IN ACCEPTING THE NEW TESTAMENT.

AND now, I suppose Mr. Newman will reiterate his charge against the author of "The Eclipse of Faith," that I affirm that we " must throw away our *moral judgment* before we can get any religion at all ;" and other trash like it. I answer, that the theory of the Christian does not at all require him to " throw away his moral judgments," only he must take care how he gets them, and what they are. His theory is perfectly consistent. He reasons thus: " I see that men have moral *capacities,* but I see also with my own eyes, and other men see it *too,* that those capacities, as they are variously developed, lead to the most various and erroneous " moral judgments," and consequently also to the most various and erroneous conceptions of the Deity. They are in every man, as is the instrument that has developed them, varying between the wide limits of a " Hottentot and a St. Paul." That which has developed mine has awakened within me an intense consciousness of its surpassing excellence and exquisite adaptation to humanity; it is in that *mirror* that my moral nature was first adequately revealed to myself; so that, comparing the New Testament with all *other* Ethical systems, I am satisfied (*in addition to other sources of evidence*) that it never came from unaided

man, and least of all from such unaided men as those
to whom I must trace it. So far, therefore, from
discarding my moral judgments, they are one of the
very elements of evidence,—though far from the *only*
element—that Christianity came from God."

Mr. Newman asks the author of " The Eclipse " to
answer a question which he fancies invincible, but which
is in fact quite easy. He asks, "How I could confute Hindooism,"* or " any authoritative system of
iniquity whatsoever ?"† I answer, " Because it lacks
both the elements of the evidence, to be sure, which the
Bible possesses,—the elevated morality and holy doctrine, and the historic credibility of having come from
God." Give me a Hindooism, or any other *ism* which
appeals in equal degree to the different sources of
evidence which converge on Christianity,—an equally
admirable morality and an equal historic credibility,—
and I will believe *that* too.

If our critic says, Nay, but he *has* proved even the
New Testament morality defective, and he knows it ;
men smile and say he is mistaken, and they know
that. If he says, that they are all wrong, and he
alone is right; they reply,—if so, so much the more
does it prove the fallacy of his assertion that men
possess the faculty of moral discernment, which enables
them to pronounce on the claims of every presumed revelation from God; if he says that they *are* convinced that
he is right after all, but only they are all " dishonest,"
I am afraid *that* would prove that they were still
worse off than if they were destitute of the "free critical
'faculty" of moral judgment altogether.

As to his proving the New Testament " morality defective," they tell him they do not admit it; that where
it *would* be so, *if* his criticism were true, they do not ad-

* Reply, p. 193.   † Ibid. p. 196.

I

mit his criticism; but, on the contrary, affirm that it is erroneous and prejudiced; — for example, when he tells us that the " moral teaching of the New Testament in relation to Patriotism, Marriage, Slavery, and so on, is essentially defective," and that Christ taught the " abrupt renunciation" of wealth to *all* his disciples.   As to the Old Testament, they acknowledge, without admitting many of his equally hasty criticisms, that its morality was *not* perfect, the New Testament being avowedly an amendment upon it; though they maintain, and with justice, that it is unspeakably superior to the systems of heathen moralists.   They admit that some things were permitted, not as the very best, but because men were imperfectly educated to moral light; and that though this may be of small account in the estimate of some speculators, who seem to doubt the very possibility of the morality of one age differing by a hair's breadth from that of another, it is unhappily a circumstance which must be taken into account, as our race happens to be subjected to the conditions of a historic development, where continuity of change is the law of " progress;" and it might surely be pardoned by one who finds even in the " old barbarism," and " the flexible Egyptian idolatry," the " law of progress in God's moral universe!"   Lastly, as to the alleged immoralities which he says the Bible attributes to *God Himself*, the Christian replies, that though he believes quite as much as Mr. Newman, that the Infinite One has moral qualities analogous to our own, yet that it is precisely here that he doubts whether he can pronounce the acts ascribed to the Deity in Scripture immoral, inasmuch as he finds precisely *analogous* acts involved in His administration of the universe; — which, as far as this point goes, brings us back to the old dilemma, which my critic is once more invited to consider and solve.

SECTION X.

MR. NEWMAN is pleased to say, in the conclusion of his Reply, that the attempt to meet the " objections " against Christianity by retorting them, and showing that the " diversities" of the objectors lay *them* open to objections, is " dishonest." He forgets one element — the magnitude and nature of the *diversities.* It is difficult to say anything in opposition to this reprover of " personal antagonisms " without being denounced as dishonest. However, as usual, let me look at his argument, and trouble not myself at all about his imputations.

He says, that it is " an impotent and dishonest defence of Christian authoritative pretensions to taunt the assailants with diversities in their positive creed;" and compares it to the attempt of the Romanist to deal similarly with Protestants. I answer, first, that I think it would be a very fair topic of argument with the Romanist, if he could prove not only " diversities " among Protestants, but, as in the present case, greater objections to their tenets than could be advanced against his own.

But, secondly; to come a little closer, I proceed to ask, with all submission, whether Mr. Newman really thinks the religion for which *he* pleads, as exhibiting the true theory of man's relations towards God, and God's aspect towards him — the *claims* on the one side, the *duties* on the other — is *authoritative* or not? If he says " Yes," then I presume the argument from objections becomes, even on his own showing, as perfectly legitimate on the one side as the other; if he says " No " (as, perhaps, considering the apologetic tone in which he speaks of " serious Atheists," who, though they do not believe " in a personal God at all," yet believe the " *more* fundamental truth of a fixed moral basis;" and his equally apologetic tone in speaking of idolatry, a crime which his definition so nearly annihilates), if, I say, Mr. Newman says, that *though* he believes his system is the true one, it is *not* authoritative, — and that it really matters very little whether a man is a " serious Atheist," a sincere Buddhist, or a Fetichist, — then, undoubtedly, it is hardly worth while to consider whether the objections against Christianity can be retorted with interest against such a theory; and for this simple reason, that it cannot, on such a theory, matter one doit whether a man be a Christian or not. Certainly, take it at the worst, he may as well remain as he is, *unless* it be contended that though a man may be anything else, it is at his peril that he remains a Christian ; or that though he may be a votary of any religion which does not claim to be authoritative, woe be to him if he professes one that does !

But I should be disposed to show the futility of this argument on yet another ground. I contend that the argument from *objections* may be, and often is, perfectly valid. I believe it is so in the controversy between Deism and Christianity. He who is persuaded of the truth of any system, even though he cannot answer all the objections against it, may most legitimately consider whether or not there are not equal or greater objections against the systems it is proposed he should adopt in its stead; and if he finds that there *are* greater, it may be quite sufficient to justify him in resolving that at least he will have nothing to do with *them*. A man may not see that his house is perfectly convenient; he may *fancy* at times that certain modifications would improve it, and perhaps be mistaken in that fancy; but as to changing it,—it is quite sufficient to decide him against that, if he be offered nothing better than a dark cellar under ground or a balloon in the air. The former is the choice residence to which Atheism or Pantheism dooms him, and the other the mansion provided by the tumid but unstable systems of our modern spiritualists.

Mr. Newman says, that I have endeavoured to "break his and Mr. Parker's heads" against one another. I should not presume; and it is quite unnecessary, for they have "broken their own heads together" with sufficient violence. In virtue of their spiritual apparatus, they have arrived, as usual, at very different conclusions on most momentous points; and though it is not of the smallest consequence as long as they are merely attempting to destroy historical Christianity, yet the moment people ask, "and what *are* we to believe?" it becomes of vital importance.

SECTION XI.

MR. NEWMAN'S CHAPTER ON THE "MORAL PERFECTION OF CHRIST."

MR. NEWMAN founds another charge of "very gross garbling" on my strictures upon his too celebrated comparison of Fletcher of Madeley with Jesus Christ. Fellowes represents Mr. Newman as having read the "Life of Fletcher" when a boy, and as having *then* thought him a more perfect man than Jesus Christ; and as having said in the "Phases," that if he were to read the book again, he should most probably still be of that opinion. Mr. Newman's exact words in the "Phases" are these. "Heroes are described in superhuman dignity, why not in superhuman goodness? Many biographies overdraw the virtue of their subject. An experienced critic can sometimes discern this; but certainly the uncritical cannot always. I remember, when a boy, to have read the 'Life of Fletcher of Madeley,' written by Benson; and he appeared to me an absolutely perfect man; and, at this day, if I were to read the book afresh, I suspect I should think his character a more perfect one than that of Jesus." *

Now, Mr. Newman says, that when he read the "Life of Fletcher" *as a boy*, he made no *formal comparison* with Jesus Christ. I thought, indeed, that the three last lines of the extract implied the contrary; but I see that that was an inadvertence of mine; he merely thought at *that* time, that Fletcher was an *absolutely*

* Phases, p. 184.

perfect man. Still that my mistake was neither " stealthy misrepresentation " nor " gross garbling," appears plainly from this, that the proposed *correction* makes nothing to the argument, but rather renders the absurdity somewhat more flagrant. I charitably supposed him, as a *child*, to have first made the comparison (which was certainly childish enough), and then afterwards, without verifying his early impressions by a reperusal of Fletcher's Life, to have proceeded to presume its accuracy on the strength of his early impressions. This would have been strange enough; but it now appears that the comparison itself was not the reflex of a childish fancy, hastily adopted, but the mellow fruit of maturer years; that, as a boy, he thought Fletcher an absolutely perfect man, and that though at a later period he did *not* think so, yet that without staying to see, by a reperusal of the Life, how far Fletcher fell short of that ideal, he presumes so far to trust his impressions as to say that if he *did* reperuse the book, he should give to Fletcher the palm over Jesus Christ! If *this* will help Mr. Newman, he is.very welcome to it, and I accept his emendation with all thanks. " When I was a child," says the Apostle, " I spake as a child, I thought as a child, I understood as a child; but when I became a man I put away childish things." How far the readers of Mr. Newman will think he did so, I leave them to judge.

I had said " Christianity is willing to consider the arguments of men, but not the impressions of boys." On this Mr. Newman remarks, " No one can possibly read this without understanding that I *recommended* my boyish impressions as something *trustworthy*, something for which I claimed *respect* from Christianity." * I answer, that the words were *intended* to convey precisely

* Phases, p. 184.

I 4

what they *do* convey, — that the unverified impressions
of boyhood had been made the basis of a most offensive
attack on the character of Christ, and that to such impressions, Christianity can hardly be expected to pay
much attention.

Mr. Newman, in reprinting the notable paragraph,
encloses the three last lines in brackets, and says that
he *now* sees that these would have been " better
omitted," as they seem to have " distracted the mind
from his argument." * Perhaps now he does see ; but
they were *not* omitted. They gave, and could not but
give, *substantially*, the impression of his sentiments,
which not only I, but I believe every other reader of
his book, entertained ; and that these impressions were
essentially correct, his most offensive chapter on the
" Moral Perfection of Christ," whom " in consistency
of goodness " he places " far below vast numbers of his
unhonoured disciples," proves *ad nauseam*.

As to the bracketed lines distracting my mind from
his " argument," as he calls it, and from the occasion
on which he gave expression to his sentiments in the
" Phases," I answer that I had nothing in the world to
do with either. It was with the *fact* merely that I
had then to do ; — that a person had avowed the preposterous sentiments in question. The Author of " The
Eclipse" and Mr. Fellowes were discussing the " Evi‑
dences of Christianity," among which it is mentioned
that the entire character of Christ, but especially as the
Moral Ideal of Humanity, was not likely to have been
of human origination, least of all among those to whom
history restricts the problem. Mr. Fellowes replies,
" that it is not so clear to everybody that Jesus Christ
is a perfect ideal of humanity," and instances Mr.
Newman. This *fact* is sufficiently substantiated in the

* P. 186.

above paragraph; and it was with that *fact* alone I had to do. That I was bound to follow Mr. Newman into all the circumstances under which he had formed or might advance his singularities of opinion, I deny: it is enough to have to do with the singularities themselves. A man, I suppose, might refer to Baxter's well-known belief in witches, or some modern's crotchet about table-turning or spirit-rapping, without entering into the question as to how he came by it, or the occasions on which he advanced it. Mr. Newman's notion seems to have sprung from the fallacious idea, already referred to in the Introduction, that "The Eclipse of Faith," instead of being an examination of certain prominent opinions of himself and others, was designed to follow "The Soul," or the "Phases," or both, step by step. I hope I have some better employment than to track all the tortuosities of his too eccentric logic.

Whether, in the present instance, he has made out his case of "very gross garbling," I now leave to the calm decision of the reader.

Mr. Newman is pleased to say, as if the occasion on which he gave utterance to the sentiment in question must come into consideration, "that I have here intruded into a controversy with which I have no concern." I think it plain, by his own confession, that I have *not* intruded into it, as in truth I had no concern with it; I was only concerned with the sentiment itself. His very complaint is, that I have *not* referred to the controversy in connexion with which the offensive passage occurs.

As to the charge of "intruding," I beg to say that when a man gives utterance to such sentiments respecting Christ, no matter in *what* connexion, it is quite sufficient warrant for the disciples of the Master they revere and love to "intrude" into the controversy; and

for myself, I beg to say very distinctly, I shall intrude
into this or any other public controversy on which I may
humbly hope to say anything to the purpose, without
asking Mr. Newman's leave, or any body else's, for so
doing. For this reason, I shall now "intrude" a little
more into this controversy, by making some remarks on
Mr. Newman's new chapter on " The Moral Perfection
of Christ."

Mr. Newman seems to think his repulsive statements may be, in some respects, made less so, if it
be borne in mind that they are especially founded on
the views of the Rev. James Martineau. I am quite
willing to give him the benefit of any such fact. The
dubiety of that eloquent gentleman as to how much
historic worth there may be in the evangelical narratives, and the latitude of his canons of historical criticism — which, if we mistake not, have fairly made his
co-religionists stand aghast — do no doubt render it very
precarious to defend Christ's moral perfection as a *fact*,
— whatever it may be as a myth,—or, in short, to prove
his very existence. His system may well be called what
Mr. Newman terms it — " a reconstruction of Christianity," of which Mr. Martineau supposes we have the
singular felicity of knowing more than the Apostles
themselves! Mr. Newman remarks : —

" I have to give reasons why I cannot adopt that modified
scheme of Christianity which is defended and adorned by
James Martineau; according to which it is maintained that
though the Gospel Narratives are not to be trusted in detail,
there can be yet no reasonable doubt *what* Jesus *was*; for
this is elicited by a ' higher moral criticism,' which (it is
remarked) I neglect. In this theory, Jesus is avowed to be
a man born like other men ; to be liable to error, and (at
least in some important respects) mistaken. Perhaps no
general proposition is to be accepted *merely* on the word of

Jesus; in particular, he misinterpreted the Hebrew pro-
phesies. 'He was not *less* than the Hebrew Messiah, but
more.' No moral charge is established against him, until it
is shown, that in applying the old prophecies to himself, he
was *conscious* that they did not fit. His error was one of
mere fallibility in matters of intellectual and literary estimate. On the other hand, Jesus had an infallible moral
perception, which reveals itself to the true-hearted reader,
and is testified by the common consciousness of Christendom.
It has pleased the Creator to give us one sun in the heavens,
and one Divine soul in history, in order to correct the aber-
rations of our individuality, and unite all mankind into one
family of God. Jesus is to be presumed to be perfect until
he is shown to be imperfect. Faith in Jesus, is not reception of propositions, but reverence for a person; yet this is
not the condition of salvation or essential to the Divine
favour. Such is the scheme, abridged from the ample discussion of my eloquent friend." *

And now what answer does any Christian make to
this plea of Mr. Newman, that he is opposing Mr.
Martineau? Why, in the first place, just this: that
whatever Mr. Martineau's opinions may be, — that supposing Jesus Christ to have been only a man — not even
a *great* man, but only an ordinary man, who, nevertheless, had enjoyed some *little* reputation of being a
good man, — Mr. Martineau, and the Unitarians, and
the Trinitarians, and all the world, have just reason
to complain of Mr. Newman's contempt of all the
commonest maxims of historic criticism in judging him.
He does not treat Jesus Christ even with the justice
and candour due to the most common historic personage. He puts *impressions* for *facts*, *fancies* for *arguments*; speaks when the documents are silent, silences
them where they speak; imagines evidence where he
pleases, and ignores it where he pleases; — and all for

* Phases, pp. 140, 141.

the delightful purpose of proving Christ morally imperfect! And now for an example or two.

Take his account of Christ's answer to the Pharisees who came to entrap him by their question respecting the tribute-money, and whose insidious villany He baffles by saying, " Render unto Cæsar the things that are Cæsar's, and unto God the things that are God's." On this answer (though not one syllable is added by Christ himself, nor by the historians who record it, that can for a moment countenance the fancy,) Mr. Newman ventures to say that he cannot but think our Lord " shows a vain conceit in the cleverness of his answer;"* and adds that he cannot regard his " error" as a merely intellectual " error," since " blundering self-sufficiency is a moral weakness." What can for a moment justify this most gratuitous imputation of " vain conceit" and "blundering self-sufficiency,"† where there is not one syllable *on the face of the history* — not the faintest shade of expression — to justify it? Mr. Newman may perhaps say, as he elsewhere says in reference to other points‡, that he is only giving his *impressions* — " a statement of fact concerning his own mind, and that is all. *Valeat quantum!* " Whereupon the reader will say, of course, who cares for a million of his *impressions*, without evidence for them?. and to *that* question I, for one, should not know what answer to give. This sort of criticism is not to do justice

* Phases, p. 152. See the entire passages in the Appendix, No. II.
† Some of the words so liberally bestowed on our Lord in this chapter will inevitably suggest to every reader an application of which the writer was little conscious. A man may shoot his arrow with exact perpendicularity over his own head. It smites the invisible and impassive air, and does no harm to *that;* but the missile descending, according to the law of gravity, with the exact force with which it has been projected, may smite full sore the unhappy archer himself.
‡ Phases, p. 176.

to Christ, even if he were nothing but an ordinary character of history; for it is to *fancy* evidence, not to produce it or sift it.

Nothing, again, can exceed the eccentric criticism with which Mr. Newman introduces these strictures. He says that to "imagine that because a coin bears Cæsar's head, *therefore* it is Cæsar's property, and that he may demand to have as many of such coins as he chooses paid over to him, is puerile and notoriously false. The circulation of foreign coin of every kind was as common in the Mediterranean then as now, and everybody knew that the coin was the property of the *holder*, not of him whose head it bore. *Thus*, the reply of Jesus, which pretended to be a moral decision, was *unsound and absurd;* yet it is uttered in a tone of dictatorial wisdom, and ushered in by a grave rebuke, ' Why tempt ye me, hypocrites ?'"*

The meaning here imputed to our Lord's words is " puerile" enough, but the puerility is in Mr. Newman's criticism, not in Christ's answer. How far-fetched is this gloss, (yet needful to make Christ's decision " *unsound*,") compared with the obvious interpretation generally put on his words; " Since you thus recognise, in fact, Cæsar's political authority by receiving the current coin which bears his image, render to him the political allegiance which you thereby acknowledge; and ' to God the things that are God's.'" This Mr. Newman calls *evading* the question; he has heard " the interpretation," he says, " from high Trinitarians, which indicates to him *how dead* is their *moral sense* in every thing which concerns the conduct of Jesus." Polite words! But Mr. Martineau tells him that Unitarians are involved in the same condemnation! What modest confidence there must be in a criticism which will not

* Phases, p. 152.

only have Christ in the wrong, but, to make it out, is
ready to affirm that the *moral sense* of almost all Christians must be half dead into the bargain! This, surely,
is not to weigh evidence, but to assume oneself infallible
in the matter, though to do so would imply that not
only Christ, but nearly every body else, was not merely
fallible, but grossly defective in moral sensibility! The
whole passage (that Mr. Newman may not accuse me
of not quoting enough) the reader will find in Appendix (No. II.), where he will see with what complacency
our critic proposes for Christ a *better* answer than Christ
gave; as well as with what humanity he apologises for the
innocent Pharisees, by asking, was it not their " duty"
thus to prove, by their questions, the wisdom of one
who professed to be an " authoritative teacher"? Here,
again, we see fancy at work, and the history ignored;
if the history was to be supposed faithful at all, why
should it be assumed that the answer of Christ is correctly given — it assuredly is not correctly *interpreted*
—while the account of the Pharisees is quite a mistake?
The only answer one can conceive is, that if Christ
must be proved in the wrong, then the Pharisees must
be presumed in the right. The critic can imagine conceit
in Christ when the history is wholly silent; he silences
the history when it speaks against the Pharisees. He
imagines they came, simple, innocent souls, in pure
good faith, to try the wisdom of Christ as a teacher
sent from God !

Take another example of the injustice done to Christ
by this style of criticism. After Christ on a certain
occasion had been inculcating the duty of " watchful-
ness" by a striking parable, Peter asks, " Lord, speakest
thou this parable to us or also unto all?" Mr. Newman says, " who would not have hoped an ingenuous
reply — ' To you only,' or ' To everybody ?' Instead

of which, so inveterate is his tendency to *muffle up* the simplest things in mystery, he replies, ' Who then is that faithful and wise steward,' &c. &c., and entirely evades reply to the very natural question." * The answer is, first, that the parable in which our Lord " evades reply," is itself, to most understandings, a sufficient indication of the way in which our Lord intended the question should be answered, namely, that he *did* speak to all, and not to some only; but, secondly, in the last verse of the thirteenth chapter of Mark, after the same or a similar parable, he gives that very categorical decision demanded, " And what I say unto *you* I say unto *all*, watch." This supplemental confirmation of one gospel by words found in another, is, as in so many other cases, a strong indication of the reality of the events, and the fidelity of the narrative. The haste with which Mr. Newman pronounces his judgment on Christ's " tendency to muffle up the simplest things in mystery," requires no comment. Without sufficiently examining facts, or ignoring them when it meets with them, " free criticism " has an easy task indeed.

Take another example of the precarious criticism by which Mr. Newman does injustice to the character of our Lord, — still viewed as a *mere* man. He affirms that Jesus Christ intended to proclaim absolutely and indiscriminately the first principle of communism — a total " and abrupt renunciation of wealth ; " that what other men regard as general principles, which, like all other general principles, must be interpreted by the spirit, not by the letter, are to be pressed to the utmost rigour of literal interpretation — which those of *no* moralist will bear ; — or even that what was Christ's demand on his first personal emissaries, who were to go forth in the strength of their miraculous mission, " with-

* Phases, p. 155.

out scrip or purse," He designed should rule the conduct
of all his disciples then and through all time! The
answer to the "rich young man," whose self-righteous
conceit assured him that he had kept " *all* the commandments from his youth up," and whose demand of a
more rigid test was well met by a reply which disclosed
to him his weak point, and showed that he was mistaken
in supposing himself willing to pursue " eternal life" at
all hazards, Mr. Newman thinks was the answer which
Christ *would* have given to every inquiring disciple;
and that the maxim, " Sell that ye have, and give alms,"
Christ designed absolutely for every Christian and for
ever!*   Mr. Newman may say, perhaps, that he is
right in his criticism, and that the generality of the
world are wrong; but even then, what man but Mr.
Newman would proceed to assail the moral character,
even of a mere man, on a criticism so precarious that
not one out of ten thousand can see its force?   And
that they with good reason demur to it is plain
enough: for, if this astounding principle were the
corner-stone of Christ's teaching (as it must have been,
if a principle at all), how is it that Jesus Christ does
not uniformly mention it on the many occasions on
which he receives his disciples? how is it that when
Zaccheus declares he is going to give " the half of
his goods," in reparation of the wrongs inflicted by his
rapacity, Jesus Christ does not tell him that *that* was
not enough, and that he will not be let off without
giving the whole? how is it, that when " Rulers " believed on him, how is it that in his interview with
Nicodemus and others, he says nothing about this
grand prerequisite of discipleship? how is it that the
" rich Joseph of Arimathea " was still rich at Christ's
death, and had not long before become a " Christian

* See Appendix, No V.

socialist ? " how is it, when advising the rich men rather
to make choice as their guests of the " poor " than the
" rich," that he does not tell them that they have no
business to have any choice in the matter ? that all
their money was to be thrown into a common stock,
and that " no man was to call anything his own ?"
How is it that he says " The poor ye have always with
you," when he ought rather to have said, " There is to
be neither poor nor rich ?" How is it, when he reproved Martha " for being cumbered with much serv-
ing," that he does not also reprove her for wasting
the " joint-stock?" Our critic may, perhaps, say : —
" Oh! all this is rubbish — legend — no part of the true
history." Then how does he know that just the precept,
" Sell that ye have, and give alms," is the only part
that *is* true history ? Why does he retain just so much
as he thinks will make for his unenviable thesis, and
ignore all that makes against it ? Is *this* historic
criticism ?

But Mr. Newman imagines, as some others have
done, that his theory derives support from the conduct
of the Apostles and the Disciples at Jerusalem, at and
just after the Day of Pentecost. The generality of
commentators and critics (Neander among them) see in
this nothing but a temporary provision. It seems to
have been to meet the wants of the multitude of
" strangers," (then brought from all parts to Jerusalem)
just converted to the faith ; for whom the resident
Christians, in the ardour of their Christian love, dis-
solved for a time the connection of *meum* and *tuum*, and
" had all things common." That this is the common
sense view is seen by this, that nothing of the kind appears in the " New Testament" itself when the emer-
gency had passed away. It is also to most minds
conclusively proved to be the right view by Peter's

K

question to Ananias, — acknowledging his right to the
estate he had sold, *though* he was a professed Christian:
" Was it not in thy own power?" which it would *not*
have been had the fundamental principle of Christianity
demanded its surrender.

But at all events, with such a mass of evidence
against him, with the all but unanimous assertion of
critics and commentators on the other side, who but
this critic would feel sufficiently secure of his judgment
to found upon it a charge of "*moral* unsoundness" in
the Founder of Christianity?

And lastly, looking still at Christ as a mere man,
who but our critic — even if Christ *had* proclaimed
the principle of the community 'of property — would
have founded upon it grave inferences of moral imperfection? I think the principle politically as pernicious
and mistaken as Mr. Newman can do, and that far, far
less than the *human* wisdom of Christ can see it to be so.
But does it necessarily follow that men who have maintained any such mistaken principle are morally unsound?
Would he deal out the same measure to all the philosophers who have maintained this or similar false *political*
notions? Would he so deal with Plato, who so zeal-
ously maintained this very dogma?

Again; still looking at Christ merely as a *man*, how
shall we characterise the charges, the odious charges,
connected with the circumstances of his death, where
not one syllable of the history justifies the interpretation which Mr. Newman puts upon Christ's character
and actions? In order to give a colour to them at all,
we must ignore all the history, and re-write it; but
then, if we thus cast aside all the history we have,
what sort of historic criticism is it which decides against
the character of Christ? If what is *said* for him be assumed false, what right have we to assume that what is

not even said, but simply fancied, on behalf of his per-
secutors, is true? Not contented with his previous
charges of " vain conceit," " arrogance and error combined;" " fanatical and mischievous precepts;" and
" mistakes which indicate moral unsoundness," Mr.
Newman further represents our Saviour as denouncing
the atrocious wickedness of the rulers, not because the
charges were true and the condemnation just, but as
guiltily and of set purpose exasperating them to murder
him in order that he might escape the difficulty of
maintaining his claims to be the Messiah, which, it
seems, he had long *hoped* he was(!), but of which he
had recently had great misgivings, and now felt to be
untenable! I defy any one to produce from all the
literature of Europe a passage so luxuriant in extravagance as the following:—" The time arrived at last
when Jesus felt that he must publicly assert Messiahship; and this was certain to bring things to an issue.
I suppose him to have hoped that he was Messiah, until
hope and the encouragement given him by Peter and
others grew into a persuasion strong enough to act
upon, but not always strong enough to still misgivings.
I say, I suppose this, but I build nothing on my supposition. I however see, that when he had resolved to
claim Messiahship publicly, one of two results was
inevitable, *if* that claim was ill-founded; viz., either he
must have become an impostor in order to screen his
weakness, or he must have retracted his pretensions
amid much humiliation, and have retired into privacy
to learn sober wisdom. From these alternatives *there
was escape only by death,* and upon death Jesus purposely
rushed."*

Here I do not stay to ask what are the *grounds* for
the pleasant " suppositions " above; for our critic says

---

* Phases, p. 158. For ample extracts see Appendix, No. VI.

he " builds nothing on them;" and it is well, for
nothing can stand on such mere quicksand. To write
thus is to indulge fancies, not to criticise history : but I
ask, first, how does all this imputation of low and gross
villany harmonise with the impressions drawn from the
whole of the only accounts we have? and, secondly, if
we *reject* those accounts, then, as before, what right
have we to form even a conjecture to the prejudice of
Christ? But the crowning absurdity of the whole is,
the fine dilemma which Mr. Newman has constructed,
and which, like most of his dilemmas, are dilemmas from
which no one is in danger but himself. He says, " One
of two results was inevitable if that claim was ill-
founded ; viz., either Christ must have become an
impostor, in order to screen his weakness, or he must
have retracted his pretensions amid much humiliation,
and have retired into privacy to learn sober wisdom."

Mr. Newman, perhaps, does not like to say that
Christ was an *impostor* at the *time* he thus planned this
curious suicide at the expense of other people's guilt ;
and so he tells us, that if he had lived he must have
become an impostor, or retracted his claims to Messiahship; *therefore* he resolved to die in order to escape the
alternative ! Did ever any man but Mr. Newman suppose that *this* was escaping the alternative? Would
not the mere fact of his dying to escape the alternative
of *becoming* an impostor (if any man ever did, would,
or could die for any such purpose) convict him of
already *being* an impostor? Is it not very much as if
we were told that a man committed suicide in order to
escape the alternative of *becoming* a thief, which he felt
that he must be, if he did not turn an honest man ?
Would not the very act prove, if it proved any thing
but sheer idiocy, that the man was already in heart *such*
a thief that he would sooner die than *not* be one?

However, such is the theory which Mr. Newman thinks is fairly *extractible* by " free criticism " from the history, which, however, must be all set aside, and a pure romance substituted in its place, to give the faintest colour to it. " Clearly," (to use a favourite formula of Mr. Newman's, but I hope with more reason,) if we thus throw aside the history, then we are simply reduced to silence. As before, we cannot reject all that makes for Christ, and substitute fancies that make against him. I deliberately say, that if we look at Christ as a mere man, — as one of whom we know nothing but what the Evangelical narrative, restricted to the purely human element, discloses to us, — there is not a man who has any pretensions, — I do not say to Christianity, but to candour or common sagacity, — who will call this (I will not say *probable*, but even the flimsiest plausible) historical criticism; and that if there is one thing which, even rejecting all Christ's supernatural claims, the narrative of his life rivets on the soul, it is that Jesus Christ was utterly incapable of the mingled atrocities and absurdities here attributed to him!

Once more : let Jesus Christ only have been a great sage, will any one say that the criticism on the Parables — those wonderful compositions, which have fixed the admiration of all ages, — which condense more meaning into smaller compass than any of the apophthegms of sages and philosophers, — wisdom clothed at the same time in the selectest, yet the simplest imagery, — is conceived in the spirit of common justice and candour? — " Strip the Parables," says Mr. Newman, " of the imagery, and you find that sometimes one thought has been dished up four or five times, and generally, that an idea is dressed into sacred grandeur. This mystical method made a little wisdom go a great way with the multi-

tude; and to such a mode of economising resources the
instinct of the uneducated man betakes itself, when he is
claiming to act a part for which he is imperfectly prepared."*

Of Christ's parabolic style generally Mr. Newman
speaks thus:—" But not to be tedious, in general I
must complain that Jesus purposely adopted an enigmatical and pretentious style of teaching, unintelligible
to his hearers, and needing explanation in private . . . . .
Christian divines are used to tell us that this mode was
peculiarly instructive to the vulgar of Judæa: and they
insist on the great wisdom displayed in his choice of the
lucid parabolical style. But, in Matthew, xiii. 10—15.,
Jesus is made confidentially to avow precisely the opposite reason; viz., that he desires the vulgar *not* to
understand him, but only the select few to whom he
gives private explanations. I confess I believe the
Evangelist rather than the modern divine."†

We here see Mr. Newman stumbling at the apparent
paradox that parables were used clearly to *convey* the
meaning, and yet parables were used to *veil* the meaning. If both purposes had been affirmed of the very
same parables, one could have understood the objection.
Who but our critic could have any difficulty in seeing
that a parable, like any other form of figurative language, may be aptly used for both purposes, and often
has been so in other compositions besides those of the
New Testament; it may be used either to illustrate a
truth, or to give it in outline; to make it clear, or to veil
it. But this, involving a twofold aspect of the same
thing, seems a troublesome perplexity to our critic's
simplicity of understanding, and he must therefore have

---

* Phases, p. 154. For the entire passage see Appendix, No. III.
† Phases, p. 153.

the parable always clear or always obscure,—always
light or always darkness !

But enough of what Mr. Newman says of the Parables; the mere memory of some of them will at once
show the reader the vanity of his criticism. The parable of the Prodigal Son," or the " Good Samaritan,"
shivers it all to atoms. Not all the petty carping in the
world can prevent or will prevent the effect they have
produced, and will ever produce, not only on the
humblest but the greatest minds; on philosophers and
peasants, on age and childhood, on all imagination and
·all sensibility;—in a word, on the heart of humanity.
Mr. Newman's criticism may make men wonder at his
taste, or the want of it, but it will not make them.
despise the parables of Jesus Christ.

Again, take the alleged inconsistency of the statements respecting Christ's unwillingness to perform miracles, on some occasions when challenged to do so.
Surely no reader of the New Testament will deny, that
miracles enough are *recorded;* and that therefore, if
really performed, and unbelief asked for *more,* our
Saviour might well be offended at such obstinacy of
unbelief. If Mr. Newman says, " Yes, but none of
these miracles *were* performed: they were all fables;"—
then, as before, if he rejects the mass of the records, how
is he so sure that the narrative respecting Christ's being
challenged to perform the miracles, and being unwilling
to do so, is certainly true ? Why will he destroy every
thing that can explain his conduct, as purely fabulous,
and yet assume that the narrative of the actions which
it *would* explain, is trustworthy? How is it that he
thus ignores every thing that can make for Christ as
fabulous, but will not allow anything to be so, which, on
the supposition that it alone is retained, makes against
him ? As before, the duty of a decorous *silence* would

be the proper inference from *such* a style of historic criticism.

All this is said, and much more might have been said, upon the supposition that Christ was a *mere* man, a common historical personage, to meet Mr. Newman on his own grounds. I now proceed one step further in the argument; and remark that, to many other of Mr. Newman's criticisms, it is possible, I should imagine, for even Mr. Martineau to reply. I know not what Mr. Martineau's degree of historical scepticism in relation to the Gospels may be; how far he feels himself at liberty to pare away the historical element; to question fact, as well as explode miracle; but if he admits any special superhuman *moral* endowments in Christ at all — as his language would sometimes imply — he has, I suppose, a conclusive answer to Mr. Newman's *great* argument. If he *does* deny *every* super-human endowment, as well as a Divine Nature, then Mr. Newman's argument is of force; otherwise, hardly so. Mr. Newman reasons, that if any one contends that Christ is a mere man, then he *must* hold that Christ must be morally imperfect; in other words, that God either *could* not or *would* not endow any human creature with capacities for exhibiting a perfect human virtue! Truly it is a nice little metaphysical theorem; but, like Mr. Newman's theories of the " origin of evil," will seem to the world but scant in proof.

Mr. Newman (as is too often the case) wraps up his meaning in language quite as " enigmatical " as that he attributes so freely to Christ. He expressly affirms that Christ, if merely man, *could* not exhibit a " perfect morality," because being man, he would be *essentially* imperfect, morally and in all respects. But he also uses the expressions (as if they were equivalent), that, being *finite*, He is to be assumed not to " *exhaust all*

perfection" (p. 143.),—that, being "finite" in every
other respect, he could not be "*infinite* in moral perfection." (p. 142.) To most persons, the idea of a Being,
just what man *ought* to be,—a model of human virtue,
—would be very distinct from that of one "exhausting
all perfection," and being "*infinite* in moral perfection."
Mr. Newman always speaks just as if they were the
same thing. Just add to this what he calls "a first
principle of thought with him,"—that "no sort of perfection is possible to man,"—no matter, I suppose, how
God may create or endow him,— and you have an easy
demonstration that Jesus Christ *could* not be "morally
perfect" as man. Whether God *has* ever created such
a Being of course depends on proper historical evidence;
Mr. Newman contents himself with the "high *à priori*
road." The species in general are morally imperfect,
as *finite; therefore* Christ *must* have been so! There
is a delightful and cheerful little corollary, which Mr.
Newman ought to have appended to his strange metaphysics of the finite and the infinite; namely, that
there neither is, can, nor will be in this or any world a
single created being who is, even within the limits of
such created nature, "perfect," or free from sin and
frailty. For being "finite," he could not exhibit
"infinite moral perfection," or "*exhaust all perfection.*"
A pleasant look-out for the universe! With most men,
the idea of a "Perfect Man," who is not *necessarily* an
Infinite God also, will be tolerably distinct.

This argument, he says, is what a Trinitarian would
employ.*

The Trinitarian's argument is mainly founded, first,
on the whole evidence, internal and external, that Christianity is of Divine origin; and secondly, admitting that,

* Phases, p. 141.

— that we cannot fairly account for the whole strain of what its Founder says of himself, or what others say of him, without coming to the conclusion that he is neither like any other man, nor exclusively man at all.   Most Trinitarians, I fancy, would hesitate to affirm that it is impossible for God to endow a human being with capacities to exhibit a perfect human virtue.

On the most attenuated theory, which admits any special endowments in Christ, the illustration of Mr. Newman appears absurd.   He asks, whether, if any one claimed "moral perfection for his old schoolmaster, or his parish-priest," he would not have a right to resent his claims! He might have waited till some one *had* claimed perfection for "his old schoolmaster or parish-priest." Meantime, it would be well for him to consider that it is very curious, and deserves some solution, that so many millions of Trinitarians and of Unitarians, amongst them so many men of the highest order of intellect and the largest culture, should have claimed moral perfection for Jesus Christ, while, it seems, there is not the smallest danger of their ever claiming anything of the sort for "any old schoolmaster or parish-priest;" no; nor even for a James, a Peter, or a Paul, or any other of the sons of men! And this consideration alone might have led him to suppress any such comparisons; the question, to any one who admits a special commission, is as regards a Being, at all events, preternaturally endowed, even if not superhuman himself, "and not about some old schoolmaster or parish-priest!"

To the *ordinary* Unitarian, of course, — whatever becomes of Mr. Martineau and his hypothesis, — and still more to the Trinitarian, the argument between these two gentlemen ceases to have any interest, except so far as it is manifestly unjust to Christ, even as an ordinary historic personage, that any man should assail him as Mr. Newman has done; and that it fills them with disgust and horror to reflect that this gratuitous odium is cast on one whom they do *not* regard as a common historic personage. The *ordinary* Unitarian believes, at all events, that Christ was preternaturally endowed as no man ever was before, or will be again — miraculously commissioned to make good his lofty claims — and invested with the character of the Judge of all men. Any argument on the assumption that, supposing Christ to have been man only, *therefore*, however preternaturally endowed by the Father of Lights, with knowledge, wisdom, and virtue, it was *impossible* he should exhibit a perfect *human* excellence, but must have been encompassed with imperfections and foibles, because a *man*, would be to them simply ridiculous. If Mr. Newman assert it, as, by consequence, he must with his theory of the Finite, the Unitarians would do well to hold him to a full proof of this pretty little metaphysical theorem, that God either never *would* or never *could* enable a single individual of our race to exhibit a perfect human wisdom or a perfect human virtue! It will last *his* time.

To the Trinitarians, of course, such an argument would be of no avail; and with them, therefore, Mr. Newman does not urge it. Yet he cannot avoid caricaturing their doctrine. Speaking of Christ's death and his relation to the instruments by whom He suffered, he says, — " If any one holds Jesus to be not amenable to the laws of human morality, I am not now reasoning with such a one. But if any one claims for him a human perfection, then, I say, that his conduct on this occasion was neither laudable nor justifiable: far otherwise."* They do not af-

* Phases, p. 159. Appendix, No. VI.

firm that, considered as man, he was not amenable to human morality. How can they, when they believe that he was the great ideal of human morality? But believing him not merely man, nor only man, they do not think that all his acts are to be measured by what all men may do; and in *that* they are no more inconsistent than in affirming that fathers and their children, kings and their subjects, are alike " amenable to the laws of human morality," though the difference of their relations will make *that* rightful authority in the one which would be simply insolent contumacy and lawless arrogance in the other. Carry this principle fairly out to the modifications which not only a difference of *relations,* but a superiority of *nature,* would impose, — apply them to Him who is believed to be Son of God as well as Son of Man, and the supposed anomalies disappear.

In relation to Christ's death, Mr. Newman's redoubtable dilemma is easily met by both Unitarian and Trinitarian. If Mr. Newman affirm that *nothing* could justify Christ in assailing the rulers, supposing him merely Man, the answer is, that He denounced their crimes, and righteously denounced them, — did the truest and the justest thing, — regardless of the consequences. If it be said, that even though he were the Son of God, *foreknowing* the results, it was a crime to do this, — the answer is the same; " fiat justitia, ruat cœlum." If it be made a difficulty at all, it will carry us one step further, and bring us to one of those metaphysical theorems, which Mr. Newman is too apt to forget, but which will last our day, — namely, how it is that God, foreseeing that the punishment which He inflicts will exasperate men, and make them worse, nevertheless inflicts it, and equitably works out the results of His Providence, by means of the crimes and follies He infallibly foresees, and yet does not prevent. If Christ was merely man, He was a martyr to "loving righteousness and hating iniquity;"—if God as well, He did no more than God does! When Mr. Newman has reconciled the absolute prescience of God with the free will and responsibility of his guilty creatures, it will be time to consider the difficulties in this last problem.

And now, what, after all, does all the carping criticism of this chapter amount to? Little as it is in itself, it absolutely vanishes,—it is felt that the Christ here portrayed *cannot* be the right interpretation of the history,—in the face of all those glorious scenes with which the Evangelical narrative abounds, but of which there is here an entire oblivion. But Humanity will not forget them; men still wonder at the " gracious words which proceeded out of Christ's mouth," and persist in saying, " Never man spake like this man." The brightness of the brightest names pales and wanes before the radiance which shines from the person of Christ. The scenes at the tomb of Lazarus, at the gate of Nain, in the happy family at Bethany, in the " upper room," where He instituted the beautiful feast which should for ever consecrate His memory, and bequeathed to His disciples the legacy of His love; the scenes in the Garden of Gethsemane, on the summit of Calvary, and at the Sepulchre; the sweet remembrance of the patience with which He bore wrong, the gentleness with which He rebuked it, and the love with which He forgave it; the thousand acts of benign condescension by which He well earned for Himself, from self-righteous pride and censorious hypocrisy, the name of the " friend of publicans and sinners;" — these, and a hundred things more which crowd those concise memorials of love and sorrow with such prodigality of beauty and of pathos, will still continue to charm and attract the soul of humanity, and on these the highest genius as well as the humblest mediocrity will love to dwell. These things lisping infancy loves to hear on its mother's knees, and over them age, with its grey locks, bends in devoutest reverence. No; before the infidel can prevent the influence of these compositions, he must get rid of the Gospels themselves, or he must supplant them by *fictions* yet more wonderful! Ah! what bitter irony has involuntarily escaped me! But if the last be impossible, at least the Gospels must cease to exist before Infidelity can succeed. Yes, before infidels can prevent men from thinking as they ever have done of Christ, they must blot out the gentle words with which, in the presence of austere hypocrisy, the Saviour welcomed that timid guilt that could only express its silent love in an agony of tears; — they must blot out the words addressed to the dying penitent, who, softened by the majestic patience of the mighty Sufferer, detected at last the Monarch under the veil of sorrow, and cast an imploring glance to be " remembered by Him when He came into His Kingdom;"—they must blot out the scene in which the demoniacs — or the maniacs, if the infidel will, for it does not help him, — sat listening at his feet, and "in their right mind;"—they must blot out the remembrance of the tears which He shed at the grave of Lazarus, not surely for him whom He was about to raise, but in pure sympathy with the sorrows of humanity, for the myriad myriads of desolate mourners, who could not, with Mary, fly to Him and say, " Lord, if Thou hadst been here my mother,—brother,—sister had not died!" —they must blot out the record of those miracles which charm us, not only as the proofs of His mission, and guarantees of the truth of His doctrine, but as they illustrate the benevolence of His character, and are

types of the spiritual cures His Gospel can yet perform; — they must blot out the scenes of the Sepulchre,
where love and veneration lingered, and saw what was
never seen before, but shall henceforth be seen to the
end of time, — the Tomb itself irradiated with angelic
forms, and bright with the presence of Him " who
brought life and immortality to light; "— they must blot
out the scene where deep and grateful love wept so
passionately, and found Him unbidden at her side, —
type of ten thousand times ten thousand, who have
" sought the grave to weep there," and found joy and
consolation in Him, "whom though unseen they loved; "
— they must blot out the discourses in which He took
leave of His disciples, the majestic accents of which
have filled so many departing souls with patience and
with triumph; — they must blot out the yet sublimer
words in which He declares Himself " the Resurrection
and the Life," — words which have led so many millions
more to breathe out their spirits with child-like trust,
and to believe, as the gate of death closed behind them,
they would see Him who is invested with the " keys of
the invisible world," " who opens and no man shuts,
and shuts and no man opens," letting in through the
portal which leads to immortality the radiance of the
skies; — they must blot out, they must destroy, these
and a thousand other such things, before they can prevent Him from having the Pre-eminence, who loved,
because He loved *us*, to call Himself the " Son of
Man," though angels called Him the " Son of God."

It is in vain to tell men it is an *illusion*. If it be an
illusion, *every variety of experiment* proves it to be *inveterate*, and will not be dissipated by a million of
Strausses and Newmans! *Probatum est.* At His feet
guilty humanity of diverse races and nations for eighteen
hundred years has come to pour forth in faith and love

its sorrows, and finds there " the peace which the world can neither give nor take away." Myriads of aching heads and weary hearts have found and will find repose there, and have invested Him with veneration, love, and gratitude, which will never, never be paid to any other name than His.

Nor let it be said it is the moral necessities of man — his guilt and sorrows — which thus attract him to the Saviour. As a *fact*, it matters not; the illusion, if *illusion* it be, cannot be dispelled by that consideration; for the moral necessities of the human heart—its guilt and sorrows — are not likely to cease in a hurry, nor to be met in any other or better way, than the comprehensive sympathy of Him who " was in all points tempted like as we are," and can be " touched with the feeling of our infirmities, though without sin." As long as the memorials of His acts and words remain, so long will He continue to exert His strange power over humanity, and until infidelity *destroys* them, there is no hope of its success.

But, in fact, the plea is not true. Multitudes of the loftiest minds have deeply investigated His claims, and admitted them; genius of the highest order in science and poetry, and art, has brought its richest trophies, and humbly laid them at His feet; the very chiefest of the western sages, like those of the east, have come to offer Him " frankincense, and gold, and myrrh," the noblest offerings of intellect, the divinest performances of art. Genius, true to its instincts after the beautiful and the sublime, even when it has not been constrained to pay a homage yet better than that of the intellect and the imagination, has not been insensible to His claims; it has poured forth a richer tribute to His honour than all the mythologies of antiquity could boast. He it is whose character and image have chiefly weaned men from their base idolatry of mere Power and Intellect, and made them see that in moral greatness, there is a radiance brighter still. He it is who has chiefly made them recognise the essential identity of the " beautiful and the good." No one of the human race has exerted one thousandth part of the power, directly or indirectly, in moulding the thought and feeling, in developing the practical energies of the most various and cultured nations of the earth. And if it be said, " And have not other religions, besides that dedicated to Christ, called forth the homage of the intellect and the tributes of genius?" I answer, Yes, though not in so great a measure, nor anything like it, nor from half the various races that have paid homage to His name. But in relation to the present point—the probability of this illusion, if illusion, being dispelled, — *here* is the difference. Those other and false religions have never stood the tests of Christianity, — nay, have never even waited to come fairly in contact with them. *That* is the great difference in calculating whether the influence of Christ is likely now to be destroyed. *They* perish before the influences which Christianity resists and surmounts; cradled in barbarism, nurtured by local and national genius, they are *hybrids* of the religious instinct and poetic fancy, and, like other hybrids, they cannot propagate. Military conquest, political revolution, shatter them to pieces; they do *not* pass from race to race, nor emigrate from clime to clime. What is still more fatal to them, is advancing science: these things of darkness are at once transfixed by the shafts of light; the mythologies of Greece and Rome were laughed at long before they were finally extinguished; a score of mythologies more have perished since that day; at this moment Brahma and Vishnu are quaking on their precarious thrones; and Old Buddha lies sprawling on the rivers

L

of China. It is not so with the religion of Christ; in the midst of the most literate and cultured ages which the world has yet seen, and which Christianity itself has tended to produce (for they have sprung up contemporaneously with its influence, and its realms still mark, with more distinctness than anything else, the frontiers of intellectual day and night, being brightest where it is brightest, and usually brighter than elsewhere even where it is comparatively dim), in *these* ages, Christ still holds his own; and though in the very midst of His church, arise from time to time an endless succession of adversaries, they cannot prevail. Its followers retain their faith; genius, large, cultured, comprehensive, soberly declares its evidence impregnable. Pascal and Butler, and men like them, endowed with the most comprehensive minds, after the profoundest study, have bowed at the Redeemer's shrine; and the greatest master of Epic song, rich with all the culture of all ages, " rich with the spoils of time," — whose strains so emulate that still sublimer poesy, on which his lofty muse was modelled, *believed* when he wrote his " Paradise Lost," not merely that he was " adorning a poetic theme," but that he was celebrating fact; — the conflict of Immortal Hate and Immortal Love. Who shall dissipate this deep illusion, thus inveterate, and solicited by every means of cure, but in vain?

And is this Personage, who has so taken captive the sons of men, and so inscribed His image on the soul of humanity, likely to be injured by a little bit of carping and captious sophistry? The critic might as well stretch out his hand to pluck Orion from his sphere.

SECTION XII.

CHARGES OF "PROFANITY," AND SO FORTH.

MR. NEWMAN says, " The sceptic whom he (the author
of the ' Eclipse') sets at me is essentially a profane intellect, free to ridicule the most fundamental principles of
the New Testament. He can, at pleasure, not only disown
— ' God hath chosen the poor of this world, rich in faith,'
— and ' not many wise are called : ' he also assumes that
acuteness of understanding, without sanctity of heart,
opens divine knowledge to us, and that a man who
blunders in questions of history and of literature ought
to be despised in religion. Such pleas are vehemently
pressed against me by this Mr. Harrington, and (unless
the author is most grossly iniquitous) are believed by
the author." * Is it not strange to hear Mr. Newman,
who has written the chapter on the " Moral Perfection
of Christ," — who rejects everything that is preternatural in Christianity, — who would deal with the
New Testament just as cavalierly as with Cicero —
nay, more, so one would think, for he affirms that " the
Latin moralists effected what (strange to think !) the
New Testament writers alone could not do ; " † — who
retains no one knows how small a modicum of what is
found between the covers of that book, and interprets
even that in an esoteric sense, — is it not strange,
I say, that he should feel himself in a condition to
rebuke a " profane intellect as free to ridicule the most

* Phases, p. 187.   † Phases, p. 97.

L 2

fundamental principles of the New Testament?" Or
does he expect a *sceptic* to be more ceremonious with
modern spiritualism than Mr. Newman is with Christianity? or, lastly, does he think that even a sceptic
cannot discern the difference between ridiculing modern
spiritualism and ridiculing Christianity? However,
he is quite mistaken in supposing that I think, or
that Harrington thought, that "acuteness of understanding, without sanctity of heart, opens divine
knowledge to us, and that a man who blunders in
questions of history and of literature ought to be despised in religion."

In the absence of citation and reference here, it is
rather hard to know on what Mr. Newman founds his
allegation; but if he means that Harrington may be
suspected of "despising men in religion because they
have blundered in questions of literature and history,"
on account of his stating that, on the *spiritualist hypothesis*, the Apostles must have been either the most
"abominable impostors, or the most miserable fanatics," *
one cannot but admire the candour and discernment of
Mr. Newman. Mere "blunders in literature and history!" No, I here "endorse" every word that Harrington says. If the Apostles "*untruly* affirmed that
they saw and did the things they *say* they saw and did,"
they *must* have been either the vilest impostors or the
most visionary of fanatics. They may well be "despised in religion," for they were fit only for Newgate
or Bedlam. The reader will not forget that it is on
the spiritualist hypothesis that Harrington is, as usual,
arguing.

Nor am I of opinion that "acuteness of intellect without sanctity of heart will" effectually "open divine
knowledge to us." But, I think, — and I rather think I

* Eclipse, p. 43.

am still likely to think,— that if there be, as Mr. Newman
contends and I concede, a religious element in Man, —
not in this man or that man, not in one here and there,
but in Man,— then that the evidence which substantiates
any *true* theory of religion must be, at least, tolerably
appreciable by every man who sincerely examines it.
The theory of "The Soul," if *true*, surely must be addressed to all, not to a few happily constituted minds; or
would Mr. Newman say that he wrote only for those who
were already of his mind? If so, why did he write at
all? If not, why does he wonder that men think themselves competent to criticise? What would be thought
of Christianity, if, addressing all men, it should not only
say (what it *does* say), that only those can fully comprehend it who embrace it, and so *experience* its power to
make good its claims, but that its evidence could not be
at all appreciated by any but such? that, if accepted, it
had nothing, *before* its acceptance, to convince the intellect of those who as yet had not embraced it, and who,
before embracing it, could not have that evidence which
experience alone can give? nothing to rebuke those who
would not examine it, or, examining it, rejected it? This
is not the case with Christianity, I trow; nor can it be
the case with any other system of religion which addresses Man as Man, and gives the true theory of our
religious nature. Harrington himself has so truly stated
the point, that I am surprised that Mr. Newman should
thus have mistaken either the sceptic or myself.

"What title has Mr. Newman, when avowedly explaining the phenomena of the religious faculty, which
he asserts to be inherent in *humanity*—though how they
should need explaining, if *his* theory be true, I know
not, —what title has he, when men deny that they are
conscious of the facts he describes, to take refuge in his
own private revelations and that of the few whose pri-

vilege it is to be 'born again' by a mysterious law
which he says it is impossible for us to investigate?
. . . . . This is not to delineate the religious
nature of humanity, — but to reveal — yes, and to
reveal *externally* — the religious nature of the elect
few, — and few they are indeed, who, by a mysterious
infidel Calvinism, are permitted to attain, by direct
intuition, and independent of all external revelation,
the true sentiments and experiences of spiritual insight.
. . . . If the answer merely respected the
practical value of a theory of spiritual sentiments,
. . . . . then Mr. Newman's answer might have
some force; for, certainly, only he who reduced that
theory to practice, or attempted to do so, would have a
right to conclude against the experience of him who
did. But it is obvious that the question respects the
theory itself, and especially the consciousness of those
terms of possible communion with God, those relations
of the soul to him, on the reception of which all the
said spiritual experience must depend."

My opinions are so far from being those attributed to
me by Mr. Newman, that though I believe that the
evidences of Christianity are appreciable by all who
will honestly examine them, yet its plenary proofs
are only for those who embrace it, live it, practise it;
and, for that very reason, I believe it is indestructible
on earth, for it *is* thus apprehended and cherished by
millions who know but very little of its evidences,
technically so called; who, surrendering themselves to
that great Teacher and Example it sets forth, and realis-
ing the peace which the world cannot give nor take
away, feel an invincible persuasion that the religion of
Christ comes from God and leads to Him; — a species of
evidence which no subtlety of reasoning will ever be
able to subvert. He who knows by this experimental

knowledge, can say to the most learned advocates of Christianity, "Now we believe, not because of thy saying, for we have seen Him ourselves."

In one of the voyages to discover a north-east passage — a course often tried before the still more numerous attempts to find one by the north-west (that enterprise so long pursued, and now so happily accomplished, and signalising, like so many other wonderful things, this eventful age), Barentz, a Dutch mariner, wintered on the eastern coast of Nova Zembla. It was the first party of Europeans that had ever spent the long polar night on those desolate shores. One day some of his crew came joyfully to Barentz, and declared they had seen part of the sun's disk grazing the horizon. He declared, on *scientific* grounds, that it was impossible. He assured them it *could* not be: they told him it *was*. The next day, and the next, fogs obstinately filled the sky, and the argument went on. On the third day the atmosphere was clear, and going out they saw the whole of the glorious orb above the edge of the horizon, and "rejoiced in its beams." They say that Barentz still declared that it could not be, or *ought* not to be. But did they heed him? No; what he said *could* not be, they saw, *was;* that was sufficient. The Christian can, in like manner, say: "I have *seen* the 'sun of righteousness' rising on the deep polar night of guilt and sorrow, and there is not only radiance, but warmth and 'healing in his beams.'" But, I suppose, even Barentz was competent to judge of the evidence, and might have preferred his eyes to his prepossessions. And even in like manner may the infidel be summoned and entitled to examine the evidences of Christianity. How much more may a sceptic freely canvass the doctrines of "The Soul!"

Mr. Newman quotes, with vivid indignation, the passage in which Harrington rebukes (as I conceive with merited severity) the use, by such "spiritual infidels" as Mr. Fellowes, of scriptural language, in a sense which the sacred writers would have utterly protested against.

"I cannot suspect *you* of hypocrisy," says Harrington, "but I confess I regard your language as *cant*. As I listen to you I seem to see a hybrid between Prynne and Voltaire. So far from its being true that you have renounced the letter of the Bible and retained its spirit, I think it would be much more correct to say, comparing your infidel hypothesis with your most spiritual dialect, that you have renounced the spirit of the Bible and retained its letter." "But are you in a condition to give an opinion?" said Fellowes, with a serious air. Mr. Newman says, in a like case, "'The natural man discerneth not the things of the spirit of God, because they are foolishness unto him:' it is 'the spiritual man only who searches the deep things of God.' At the same time, I freely acknowledge that I never could see my way clear to employ an argument which *looks* so arrogant; and the less, as I believe, with Mr. Parker, that the only true revelation is in all men alike." So far in the "Eclipse."

"Now," says Mr. Newman, "I will not here farther insist on the *monstrosity* of bringing forward St. Paul's words as mine, in order to *pour contempt* upon them; a monstrosity which no sophistry of Mr. Harrington can justify."*

I think the *real* monstrosity is, that men should so coolly employ St. Paul's words — for it is a quotation from the treatise on "The Soul," — to mean something totally different from any thing he intended to convey by them, and employ the dialect of the

* Reply, p. 182.

Apostles to contradict their doctrine;— *that* is the monstrosity; and that is it which the citation from Paul is designed to exemplify; it is not to pour contempt on *his* words, but on a "monstrous" perversion of them. It is very hard to conceive that Mr. Newman did not see this; but rather than suspect him of the meanness of doing what he so freely imputes to me— of wilfully suppressing a passage which would at once have explained the meaning — I will suppose it. But had he gone on only a *few* lines, the reader would have seen Harrington saying: — "Those words you have just quoted were well in Paul's mouth, and had a meaning. In yours, I suspect, they would have none, or a very different one. *He* dreamt that he was giving to mankind (vainly, as it seems) a system of doctrines and truths which were, many of them, transcendental to the human intellect and conscience, and which, when revealed, were very distasteful, and not *least* to you."*

Similar observations apply to another of Mr. Newman's particularly solemn rebukes.

In " The Eclipse " Mr. Fellowes says :—" *We* separate the dross of Christianity from its fine gold. ' The letter killeth, but the spirit giveth life. The fruit of the spirit is joy, peace, not ' "——

" Upon my word," said Harrington, laughing, " I shall presently begin to fancy that Douce Davie Deans has turned infidel, and shall expect to hear of right-hand fallings-off and left-hand defections."

" I request," says Mr. Newman, " the reader to consider whether, if we blot out the names *Fellowes* and *Christianity*, and put instead *Paul* and *Judaism*, Mr. Harrington's scoffs would not have equal weight." I answer, No; *because* the very gist of Harrington's ridicule is directed, not against *Paul*, but against Mr. *Fellowes*

* Eclipse, p. 46.

— against his abuse of Paul's language to express views
from which Paul would have recoiled with horror and
indignation — against the practical absurdity (calling it
by no harsher name) of using apostolic language while
utterly abjuring apostolic doctrine, — it is against *that*
that Harrington's sarcasm is directed ; — against a
" gospel" which Paul would utterly have disowned —
" another gospel" which is truly " *not* another," but
often a jumble (as I can bear witness in many instances)
of the most incongruous dogmas of private fanaticism,
stamped with the Christian mark, and so foisted into
current circulation.   This old custom-house practice of
" kissing the book " for the purpose of passing a con-
traband theology, has become too common among many
who utterly deny every distinctive feature of Christianity ; and, if carried out to its legitimate issue, would
lead to a state of mind just like that of Strauss, who,
having translated Christianity into a chaos of Hegelian
Pantheism, gravely discussed the question whether a
man in such a case might not still remain a clergyman,
and preach historical Christianity in the letter to please
his hearers, only taking due care not to let *them* understand that *he* understood it to be a thing of myths !
Mr. Newman tells me that " I clearly have a *profound
unbelief* in the Christian doctrine of Divine influence,
or I could not thus grossly insult it."*   I answer, God
forbid that I should " insult" it, whether it be the more
special influence — sometimes direct illumination, sometimes mere superintendence, which, as I fully believe,
presided over the composition of the sacred Scriptures —
or the ordinary, though mysterious action by which God
aids those who sincerely seek him, " in every good word
and work."   That which Harrington ridiculed — as the
context would have shown Mr. Newman if he had had

* Reply, p. 178.

the patience to read on, and the calmness to judge—is the
chaotic view of inspiration *formally* held by Mr. Parker
(who is *expressly referred* to *), to which Mr. Fellowes
is represented as adhering; a proof again, if any were
wanting, that Mr. Fellowes was not designed to be the
counterpart of Mr. Newman. Mr. Fellowes, indeed,
naturally enough, invests Mr. Newman with such inspiration, as he must, on Mr. Parker's theory, concede
it to everybody else, from whom he professed to derive
any "spiritual" benefit at all. And surely, according
to that theory, he is quite right; for *if* Minos and
Praxiteles, and Numa and Titian, are inspired in the
same sense as Moses and Christ—and Benjamin Frank-
lin as truly as any of them—lawgivers, artists, poets,
and painters — there are few men that might not put
in a claim; — nay, I think that the "Inventor of
Lucifer Matches" (at the introduction of whose name
Mr. Newman is so indignant) as well as the inventor
of "Eureka Shirts," and a good many more, must
also be admitted. As to the inventor of lucifer matches
in particular, I am thoroughly convinced he has shed
more light on the world, and been abundantly more
useful to it, than many a cloudy expositor of modern
"spiritualism." Mr. Newman further says: "I am
sorry to add, that in order to avert the indignation
of his readers, and pretend it is some conceit and
vanity of mine which he is ridiculing, he endeavours,
in pages 10. 14. 46., and elsewhere, to instil into the
reader that I make exclusive claims of inspiration for
my single self. I wish I could think that he has sincerely mistaken me."† He has what is *tantamount* to
his wish then. In the above case I was speaking, as
the context shows, of Mr. Parker's theory of inspiration,
and not his, which, in truth, I do not comprehend.

* Eclipse, p. 81. † Phases. Reply, pp. 178, 179,

Assuredly in none of the cited pages, nor "elsewhere," is he represented as doing what he states. I never thought he made *exclusive* claim to "Inspiration;" rather I thought that, whatever he deemed it, he made it only too cheap. He further says: "I have already noted how *falsely* he insinuates that I claim some exclusive inspiration, whereas I only claim that which all pious Christians and Jews since David have always claimed." * Does Mr. Newman mean that he claims as much as the Apostles claimed, whether they did so rightfully or not? If so, he claims enough, and a good deal more than I should be disposed to grant him. The latest utterance of Mr. Newman on this subject that I have read, occurs in his preface to the second edition of his " Hebrew Monarchy," where he tells us that he believes it is an influence accessible to all men, *in a certain stage of development!* Surely it will be time to consider his theory of Inspiration when he has told us a little more about it. To my mind, if the very Genius of Mystery had framed the definition, it could not have uttered anything more indefinite.

* Phases. Reply, p. 182.

SECTION XIII.

**MR. NEWMAN'S REPLY TO THE NOTES RESPECTING "SLAVERY"
AND THE "EARLY PROGRESS OF CHRISTIANITY."**

ANOTHER remarkable passage in the new edition of
" The Phases" deserves notice. Mr. Newman had
asserted that the New Testament sanctioned slavery,
and was, in fact, the "argumentative stronghold of
the accursed system." I endeavoured to show that it
does *not* sanction slavery ; that it simply does *not*
denounce it ; — that this caution, in the then condition
of the world, was *necessary*, if the Apostles were to
gain a hearing at all ; and *wise*, since they would do
more by quietly diffusing the principles which, if triumphant, must exterminate slavery, than by passionately denouncing it ; — that experience has shown that
only amongst Christian nations is there any extensive
or combined movement against slavery ; — that hatred
of it becomes more and more active-in proportion as
people become more and more Christian. I remarked
that this was the only way, without perpetual miracle,
by which any religious reformer could propagate his
system ; and that if any one were sufficiently in love
with the new systems of spiritualism to go as missionary to the East to preach them, he would not,
in addition, publicly denounce " the social and political
evils under which the nations groaned ; or that if he
did, his spiritual projects would soon be perfectly understood and summarily dealt with." I added, addressing Mr. Fellowes, " It is vain to say, that if commis-

sioned by Heaven, and endowed with power of working
miracles, you would do so; for you cannot tell under
what limitations your commission would be given: it
is pretty certain, that *it would leave you to work a
moral and spiritual system by moral and spiritual means,*
and not allow you to turn the world upside down, and
mendaciously tell it that you came only to preach
peace, while every syllable you uttered would be an
incentive to sedition."* On this Mr. Newman comments as follows: "This writer supposes he is attacking
me, when every line is an attack on Christ and Christianity.   Have *I* pretended power of working miracles?
Have I imagined or desired that miracle should shield
me from persecution?   Did Jesus *not* 'publicly denounce the social and political evils' of Judea?   Was he
not 'summarily dealt with?'   Did he not know that his
doctrine would send on earth 'not peace, but a sword?'
and was he *mendacious* in saying, 'Peace I leave unto
you?' or were the angels mendacious in proclaiming
'Peace on earth, good-will among men?'   Was not
'every syllable that Jesus uttered' in the discourse
of Matt. xxiii. 'an incentive to sedition?' and does
this writer judge it to be *mendacity*, that Jesus opened
by advising to *obey* the very men whom he proceeds
to vilify at large as immoral, oppressive, hypocritical,
blind, and destined to the damnation of hell?   Or, have
I anywhere blamed the Apostles because they did
not exasperate wicked men by direct attacks?   It is
impossible to answer such a writer as this; for he
elaborately misses to touch what I have said.   On the
other hand, it is rather too much to require me to
defend Jesus from his assault."†

My assault!   I trust that that Name is safe enough

* Eclipse, p. 419.   † Phases, 2nd ed., pp. 106, 107.

from my assault. I must beg Mr. Newman to recollect that *he* wrote the preceding paragraph, not *I.* I admit, however, that "it is rather too much to require *him* to defend Jesus" from *any* assault; since his chapter on the "Moral Perfection of Jesus" shows that he is much better skilled in assailing Him. No; I shall not repair to my critic for any such purpose; if I wanted to palliate the conduct of the Pharisees, indeed, that chapter instructs me where to go.

"It is impossible," he says, "to answer such a writer as this." I think it is impossible to *answer* any writer by asking a number of irrelevant questions. But it is very possible to answer *him ;* and so now for the questions of his catechism, taken *seriatim.*

1. " Have I pretended power of working miracles ? "

Answer. Not that I know of; did I ever say he had ?

2. " Have I imagined, or desired, that miracle should shield me from persecution ? "

Answer. I cannot tell what he has "imagined or desired ;" but I am sure I hope there is no need of a miracle to shield him from persecution.

3. " Did Jesus *not* publicly denounce the social and political evils of Judæa ? "

Answer. He did *not* denounce the political evils, as is plain from His conduct with regard to the tribute-money, in which this consistent censor blames His " evasion ;" and from His answer to the man who wished Him to interfere about the " division of his inheritance :" nor did He denounce any *other* social evils than such as followed directly from the perversions of the Mosaic law by its professed administrators, — the Scribes and Pharisees. The corruptions of that Theocracy which He came at once to vindicate and to abolish, He *did* denounce, and as a religious Reformer, most consistently and justly. All the evils He denounced were directly involved in its mal-administration,—which had "destroyed the law of God by man's traditions:" and this may be seen by any one who considers *what* those evils were, from the "pretence of long prayers" and "making broad the phylacteries," to the "devouring of widows' houses" and the perversion of the fifth commandment. The Pharisees *wished* him, indeed, to go further, but He was too wise to be entrapped; a thing which it is strange Mr. Newman should overlook, since he has censured Him for His asserted evasion.

4. "Was He not summarily dealt with?"

Answer. He was; and would have been yet *more* summarily dealt with, and with less trouble to the Pharisees, if he had done that which Mr. Newman insinuates that He did, but did not.

5. "Did He not know that His doctrine would send on earth, not peace, but a sword?"

Answer. Yes; He knew that His religious doctrine would, and He told the truth.

6. "And was he mendacious in saying, "Peace I leave unto you?"

Answer. No; though Mr. Newman would insinuate that He was. He came to "bring peace," though he *also* came to "bring a sword;" He came to bring peace, and He did *not* come to bring peace; which, though it be unintelligible to a man who is resolved that the same words shall always have the same meaning, is very intelligible to millions of Christians, who have perfectly well understood that Christianity may involve "the loss of all things," and yet fill the soul with a peace which overpays them all; and it is the less excusable in Mr. Newman not to see this, since our Lord explained the paradox, by telling the whole truth, of which Mr. Newman here sophistically gives half; "*Peace* I leave with you . . . In the world ye shall have *tribulation;* but be of good cheer, I have overcome the world."

7. "Were the angels mendacious in proclaiming ' Peace on earth, good-will among men?'"

Answer. No; for a similar reason.

8. "Was not every syllable that Jesus uttered in His discourse of Matt. xxiii., an incentive to sedition?"

Answer. No; it was a just denunciation of the most horrible moral and religious delinquencies on the part of the most odious traitors to God and man, pronounced by One (as we believe) divinely authorised to pronounce it, and which, though it might indirectly lead to sedition, He was bound to pronounce.

9. "And does this writer judge it to be mendacity that Jesus opened by advising to obey the very men whom he proceeds to vilify at large as immoral, oppressive, and hypocritical?"

Answer. No; though again Mr. Newman takes care to insinuate that Christ was mendacious; as if Christ enjoined his disciples to obey these men in the very points in which he told them not to obey them. He tells them they are to " obey " their spiritual rulers in the things they enjoin, " as sitting in Moses' seat," and proclaiming *his* precepts; but that they are *not* to do after their works, " since they say, and do not." Nor did He " vilify " the Pharisees, whom Mr. Newman seems disposed to pet, but justly characterised them.

10. " Or have I anywhere blamed the Apostles because they did not exasperate wicked men by direct attacks?"

Answer. What does he mean by "*direct*" attacks, and what does he mean by "*wicked*" men?

I only know that he found fault with the " New Testament " for *not* denouncing slavery as an immorality; to denounce it, I suppose, would have been a *direct* attack upon it. Mr. Newman certainly appeared to infer that this silence implied a justification and sanction of slavery;—which is denied. He now says, " I merely pointed out what it was that they (the Apostles) actually taught, and that, *as a fact*, they did *not* declare slavery to be an immorality, and the basest of thefts. If any one thinks their course was more wise, he may be right or wrong, but his opinion is in itself a concession of my fact."* Passing by the confusion of expression about "pointing out what the Apostles actually taught," which, in point of fact, turns out to be something they did *not* teach, few persons would have complained of the representation. No doubt the Apostles did *not* denounce slavery as the " basest of thefts," but the question is, whether that non-denunciation sanctions it, or fairly makes the New Testament the " argumentative stronghold of the accursed system;" for this Mr. Newman asserted it to be.

A religious Reformer must, of course, by that very fact that he is one, denounce the moral and spiritual vices opposed to what he conscientiously believes to be religious truth; and like the Apostles, or Luther in later times, will brave (as these did) all the opposition which may meet him on that score, and even all the indirect possibilities of civil commotion which may ensue from this necessary proclamation of the truth. But it is absurd to suppose, that *therefore* he is bound to denounce the social and political abuses of the community he addresses: this may not be *possible* if he is to gain a hearing for the principles he teaches, or even if he wisely calculates for the extinction of those evils themselves. For this reason, it does not follow that he will even denounce

* Phases, p. 107.

all those evils which his *followers* may very properly denounce, and the condemnation of which may be involved in the very principles he proclaims; as I firmly believe slavery is condemned by the principles of the " New Testament." He will not denounce these things, that his mouth may not be shut at once; that his doctrine may not be justifiably accused of seditious tendencies, and thus " summarily " put down. As this is the course which common sense points out for the religious Reformer, so it has been the course acted on, not by Apostles only, but by the wisest of all time, and in proportion to their wisdom. And as thus it must be, if success is to attend any such enterprises at all, so I put it on a practical issue. I ask, as I asked Mr. Fellowes, whether, if any one should have the compassion to go and preach that "spiritualism," which, if we may believe Mr. Newman, *might* convert Hindoos and Mahometans *, and, it seems, does *not* very readily convert Englishmen, — and really it seems hard not to enlighten mankind, where they are willing to be enlightened, and to persist in enlightening them where they are not, — I ask, I say, in that case, whether the said missionary would denounce political and social evils as well as all else he denounced? If he says, Yes; I say then, his system of religious reformation will be summarily dealt with, and his hopes of any success brought to a sudden termination; if he says, No; then he need not wonder that the " New Testament " is silent on these topics too.

I had said that Mr. Newman proclaims " his hatred of despotism and slavery, where such magnanimity is perfectly safe and perfectly superfluous." Mr. Newman takes this as an affront. I *did not* mean to question his

* Soul, pp. 244. 258.

courage (about which I knew nothing); since to act as
he seems to think the Apostles *ought* to have acted would
not be *courage* in my estimation, but mere fool-hardiness.
I simply meant to imply, by the sarcasm, that not even
he can carry out, or would carry out, the theory which
blames the Apostles for not adding to the proclamation
of what they believed religious truth, a crusade against
slavery, despotism, and other political and social evils.
Mr. Newman indignantly denounces the crimes of the
House of Hapsburg,—long may he be able and willing
to do so;—but it would be no " magnanimity " in him
to proclaim the same sentiments in the " market-place "
of Vienna, or from the "house-tops " of St. Petersburg,
but sheer idiocy. Now, when I find any religious Reformer proclaiming the new spiritualism, or any other
modification of Deism, and neglecting the same practical
regard to common sense as to what and where they
speak, then I shall be willing to allow that they are at
least consistent in the theory in virtue of which they
censure the Apostles; but I can hardly hope that they
will get any one to listen to them.

Mr. Newman, indeed, thinks it probable that the
Apostles might as harmlessly have denounced slavery
as the Quakers have done in America. " It is matter
•of conjecture, whether any greater convulsion would
have happened if the Apostles had done as the Quakers
in America. No Quaker holds slaves; why not?
Because the Quakers teach their members that it is an
essential immorality."* Yes, it is matter of conjecture;
and therefore the Apostles, I should imagine, living at
the time, and required to act in the case, were the only
proper judges. In the meantime, *we* are tolerable
judges of Mr. Newman's parallel. Quakers teach their

* Phases, p. 107.

— *members!* Yes; but not to insist that they live under
a constitutional government, (where the bulk of the
people are themselves Christians,) if they were to take
a tour through the southern states, to *proselytize*, and
proclaimed that slavery was immoral in every body, and
ought to be abolished, I suppose no very remote experience would sufficiently show the precariousness of all
" conjectures" as to the consequences.

Mr. Newman says, " The Romans practised fornication at pleasure, and held it ridiculous to blame them.
If Paul had claimed authority to hinder them, they
might have been greatly exasperated; but they had not
the least objection to his denouncing fornication as immoral to Christians. Why not slavery also?" *   There
are no doubt false analogies and true analogies. Whether
this is one or the other, we shall soon see. The question, I presume, is about denouncing slavery as a thing
criminal *in itself;* not as an immorality to *Christians*
only, but as wrong in anybody. Fornication they *did* so
denounce; it was an immorality, whether practised by
Christians or any one else. Now the fallacy of any
such analogy, when thus fairly stated, becomes clear
from this argument, which is the counterpart of Mr.
Newman's.

" The Romans practised idolatry at pleasure, and
thought it ridiculous to blame it. If Paul had claimed
authority to hinder them, they might have been greatly
' exasperated.' (I should think so.) But they had
not the least objection to his denouncing idolatry as
immoral to Christians, or to *any body;* for thus he denounced fornication." — Does it follow now that they
would have *no objection?* Let his own history, let the
thousands of martyrs who, before long, died because they

* Phases, p. 107.
M 3

would not burn incense on heathen altars, answer the question!

As to whether Christianity is or is not unfavourable to slavery, I am quite willing, as before, to remit the decision to the practical test. I defy any man to discover in any age, or in any nation, any considerable body of men who breathed a word of disapprobation of slavery *as such*, till Christianity came into the world; nor then, except amongst those nations that have been brought into contact with it. The apathy of all the nations of antiquity, and all nations not Christian at the present day — the utter unconsciousness of the best moralists of antiquity, of there being any harm in slavery, confirms the conclusion that the origination of right sentiments on this subject has been the work of Christianity. Nothing really avails against this gigantic evil, except the influences that have abolished both the slave trade and slavery amongst ourselves; that is, a deep persuasion that slavery is utterly opposed, if not to the letter, yet to the entire spirit of Christianity, and that it and the Gospel cannot coexist in perpetuity. It may last long, for human cupidity is not more easily subdued than slavery; but where Christianity enters, the fray is sure to begin, and will never terminate but with the extinction of slavery itself. Since " The Eclipse of Faith" was first published, there has appeared among us a book which has done more to awaken the hatred of the world against slavery than perhaps anything that was ever written before, or is likely to be soon written again. Now what was it after all that gave to its exposure of the evils of slavery such intense interest, and so deeply stirred the heart of America and of Europe as they read? What was it but the Christian sentiment which inspired it? What was it but the bond which was felt to connect poor

Uncle Tom and the little Eva with Him whose love
knows no distinction of colour; who welcomes both
alike to His feet, and in whom "all the families of the
earth are to be blessed;" who came to open "the
prison doors to them that are bound;" and even where
He does not do that literally, yet can enfranchise degraded humanity with a freedom so much more glorious,
that it must make the cheek of every conscientious
Christian tingle to think that any inferior freedom
should be withheld?   Let our philanthropic Deists
write a book which, freely resorting to their sources of
interest — to the abstract rights of man — shall produce half the same effect which this does by combining
with all such topics (which are equally those of *both*
parties) the nobler sentiments which Christian philan-
thropy alone can inspire.

And now as to the "early progress of Christianity."
Mr. Newman had represented the Christians, previous
to the age of Constantine, as a "small fraction;" and
yet declared that it was the Christian soldiers of Constantine who conquered the empire for Christianity." If
all the Christians in the empire were but a small fraction,
those in the army — considering that it was not a very
likely place for the primitive Christians to harbour in
—must have been a very small fraction of "a small
fraction;" and the question returns, how it came to
pass that a small fraction of a "small fraction" managed
to conquer the colossal strength of a hostile or indifferent empire *for* Christianity.

Mr. Newman, omitting this part of the subject — it
was as well omitted—affirms, as usual, that I have misrepresented him, and thus he endeavours to show it: —
" The Author of 'The Eclipse of Faith' has derided
me for despatching, in two paragraphs, what occupied

Gibbon's whole fifteenth chapter; but this Author, here
as always, misrepresents me.   Gibbon is exhibiting and
developing the deep-seated causes of the spread of
Christianity before Constantine; and he by no means
exhausts the subject.   I am comparing the ostensible
and notorious facts concerning the outward conquest of
Christianity with those of other religions."*

I consider that in this very paragraph, Mr. Newman
distinctly shows that I have *not* misrepresented him;
nor is it true that I have overlooked his novel hypothesis.   He says that "Gibbon is exhibiting and developing the deep-seated causes of the *spread* of Christianity
before Constantine"—which Mr. Newman says had *not*
spread!   On the contrary, he assumes that the Christians
were a " small fraction," and thus *does* dismiss in two
sentences, I might have said three words, what Gibbon
had strained every nerve in his celebrated chapter to
account for.   As to Gibbon's not " exhausting" the subject, I have here the happiness of entirely agreeing for
once with Mr. Newman ; though, if Mr. Newman's view
of the early condition of Christianity be correct, I should
have thought he would more likely have said that
Gibbon more than exhausts it.

In relation to Mr. Newman's hypothesis, the question
still returns,—supposing the Christians in the time of
Constantine a small fraction, and the soldiers a small
fraction of that,—how Constantine came to be fool
enough to endanger his cause by implicating it with
their own, and they heroes enough to conquer the empire for him and themselves ; especially since Julian
would undoubtedly have liked to reverse the trick, and
very signally failed?

Mr. Newman has added a little and altered a little in

* Phases, p. 101.

his statements on this subject in his present Edition,
but, as in so many other cases, manages to assume what
ought to be proved. He says, after repeating that the
Christians were but a small fraction of the empire, that
" Christianity was adopted as a state religion because of
the great *political* power accruing from the organisation
of the churches, and the devotion of Christians to their
ecclesiastical citizenship." If they had *not* been a small
fraction, we should still, of course, have demanded
something more than this free and easy way of disposing
of this matter; for the bare assertion of such a critic as
Mr. Newman will hardly pass without proof; as also,
how it was that *such* organisation as the primitive
Churches could be so obviously suited to *political* and
military purposes.   But, since they were a " small fraction" of the empire, it is still less obvious how a great
political power could suddenly " accrue from their
Church organisation."

In the same passage, Mr. Newman says, " the bra-
very and faithful attachment of *Christian regiments* " —
who would not have thought that it was one of Constantine's *aides-de-camp* that was speaking? — " was a
lesson not lost on Constantine ; " but how there came
to be " Christian *regiments,*" when all the Christians in
the empire were " a small fraction," and the camp about
the last place wherein to seek them, is, as before, the
main question.

SECTION XIV.

SOME MISCELLANEOUS TOPICS.

NOT to omit any thing, however incidental, which
Mr. Newman has said in reply to " The Eclipse," I
will make a remark or two on a note* in which he evidently refers to the work, though he does not name it.
Mr. Newman had admitted in his " Phases" the " very
complete establishment which Paley's ' Horæ Paulinæ'
gives to the narrative concerning Paul in the latter half"
of the " Acts," and which appeared to him " to reflect
critical honour on the whole New Testament." The
author of " The Eclipse of Faith " says (" Dilemmas of
an Infidel Neophyte "), that on renouncing Christianity
Mr. Newman does not attempt to *account* for this, " as
he surely ought." Mr. Newman cannot see that he
has to account for any thing! He says in his recent
edition, " A critic absurdly complains that I do not
account for this." I do not " absurdly " complain that
he does not account for it, because I am perfectly well
aware that it is impossible for him to do so. But I,
not absurdly, complain that, admitting the facts, he does
not *attempt* to account for them. He says, " Account
for what? I still hold the authenticity of nearly all the
Pauline Epistles, and that the *Pauline* Acts "—we see
how fine his criticism can cut, but no reasons given,—
" are compiled from some valuable source—from
chap. xii. onward; but it was gratuitous to infer that

* Phases, p. 14.

this could accredit the Four Gospels." Precipitate
again. It is "gratuitous" of him to suppose that I was
saying "that the coincidences could accredit the Four
Gospels," though I think they will indirectly go a great
way towards that; but it does not follow that, if they
do not accredit the Four Gospels, there is not still
something to be accounted for. *Supposing*, as this
admission does, the Pauline Epistles to have been
written under the circumstances related in the "Acts,"
it is natural that he who rejects Christianity should
seek to give some plausible account at least, of the
ready reception of Paul's extraordinary pretensions in
so many widely different communities; — an explanation
especially, not simply of his preternatural claims, but
of such a prompt submission to them; — to let us know
whether he was a fanatic or an impostor; — how if the
latter, he managed to hoodwink the people, and how if
the former, they managed to hoodwink themselves?
How it was that they contrived to surrender at so early
a period, and in so many distant places, their various
national and local prejudices in favour of these novel
and (if false) not very attractive extravagancies?
I rather think that most people will think there is
something to be accounted for, if a man admits what
Mr. Newman admits, and yet rejects the miraculous
órigin of the Gospel. In the meantime, and since Mr.
Newman thinks any inference in favour of Christianity
from such a source so precarious, I recommend him to
do what Johnson said had never been done nor was
likely to be done, — refute Lord Lyttleton's argument
for Christianity from the life and labours of Paul, or
the inferences which Paley so forcibly draws at the
close of the "Horæ Paulinæ," from the historical facts
there established, to the preternatural origin of Christianity.

In general it may be remarked of that singular book
the " Phases," that ordinarily such is the oblivion of all
that does not make for a present assertion or of almost all
that makes against it, that an amusing book might be
written by reversing the whole process of the " Phases,"
and supplying the evidence omitted from point to point.
For example ; Mr. Newman proposes to get rid of the
testimony of Peter to the Resurrection. He has already
successfully eliminated that of Paul, John, and others,
by processes equally summary.   Well, and how does
he get rid of Peter ? — Nothing more easy : — " Peter
does not attest the *bodily*, but only the *spiritual* resurrection of Jesus, for he says that Christ was ' put to
death in flesh, but made alive in spirit.' (1 Peter, iii. 18.)
Yet if this verse had been lost, his opening address (i. 3.)
would have seduced one into the belief that Peter taught
the bodily resurrection of Jesus."*

Let us suppose — if we *can* suppose — some disciple of
Mr. Newman acquiescing in this view, till he came to
look a little into the evidence here quietly ignored.   I
fancy he would say, " Manifestly, I had no right to assume that Peter i. 3., which asserts the fact of Christ's
resurrection with such literal plainness, was not to be so
interpreted, because there was another passage the meaning of which was disputed.   Was not this to interpret
the plain by the obscure?   And then again, it was
clear that I had overlooked *other* passages, which, like
i. 3., spoke as plainly of the resurrection — as for
example, iii. 21. — What right had I to say that these
plainer texts were to go for nothing, and be interpreted
by the more *obscure?*   And after all, even that
obscure verse,—what could be made of it but the bodily
resurrection? and though I once believed Mr. Newman, that the " received version" was " barely pos-

* Phases, p. 123.   Second edition.

sible," yet I now see, in fact, that there is a respectable
weight of evidence in favour of it. And whether there
be or not, what can be meant by Peter's testifying to
Christ's ' spiritual resurrection?' Clearly, it was the
greatest extravagance to suppose that Peter believed
the soul of Christ had *died*, and yet how else could
it have been ' raised?' Again; I saw that the whole
language of the New Testament so plainly implies
that the bodily resurrection of Christ was really believed in and affirmed — whether truly or falsely —
that it was mere interpreting for the *nonce* to suppose
Peter an exception, and to mean something totally
different. And then, how was it possible to dispose of
those passages in Peter's address on the Day of Pentecost, in which he affirms so expressly Christ's *bodily* resurrection? and again at the choice of the new Apostle,
when Peter expressly says that the choice must be from
among those who "had companied with Jesus," and could
" bear witness to his resurrection?" Yet Mr. Newman
does not even mention these facts; and if he says the
first part of the Acts is spurious, still he should have
shown it. Manifestly, to write in this way, is not to
" investigate evidence."

SECTION XV.

A FEW WORDS TO A PROSPECTIVE REVIEWER.

I MUST make a little pause here just to bestow a brief notice on a critic in the last number of the " Prospective Review," the organ, I believe, of what may be called the extreme Unitarian school; I suppose there can be little doubt about the authorship. The style would betray it, even if the article were not a professed defence of the " Moral Perfection of Christ " against the special criticisms of Mr. Newman. But as the critic has not revealed his name, it shall be un-mentioned here. In the prelude to that article, the writer is pleased to express himself " greatly delighted " at the " Reply " to " The Eclipse of Faith;" though one would have thought that his reason and his *taste* would have been a little startled by those curious displays of logic and rhetoric which adorn that singular performance. But I do not complain of this ; every man to his taste ; *de gustibus,* and so forth. But what I think I may complain of is, that this critic, though stultifying a previous decision of the journal in which he writes, declares that the Author of " The Eclipse " " has thrown his whole force of thought —all the power of exposition, argument, and sarcasm " (for which the critic is pleased to give him credit) " *in spite of himself,* into the irreligious scale !" In the next sentence he forgets even that qualification, and professes to be in doubt whether " The Eclipse " might not have come from the " *officina* of Atheism,"

whether " it was written in good faith," or whether it
" be not rather a covert attack on all religion !" Is
it possible, I am ready to ask, that the critic can have
read one *tenth* of the book, to have really any doubts
about the *intentions* of the author, whatever he may have
about his ability to second those intentions ? Did not
the very journal in which the critic writes declare,
only a year or so ago, that the work had its value,
specially as a protest against some of Mr. Newman's
one-sided views ; that it was calculated to give "pause
and check to many a flashy young man," and that this
was probably the " worthy and pious" purpose of the
author? Were not special commendations bestowed on
the protest against Mr. Newman's views of Christ,
which it is the very object of this critic to explode ? *

The *suspicions* of the critic offer a tempting theme
for the exercise of those same powers of sarcasm for
which he gives me credit, if I were disposed to use
them ; — which I will use, however, but sparingly, for
the reasons I shall presently assign. It seems almost
incredible that he can really *mean* what he *says*,
and unsay all that his own journal has said. I can
make allowance for a little sensitiveness at the dilemmas in Harrington's sceptical discussion, demanding, as they do, an answer from one who, on *such*
questions, practically espouses the Deist's cause ; I can
sympathise with the natural wish to pay a little com-
pliment to his friend Mr. Newman, whom he is just

---

* The obverse and reverse of this critical medal would furnish
curious contrasts : but it is hardly worth while to cite passages. The
articles will be found in the numbers for August, 1852, and Novem-
ber, 1853. The motto of the Review is, " *Respice*, Aspice, Prospice."
The editor seems for a moment to have forgotten the first word of the
three.

under the cruel necessity of opposing; I can indulge
even the little flourish of "self-deceiving partiality,"
which permits him to say, in one and the same breath,—
" How it is that these same powerful instruments"
(which have so demolished "The Eclipse of Faith"),
" when wielded in a different cause, and directed against
ourselves, appear to us to beat the air, we really cannot
tell." I can less understand how it is that just as he
is about to show, on one of the most testing questions
which can exercise the intellect and the heart of man
that *either* himself or Mr. Newman must be a very
baby in critical discernment — one, believing in the
absolute moral perfection of Christ, and the other, that
he was not only "encompassed with our infirmities,"
but "far below vast numbers of his unhonoured disciples,"—he should select just that moment to profess
" a profound deference for Mr. Newman's moral and
historical judgments!" Pity his friend, love him, wonder
at him, expostulate with him, all that is intelligible;
but only think, gentle reader, in such a case, of a "profound deference for historical and moral judgments!"
Who would not think now that it was Socrates, rather
than Protagoras, that was speaking here, and that the
critic was ironical in spite of himself? It is as if two
men were looking at the sun: "Glorious orb!" says
one, "how every meaner light fades away before thy
effulgence. Who can confound *thee* with any other of
the lamps of light?" "Do you call *that* the sun?"
cries the other; "it is but a star of the tenth or twelfth
magnitude. I see far brighter orbs than that." "My
d ar friend," exclaims the first, "I have the profoundest deference for your powers of vision, but
really ——" But I will not go on. I suppress the
sarcasms which the suspicions of my "Atheism" and
the compliments to Mr. Newman's "historical and

moral judgments" would justify, for the sake of that
effort which the critic has made, (though, as I think, on
most precarious grounds, and from a most imperfect
point of view,) to defend the moral excellence and perfection of Him who is worthy of all love and veneration.   The critic's conclusion, indeed, may surprise us,
but still he arrives at it.   He abandons seemingly
all that is preternatural in Christianity — he reduces
most of its history, all its miraculous history, to a
caput mortuum of myth and fable — he leaves us in
utter doubt how many or how few of its facts we are to
credit or reject — he believes that the " Messiah " himself was mistaken in his own Messiahship — he fancies
that he knows more of Christianity, while he denies
the integrity of the only records which inform us about
it, than the Apostles themselves; — in all this he fights
his battle under grave disadvantages, and, in fact, re-
poses his belief in the " moral perfection of Christ "
solely on an irresistible feeling.   Apart from that feeling
(for which I yet cannot but honour him), he seems to
vault upon air, or upon a rope so thin, that he seems to
a spectator to do so; and as he trips about in the
spangled dress of his somewhat too glittering rhetoric,
it is impossible to restrain the fear lest he and his thesis
should together tumble to the ground.   Still he has
defended the thesis; he avows that he sees, as he looks
on the face of Christ, the moral glory and grandeur
which beam from thence, and has endeavoured to shel-
ter Him from the rude attack which the author of the
" Phases" has ventured to make upon Him.   For that I
will so far honour him, as to give him free leave to vent
what suspicions he will of " my possible Atheism," or
my " equivocal good faith."   If He, whom he strives
on this occasion to defend, said that He would remember the most trivial act of kindness to the " least of

N

those" whom He deigns to call "His brethren;" surely
His disciples may well forgive even a greater wrong to
one who is endeavouring, though I sincerely believe
most inadequately, to defend His cause.   I trust that
this may convince the author of the critique, that "The
Eclipse of Faith" does not come from the "Atheist's
workshop," or from one who writes with "bad faith."
Or, if he still doubts it, and will attempt to justify his
suspicion, I pledge myself to examine whether his view
or mine most naturally leads to religious scepticism;
also, whether it may not be possible to give his logic a
little more exercise in showing how, with *his* premises,
he knows anything certain about Christ at all, or why
His perfection as well as His miracles may not be a
mere myth — than Mr. Newman has done by so feebly
assailing the moral delineation of Him.   I promise,
however, that I will not charge my critic as he charges
me, with "*hastening* with utmost glee to poison the
fountains of natural piety, and *relishing* the sorrows of
the believers, whose dreams he strives to dissipate!"
Such imputations should be left to those who have
reached a downright, coarse, unmitigated Deism, and
have snapped the last link which binds them in reverence to the moral loveliness he celebrates.   Nay,
I may even say they should be left to those who wield
a less graceful pen than his; for good taste condemns
them not less than good feeling.

SECTION XVI.

CONCLUSION.

At length, I have done with Mr. Newman; but I cannot resist the present opportunity of saying a few words to my young Christian contemporaries on what I deem the true position of the chief arguments on which they are generally invited to surrender their faith, as compared with those which support it; and on what, before surrendering it, they have a right to demand from those who seek to snatch that Faith from them.

At last, after much discussion in this and preceding ages, the world, I think and hope, is beginning to comprehend that it is not sufficient to discredit Christianity, or indeed any other system, to propound plausible or even *insoluble* objections; since it is a sort of weapon by which Atheism, Pantheism, and the half score systems of Deism may be alike easily foiled. And if there is any theory of religion, which is not in the same predicament as Christianity; nay, which is not exposed to yet *greater* objections, I shall be glad to be informed of it. I can only say, it is a perfect novelty to me. Certainly it is not any of the theories of Deism, the pleasant varieties of which have sprung out of the very eagerness with which the advocates of each have sought to evade the difficulties which press the abettors of every other.

Encompassed on all sides by impassable barriers, in whatever direction we speculate — and in none by loftier or more solid wall of rock than in metaphysical or moral philosophy,—we are *not* called upon to answer every objection which may be made to our tenets — for that is impossible, whatever the hypothesis that may be adopted : the only *real* question is, on which side the greatest weight of positive evidence is found, and the least weight of opposing objections.*

Christians believe that precisely one and the same principle applies both to the *works* and to the *word* of God.   In the former, every phenomenon proves His power — most of them His wisdom ; and the more, the more they are examined.   The vast *preponderance* of them also, both in the world of outward nature and in the internal world of consciousness, proclaim His goodness.   The Christian believes, therefore, that He has all these attributes ; — the last happily confirmed to him by what he deems an express and authoritative revelation, which perhaps could alone, amidst the conflicting facts of God's present administration, prove to man's tottering reason and feeble faith, that the Divine Goodness is Perfect and Infinite.   But, while on the above preponderance of evidence the Christian receives these cardinal truths, he also sees in the present condition and the entire administration of this lower world much that is utterly incomprehensible ; many things that God does, still more that He *permits* to be done, which he cannot harmonise with man's "little wisdom," and "little love ; " though he *believes* they *can* be harmonised.   He dares not make his judgment the measure of *all* that God can do in the rightful exercise of those infinite attributes of rectitude, wisdom, and benevolence, which on independent, and, as he believes, irrefragable grounds, he ascribes to Him.   The only answer that can in our present state — nay, perhaps in any state — be given to *some*

---

* See a striking admission of Hume (an unexceptionable witness *here*), and some admirable cautions of the sagacious Locke, in Appendix, No. VIII.

questions which the finite may ask of the Infinite, is
that with which God Himself, when He "spake out of
the whirlwind" to the patriarch, rebuked and silenced
at once every mutter of discontent with which human
pride and folly ventured to arraign Divine Wisdom and
Beneficence. It was an appeal, not to a *demonstration*
of Infinite Goodness, but to a Power and Wisdom which
were visibly unlimited and incomprehensible; "Where
wast thou when I laid the foundations of the earth?"

The conditions of argument are similar in relation to Christianity. The Christian believes, from an
immense variety, complexity, and convergence of proof,
that the Book which contains it, and the system it
reveals, never came from man. Particular objections to
portions of it, nevertheless — both as respects doctrine
and history — may, like the correspondent difficulties in
the outward universe, be attended with unanswerable
perplexities; but the Christian listens to them just as
he would to a judge, who, in his summing up, tells the
jury that there can be *no doubt* that the evidence —
nine parts out of ten — will justify them in bringing in
one, and only *one* verdict; though he says there may be
one, two, or three points on which the evidence is conflicting, and on which neither himself nor mortal man
can give or even suggest any plausible solution.

To any such objections — *the substantial points of
the evidence remaining* — the Christian feels himself entitled to say, " Stand by ; I cannot stop for you." In
relation to many of them, he may boldly say, when
called to solve them, " I cannot; Time may solve them,
as I see it *has* solved many ; and these, like those, may
then be transferred to the other side of the account ;
but even *now* they cannot materially affect the columns
which give the total." And, in my judgment, it is
in many cases not only wise to say this, but the only

honest course. Much mischief has often been done by
pretending to give a solution, which neither he who
gives nor he who demands it, feels to be sufficient.
There is *another* thing, however, that can be done by
the Christian; and that is to say, not only " the *mass*
of the evidence justifies my belief in *spite* of these objections, but see how easily I can transfer the war.
Come, answer a few of *my* objections;" and if the opponent says, " No, that is ' dishonest,'" he can reply,—" It
is perfectly honest, and absolutely necessary too; for
you do not wish me to believe *nothing*, I presume; you
wish me to believe you! Do for me what you say
I must do for you. Answer satisfactorily all the objections I put to you."

If that course be taken, I fearlessly say that the
argument of " objections," which has always been the
great weapon against Christianity, can be consistently
employed only by him who would drive you to absolute
scepticism : certainly not, as we have seen, by any form
of modern Deism. For how stands the argument on
that side ?

Not only has Deism its insoluble objections — and
plenty of them too,—but, in all its forms, the *main objections* must remain the same in every age; they are, in
truth, insusceptible, in the nature of things, of any alle-
viation. In rejecting all authoritative external revelation, Deism *ipso facto* proclaims itself incapable of giving
any explanation of man's chief perplexities—perplexities
which an external revelation alone can solve;—those
connected with the original condition of man, his present
position relatively to the Deity, and his future destinies.
On these Deism has a score of discordant theories; and
not a few in relation to the character of the Deity himself,
and even as to the grounds and limits of human duty !

It is in vain to say that the bulk of mankind are in-

capable of judging between the claims of Christianity
and opposing systems; because, if it be meant that only
a segment of its evidences can be made clear to the
common people, it is equally true of other subjects in
which man is *imperatively* required to take a part; as is
distinctly shown in "The Eclipse of Faith."* The
lawyer, the statesman, the physician, the political eco-
nomist, much more the common people, are compelled,
in a thousand cases, to *act* on an imperfect knowledge,
and in a great number of cases on very much less evidence than that which even the mass of the people may
comprehend in relation to the claims of Christianity.
So far as it is an objection, therefore, it does not apply
to Christianity merely, but to the entire constitution
of the world and of human nature; and applies, moreover, in full force to the theories which it is proposed
to substitute in its place. Do men dispute less about
them? Let the history of the ever-varying theories
of Deism, and those of Pantheism, Atheism, and Secu-
larism answer. And even if men be resolved, because there are these difficulties everywhere, to have *no*
religion at all, they do not escape similar dilemmas, or
rather they double them: not to mention, that it will
not avail one in a million; for if the facts of all history
prove any one thing, it is that man is so constituted
that he *will* have some religion, and the only question
is *what*.

The helpless condition of Deism, in its many forms,
we have already seen in the fourth section; its inco-
herent gabble or its dread silence on those problems in
which man feels he must have something other than
ever-varying guesses or mysterious shakes of the head;
and its endless discords even in the little sphere in

---

* Eclipse of Faith, pp. 324—327.

which it professedly dogmatises. It is simply *destructive; it constructs* nothing; its promises, indeed, are large, but it never fulfils them. It is always just *going* to prove; always in the *paulo-post* future tense. Meantime it contents itself with the more easy task of laughing at and deriding the attempts of Christianity to do what it leaves undone. It has only two faults, as some one said to the man who wished to borrow his donkey,—" He is very hard to be caught, and when you have caught him, why — he is good for nothing."

Before the young Christian yields to those who summon him to surrender his faith, I think he is justified in asking a proof (the more rigid that they renounce all *authority*) of some one of those many theories of God, man, and the universe, which they propose for his acceptance. In default of that — and I think it will be long before he will get it, — the Christian, previous to being reduced even to a preliminary scepticism, may fairly demand a *demonstration* of those principles by which so many modern Deists attempt summarily to set aside the claims of Christianity.

For example; it is confidently proclaimed by many of them that a miracle is *impossible*; this is proved, in the progress of modern science, so they say. Strauss *avowedly*, and very many modern opponents of Christianity, *tacitly* assume this principle; that is, they reduce every thing to the uniformities of present experience, and then decide, of course easily enough, that what *ex professo* presents phenomena at variance with that experience, is to be rejected. Having laid it down as an axiom that a miracle is *impossible*, Christianity, of course, must be false; and the only wonder is, that any body who believes this should enter into criticism at all to refute its historic claims, or to prove that what was impossible *per se* was not very *probable* in any other way.

It is in vain to reason in this way until the *impossibility* of miracles, which is so often assumed, has been distinctly proved; and then, no doubt, Strauss and his followers may dispense with every other argument altogether. But *then*, it is well to remind the Deist that when it *is* proved that we must take the uniformities of present experience as an invariable standard;—that we must assume that nature *never* varies, never has varied, never will vary beyond the limits of present experience;—that the antecedents and consequents we see now have always followed, and will always follow, one another;—I say it is well to remind him then that the inferences Harrington points out in the discussion on "Miracles"* fairly open on us; that the *origination* of the present system, or, in fact, any condition of things at variance with our present experience, becomes an absurdity. Every immediately *preceding* generation—the men of yesterday, the day before that, and so on, *ad infinitum* —have as much reason to argue in the same manner as we do; and there is left nothing for us but a blank Atheism or an equally blank Pantheism, "with an eternal recurrence of similar phenomena or an eternal succession of finite cycles of similar phenomena." If these, and such like consequences, follow not, I invite the Deist to a refutation of Harrington's conclusions on the supposition of the impossibility of miracles.

But the whole reasoning of those who thus appeal to present uniform experience, is really one of those fallacies against which Bacon cautioned the world so many years ago; and the philosophers who urge it belong to that class who, as Socrates says, "will not believe any thing but what they can see with their own eyes or press between their fingers." A severe examination of

* Eclipse Miracles, pp. 245—281.

whatever is at variance with the inductions of a wide
present experience, — a rigid sifting of the evidence,
is no doubt necessary; but to decide, absolutely and
à priori, that that *cannot* be true which is not conformable to it, so far from being worthy of the Baconian
philosophy, is worthy only of those New Zealand philosophers who, when their countryman, Duaterra, having visited England, told them that the Europeans had
quadrupeds so large that they could carry a man enormous distances in a day, and with incredible swiftness,
unanimously voted him a liar.   They had never seen
an animal larger than a pig — that was the " uniformity "
of their experience, — and hence their hasty inference;
some " put their fingers in their ears and begged he
would let them hear no more of his lies;" others,—experimental philosophers, no doubt,—gave a very satisfactory proof that the informant lied, by attempting to
ride the said pigs, and as they rolled off upon the sand,
asked " how it was possible to believe what was so
plainly contrary to all experience?"   There, reader, in
the New Zealand savage, rolling off his pig, you have a
lively image of him who argues that a miracle is impossible, because he avows that in the whole circle of his
very wide experience, and in the whole course of his
butterfly existence, he really never saw one !   Of course
the answer is, " My friend, I really never said you
had."   All ages and the wide universe become to these
philosophers just what his little island and his pigs were
to the ignorant savage.

Again; some folks tell us that an external authoritative revelation of moral and spiritual truth from God is
impossible to man.   I do not scruple to call it, after the
reasonings both in " The Eclipse of Faith" and the
present volume, one of the shallowest theories which
a shallow metaphysics ever attempted to impose on

mankind. But, at all events, the Christian, before he renounces his faith on any such *à priori* theory, is at least justified in demanding a rigid demonstration of it.

Similarly; he is often told that prophecy is incredible; and that if a prophecy *seem* to be minutely accordant with the facts it predicts, that is itself proof that it was composed *after* the event, and is *history* and not *prophecy!* Strauss applies this canon without a thought of *proving* it: and Mr. Newman often follows him.* Of course it is easy to prove anything at this rate, for the critic cannot miss his conclusion; if God has given a prophecy, it will be of course fulfilled; and then if it has been fulfilled, it is *ipso facto* proof that it could not have been prophecy! so that God will have confuted the prophecy by literally fulfilling it!

Now I say that the Christian is warranted in demanding, not a free and easy assumption of these "high à priori" methods of confuting the claims of Christianity, but a rigid proof of them. Let them be proved, and it will be unnecessary to say another word on the subject; and the only wonder is, that authors like Strauss should have thought it worth while to write a syllable, with such postulata, *except* to prove them. Instead of that they assume them, and then, of course, easily prove that miracles and prophecy are incredible, — for they are incredible; — God, it appears, having established Perso-Median laws of the universe, the first of which is, that it is *illegal* for Him ever after to have anything to do with them! The Christian is justified in demanding, for any such assumptions, not conjectures nor dogmatism, but the most severe proof.

There is a *third* thing which the Christian is justified in demanding of those who summon him to surrender

* Phases, p. 130, 131, 2nd ed.

his faith; but a word or two first. He will often be
told in these days of the " unmanageable and intractable" character of the Christian evidences. Now he
must not forget the still more " unmanageable and intractable character" of the hopelessly discordant theories
which he is so pleasantly invited to choose amongst instead of Christianity; nor that man, on a thousand subjects, may have sufficient evidence to determine him,
though it will vary much in different individuals, and be
comparatively superficial even in the most profound. It
is just so with the Christian evidences; they are varied
and complicated, and deep enough to engage and reward
the efforts of the most comprehensive and the subtlest
mind; and they often have done so. They are also simple
enough, as regards their great outlines, to satisfy every
man that investigates them with sincerity. The little
tract of Whately, on the Christian Evidences, contains
enough within its paper covers to baffle the efforts of
Infidelity; for it states the great facts on which Christianity has been, and is, received in the world. But the
point to which I wished to call attention is this, — that,
at all events, the Christian is justified in asking a sufficient—at least a plausible—account of the origin and
success of Christianity from those who impugn it. *How
little* they are likely to give *that,* considering the ludicrous contradictions and the self-refutative character of
the hypotheses which have been hitherto invented, may
be seen by any one who will read " The Dilemmas of
an Infidel Neophyte" in " The Eclipse of Faith."

The position of Christianity, in relation to the objections that may be urged against it, is very different from
that of all the forms of Deism. Not only has it always
its mass of *positive* evidence to appeal to, but that evidence is ever accumulating.

Nor will the young Christian hesitate, if wise, to draw

from the past a happy augury for the future, and sustain his faith by the omens derived from the failure of so many predictions of Infidelity. Whether the Scripture prophecies be true or not, certainly the predictions of our opponents have been false. We hear no more of many of the objections which towards the middle and close of the last century were so prematurely urged against the truth of the Bible. We hear little now of the inferences from the prodigious astronomical cycles of India or China, the immense antiquity of Egyptian dynasties, the *clear* confutations of the Bible which lurked in yet undeciphered hieroglyphics! Enough has been disproved to show the precarious nature of such hasty theories, while many of the assumed facts, being found to be utterly false, are already transferred to the other side of the ledger. Similarly the history of the New Testament — the Acts especially — has been found to be more accurate in proportion as the records of classic antiquity have been more diligently studied, or new fragments of them recovered. God seems to be even now enabling us to throw fresh lights on the history of the Old Testament, by unlocking the archives of Time, and revealing documents on stone and marble deposited, more securely than those in any museums, in the mounds of ancient Nineveh. Nor need we doubt that many of the lost fragments of more perishable human records may yet be dragged from secure lurking places where God has hidden them, to silence for ever many controversies, which have filled volumes with con-jecture and fable. The facts which appear to have been destroyed by Time, Time may effectually restore. The convulsions which covered Herculaneum and Pompeii, and seemed to entomb so many glories of ancient art, and destroy so many records of ancient history, did, in fact, but embalm them. They were buried only to be restored by a glorious resurrection.

It is most instructive to consider how many predictions of the enemies of Christianity between Julian and Strauss have ignominiously failed.   Take, for example, the boasted historic discrepancies and asserted "immoralities" to be found in the Bible.   Many of them have been reiterated by all infidel writers from the earliest times till now.   Many of them are just the same in the "Phases" of Mr. Newman, in the "Age of Reason" of Thomas Paine, in Bolingbroke, in Celsus.   As a *fact*, the objections *do* not prevail against the persuasion which the New Testament *somehow* inspires, that it is history, and true history, not fiction nor a lie.   "If the Bible," says Paine, "perish, from an exposure of the absurdities and errors which fill it, mind, it is not *my* fault."   Poor soul! — "'Tis sixty years since;" and in that time, the Bible has found its way into scores of new languages and dialects of man, Christianity has dotted over the earth with its missionary stations, schools, and churches, and presents a picture of unwonted activity of *propagandism* in nearly every community that professes it!

Since that time, the machinery of modern Missions and Bible Societies has been set in motion; since that time, the family of nations professing Christianity have attained an enormous expansion of power and population, and are plainly destined to exercise a preponderant dominion in the earth; while even among these, those are far, far foremost in the race of science, wealth, commercial activity, which most reverence the statute-book of Christianity, and are most eager to promote her triumph; almost these alone now colonise — their hives alone swarm.*   Since that time the teeming millions of India

---

* No doubt there are a multitude of causes which tend to produce differences among nations; but it is hardly possible for an *inductive* philosopher to ponder the facts above mentioned without *suspecting* that

have been subjected to British sway and to British
influence; and now the yet more populous China * is

Christianity has some vital connection with them. Either she tends,
by her direct and indirect influence, to create and evolve the elements
of national activity and greatness, or receives them by donation from
Heaven for some purposes subsidiary to her designs. The Christian
will have little difficulty in believing both; that, if loved and cherished,
she will create power and is dowered with it; nor, if her claims be well
founded, is it wonderful that those nations which, in any tolerable
measure, use their energies, and devote their hearts to her enterprise,
should be permitted to

"Share the triumph and partake the gale."

But it is the easiest thing in the world (though the experiment may
be a costly one) for Englishmen to bring the matter to a tolerable test.
All they have to do is to be persuaded by our modern infidels to abandon Christianity, and suffer its institutions to go to decay; to shut up
churches, chapels, and sunday-schools; demolish bible societies and
missionary societies; substitute for the Bible one or other or a dozen of
the panaceas which philosophic quackery is ever providing for the regeneration of the world, and especially that ludicrous thing called "Secu-
larism,"—which promises us the annihilation of the Deity, and the
apotheosis of man; or rather, the extinction of *one infinite* God, and the
creation of eight hundred millions of petty impotent "divinities," instead! England, at least, may then soon learn whether or not there
be any vital connection between Christianity and national prosperity;
and whether, in abjuring the Bible, her best bower anchor has not
parted. Lamentable as the result of such an experiment might be,
it might possibly be as instructive to the world as her past history.
But Heaven grant that she may never be fool enough to try it!

* It is too early for a sober man to speculate about the stupendous
revolution in China, its character, or its results. I am stating facts, and
wish to keep to them. But at all events we see thus much; that *almost*
without human effort, in comparison with the effects, this mysterious
Book—coming into most partial contact with the venerable and seemingly impregnable superstitions even of China, and subjected, as might
be expected, to all sorts of corruptions by the contact,—has had
no inconsiderable share in producing the most wonderful revolution the
world has yet seen,—in shaking and rocking that empire which was
apparently "barred and bolted" for ever against all external influence;
to whose apparently invincible and immutable prejudices, enshrined in
the mysterious hieroglyphics of an almost inaccessible language, Infidelity had so often pointed as laughing to scorn the efforts of Christianity! Mingled with much folly, wickedness, and superstition, the

opening its jealous gates to the incursions of advancing Christendom. Never did Infidelity choose a more luckless moment for uttering its prediction, that poor Christianity is about to die; never was there a moment when its disciples could more confidently repeat the invocation of the sublimest genius that ever consecrated itself to sacred song, when, celebrating the events of his time, he "snatched up an ungarnished present of thank offering" before he took his "harp, and sang his elaborate song to generations:" "Come forth from thy royal chambers, O prince of all the kings of the earth; put on the visible robes of thy imperial majesty; take up that unlimited sceptre which thy Almighty Father hath bequeathed thee; for now the voice of thy bride calls thee, and all creatures sigh to be renewed!"

Sixty years before Tom Paine, Bolingbroke and so many more had reiterated the very same historic and "moral" objections, and predicted that belief in the Old and New Testament *could* not resist the effects of the revival of literature and the progress of science. How readily such ratiocinations may be set aside even by a *sceptic*, may be easily shown in the following little dialogue, where the reader may perhaps recognise the traces of an old acquaintance.

"May I ask to look into your book?" said a young man of about thirty years of age, to a fellow-traveller who had just laid one down.

"Certainly," said the other, with a smile, handing to him an abridged edition of Strauss, which I understand has been rather widely circulated among the class of intelligent artisans, — "It is a little book which will

emancipation of 340 millions from the deepest idolatry and debasement must needs be; but the fact remains, that this ancient empire is shaken, and that the Bible (however imperfectly known) has been a most efficient instrument in the change.

soon demolish Christianity. It shows, clear as the day, that the Gospels, instead of being fact, are full of contradictions; and no more worthy of being regarded as history than Mother Hubbard's tale."

The young man looked indifferent,—perhaps felt so. The other went on.

" It is a cheap edition of that immortal writer Strauss, who, at the early age of twenty-eight, exploded for ever the historical character of Christianity, which had so long imposed on the world."

The young man continued silent, but seemed a little amused.

" What do you say to that?" said the other.

" Why, I was only thinking," replied the young man with an air of great simplicity, " if the Gospels are so full of contradictions, as you say, that it is strange these should not have been pointed out long ago; and that it was left for the promising young gentleman of twenty-eight to discover them to the world, eighteen hundred years after they were written! What fools mankind must have been!"

" You are mistaken, my friend," said the admirer of Strauss, who found the temptation to display a little of his learning irresistible,—" In the earliest ages, Celsus, Porphyry, and others"—the young man *looked* very ignorant of these learned names,—" pointed out many of these contradictions and discrepancies; many more were pointed out and insisted upon by the great deistical writers of England,—by Bolingbroke and Tindal, and Toland and Collins, and many more; and again in France and Germany, by Voltaire, and Wieland and Lessing. No, no: the contradictions were too palpable to be eighteen hundred years in being found out. It would be more correct to say, that many of them have been discovered and *exposed* for near eighteen hundred years."

o

The young man seemed overwhelmed with such a catalogue of great names.

"Why," continued the other, flattering himself, I think, that he had made an impression by all this learning on his ignorant hearer, — "So little truth, sir, is there in your observation, that a celebrated French author, Quinet, has said that there is, perhaps, hardly a single objection in Strauss but what had been repeatedly urged before; and if that is not literally true, it is certainly not far from the truth."

I was wondering whether the young man would see that our infidel friend was fast demolishing, in his eagerness to show his own erudition, the reputation of the "wonderful young man of eight and twenty," and reducing him to a retailer of other men's criticisms.

But he took another and a more effectual way of retort. He said, with great simplicity, " I do not doubt in the least, sir, that it is all just as you say; and *therefore* I conclude, from the argument with which you began — namely, that, as the Gospels must be given up on the discovery of such notorious contradictions, and, as you *now* say, that they have been discovered for many hundreds of years, — I say, I conclude that the Gospels *were* given up long ago, and have not been believed for many hundred years. I am sorry, however, upon my word, for the promising young man you mention. He had not, it seems, a fair chance of doing much; he has been saying, it appears, things which other people have said before him, and what you say he *will* do *must* have been already done!"

Our acquaintance looked a little perplexed, but he evidently began to think the chances of conversion diminished, and that the young man was not such a simpleton as he had at first taken him for.

" Why," said he, " the exposures of the contradictions in the Gospels *ought* to have led mankind to reject them long ago,—no doubt of *that;* it is certain, however, that they have not rejected them."

" Ah !" then said the young man, " I am afraid, if men have been such blockheads as to be imposed upon in spite of such *clear* proofs as you mentioned a little while ago, they will very likely be still imposed upon. I am afraid the world is too great a fool to be mended by the promising ' young man of eight and twenty.'"

" And I tell you," said the other, with some vehemence, " that Christianity, since Strauss's work, is not worth a hundred years' purchase."

" Pray how long is it since this wonderful work was first published ?"

" Only five and twenty years ago," said the other.

" About a quarter of the century is gone," said the young man, very quietly. " It is high time that Christianity should look about it. But I do not see that the book has made much impression at present. I am afraid people will still be as stupid as they were in the days of those other gentlemen you mentioned — Bolingbroke and the rest. I am almost afraid that you must say, like the prophet, ' Who hath believed our report ?'"

" Nevertheless, you will see it is as I say."

" Well, ' seeing is believing,' no doubt of that ; and we shall see what we *shall* see : but it is clear you cannot trust to any thing else than *seeing ;* for, as gentlemen of your opinion have been disappointed so often in past ages, and so many promises have come to nothing. owing to the wonderful stupidity of mankind, who *will* believe these Gospels in spite of ' the contradictions they contain,'—why, the same thing may occur again for aught I can see."

"I only know," said the other, "that the Faith which Christians tell us they are to exercise in the ultimate triumphs of Christianity, will be very necessary."

"Both parties will require it," said the young man with a half laugh. "If I may judge by the rate of your past success in disabusing mankind of their strange delusion, against which persecution and argument, criticism and wit, have been so often used in vain, I think you will require at least as much 'faith and patience' as the Christian talks about. But you seem to have got the first, if the last will but hold out. I almost think," he continued, "you will need an exhortation similar to that to the Christians, to be addressed to you, —'Therefore, beloved brethren, be ye steadfast, immoveable, always abounding in the work of'—Celsus, Bolingbroke, and Strauss;—only I fear it will end differently—'forasmuch as your labour will always be' in vain in the name of Celsus, Bolingbroke, and Strauss!"

I found it difficult to keep my countenance at this solemn counsel.

"Never mind," rejoined the other, "we shall have a good *ally* in the inconsistencies, and follies, and wickedness of Christians themselves. They are always preaching the excellence of their ethical code, but they do not practise it over much."

"There is something in *that*," said his opponent. "For my part, I have always considered the inconsistencies of Christians themselves enough to ruin them."

The other seemed pleased with this admission, and went on in a hearty tirade against the inconsistencies of Christians.

"I agree with you—I quite agree with you," said the young man, with a smile. "You can hardly say anything too strong of them in that respect."

The other, thus encouraged, proceeded to declare that the monstrous doctrines and abuses of the corrupt forms of Christianity were enough to ruin any cause.

The other still assented. " But," said he, "they have *not* dissipated this illusion."

" No," said the other; "but they *ought* to have done it."

" Ah!" then replied his opponent, " I fear that instead of giving legitimate hopes, the argument ought to have rather the contrary effect. You see how stupid mankind are! Not even what you so curiously call your *best* ally — that is, the *vices* and *corruptions* of distorted Christianity — can cure them. There is more work, my good sir, for faith and patience. You ought to pray Heaven that they may not exemplify the virtues they profess to love; or else, having been, in fact, invincible even with their follies and vices, your cause will be absolutely hopeless!"

" Joke on," said the other, who did not much relish this turn; " but it will all come in time you will see."

" I doubt whether I shall live long enough," interjected the sceptic.

" Why now," resumed his antagonist, " they talk of the Evidences, and such stuff. How can the common people judge of the Evidences? — how can they enter into the question of various readings, and Alexandrian and Vatican manuscripts, and Syrian, and Hebrew, and Greek criticism, and all that farrago of learned nonsense, which they are told establishes the truth of Christianity?"

" I dare say not," said the other carelessly; " I suppose they receive the results of the 'learned' investigations when they cannot follow them; but it is clear they do believe in spite of not being able to follow them."

"Aye," replied the other, "but when they come to understand that manuscripts are not to be trusted, or that the Greek won't bear this, and the Hebrew won't bear that; that there is one critic for *this* various reading, and another for *that*; that" —

"How!" returned the sceptic, laughing; "you do not surely think they will be better able to understand learned refutations of nonsense than learned *demonstrations* of nonsense! Or does it seem to you that if I cannot read Syriac or Greek, when I am told that it means so and so, I can read it and understand it when I am told that it does *not* mean so and so? No, no; the question of the *destruction* of Christianity will not be decided by this 'clishmaclaver' of what, if unintelligible on the one side, must be to the mass equally unintelligible on the other. As far as these learned matters go, the bulk of the common people will be led by other considerations; by arguments they *can* appreciate; and as regards what they do *not* understand, they will be decided just as they now are and *must* be — by the weight of authority derived from the presumed learning, known zeal, and *character* of those who tell them that things are so and so. Besides, if this sort of argument were sufficient, it ought to have exploded Christianity centuries ago; for, by your own confession, there has been no lack of such topics. There has been enough of citation and counter-citation, manuscript against manuscript, and learned nonsense against yet more learned nonsense; but you see it does not answer the purpose either with thousands of the learned, or millions of the ignorant. No, no; but I could tell you how," half sinking his voice to a whisper — "you *may* explode Christianity."

The other became all attention.

"Try the *positive* side," said he. "*Construct* some

system *better* than the New Testament, and *agree* about it. Exemplify it far more perfectly than the inconsistent Christians have done. Let it be expressed, too, and illustrated in such forms — so resplendent with genius, and so attractive with the graces of imagination and sensibility,— that it shall throw into the shade those gospels which, upon my word, are the things which principally do the *mischief.* Only be cautious," continued he, with a slight smile; " if you appeal, as perhaps you must, to the creations of imagination, *don't* do the thing *so* perfectly as to *deceive* the people into the belief that the embodiments of fiction are true history, as you believe to have been the case with the Evangelical narrations — or the last error will be worse than the first! "

It is surprising how little of the sceptic's arguments a Christian could, in such a case, object to; but, to be sure, it all depends on infidel premises — the prophecies of the speedy destruction of Christianity! But I must not give any more of any such dialogues, or else, having been suspected of " Paganism" by one, and half suspected of " Atheism " by a second, I shall perhaps be mistaken for a " sceptic " by a third.

This inveteracy of belief in what, if false, must be the most prodigious of all *fables* or *falsehoods*, does not cling to any other myth or lie. Niebuhr has not to do his work twice — if indeed he ever had to do it once, as regards the pure fiction of the history he exploded. Whether any one really believed, for centuries before he wrote, that Romulus was suckled by a wolf, and Numa met his divine Egeria in the sacred groves, may be questioned, but assuredly no one believes it now. Osiris and Isis, Jupiter and Juno, Venus and Bacchus, Thor and Odin, are killed but once; man looks contemptuously on, and no man tries to save them. Myths innumerable have been scattered by advancing knowledge and civilisation; they often yield even to external influences, *never* resist internal light. Yet *these* myths of the New Testament — it is strangely provoking! — are always being killed and always living again! Age after age, in the very bosom of Christianity, adversaries appear who again and again repeat the same story of the same "historic incredibilities," and make no progress. They are confronted by men fully their equals in all respects, who tell them that they are egregiously mistaken. Generation after generation of the opponents of Christianity, with their books, go to the bottom and are forgotten, and men still obstinately believe the New Testament true, its miracles facts, and its doctrines divine! You will say, "and have not their adversaries gone too?" Very likely; but that which the one attacked and the other defended remains; it still goes forth with its many voices in all languages of the earth, "conquering and to conquer." Nor can I forget that such is the interest attached to the Bible that its defenders are often still read when its assailants are utterly forgotten. Butler and Paley, Watson and Chalmers still live, though Tindall and Chubb, and Thomas Paine rest undisturbed in their dust. "And will 'The Eclipse' not be forgotten too?" I fancy I hear the reader archly ask: to be sure, I answer, and welcome; but if it last as long as the "Phases,"—and it cannot well be more ephemeral, —I shall be content.

I almost wish that the Deistical literature was not so hopelessly covered with oblivion as it is; it would show how long, how often, and how passionately have been urged the greater part of those "historic and moral difficulties" which are so often paraded in *our* day, as if they were absolute novelties.

Again; if the Christian is told, as he is very frequently

told now-a-days (and especially by Mr. Newman), that *our* "logic" is inconsistent with the "logic" of Apostles; and that unless we could renounce *our* "logic," it is in vain to attempt to resuscitate their "faith," he will do well to smile at such assumptions, and say that *our* "logic" is that of Butler, Newton, Bacon, Clarke, Robert Hall, Paley, Chalmers, and a host more who have not deemed the "logic" of "Apostolic times" incompatible with any "logic" of our own. As to this amusing presumption, he will be content to confront it with the immense homage which minds of the first order have, not in barbarism, but amidst the highest culture, and in spite of the most strenuous opposition, deliberately paid, after the profoundest study, to the truth of Christianity. — Again; should he — though I think he will hardly be troubled there, — be challenged to surrender his faith on the ground of the superior *practical* results of some other system, — he need not be afraid to appeal to that test. Grievous as are the inconsistencies of Christians, I may leave it to his own conscience to determine *that* question. In the tendency to produce individual happiness, social well-being, philanthropic activity, — in efforts to ameliorate the condition of man, to succour the distressed, to "visit the fatherless and the widow," to be "eyes to the blind and feet to the lame," to "take the wings of the morning and fly to the uttermost parts of the earth," in eager sympathy with the wretched outcasts of superstition whom no man but the Christian cares for,— that faith is yet to be found which will at all sustain comparison with Christianity.

Of all religions Christianity is that, and that alone, which never will let the world slumber. No form of it is so corrupt as not to have internal energy enough to send forth its emissaries to the ends of the earth; men

who will endure all privations and bear all perils to
persuade the nations to embrace it.   This, among many
peculiarities which discriminate Christianity from other
religions, is one of the most striking, and ought to
excite deep reflection.   No other religious system mani-
fests, or ever has manifested, this remarkable, this uniform tendency.   How would all Europe be astonished
at the appearance of Mahometan Mollahs, or Hindoo
Brahmins in London and Paris, sent to *persuade* us
to embrace *their* religions.   Not only have heathen
religions never done this ; but the *religion* which cradled
Christianity itself rather restrained than extended its
benefits.   Judaism received, but hardly welcomed proselytes.   Christianity, on the other hand, addresses all
" kindreds, people, nations, and tongues ; " and has, in
these our days especially, lifted up its voice in every
clime, and is speaking the dialect of nearly every tribe
of man.   Nothing is more certain than that man will
have *some* religion, and if none other makes conquests,
and, as is too plain, Deism neither will nor can, it is
tolerably certain that Christianity, whether true or
false, is likely to reign.

    And let us not forget what Christianity is now doing;
it has (as just said) the power to do what no other religion does, and what no form of Deism ever attempts to
do ;—it has the power to render those who believe in it
intensely anxious to make it triumphant; it sends its
agents to the uttermost parts of the earth, and supports
them there. And, by doing so, it has reclaimed barbarous
tribes to civilisation — abolished their idolatry — fixed
their language, and given them the elements of all art,
literature, and civilisation in giving them the BIBLE ;
for in the very process of giving *that* it gives them all
these also.   Only the other day, many of us saw from
the remotest isles of Polynesia, a Samoan newspaper,

printed entirely by a race who, only a few years ago, were a set of naked savages, addicted to cannibalism and infanticide, and without the elements of a written language. The paper was printed in a style which (as an English printer truly said) would do no discredit to an English printing office. Not only so; but the same Christianity has the power of immediately inspiring those who receive it, again to aid in its further diffusion, and to hand on the bright torch which has kindled the hallowed fire on their own hearths and altars. Only last year, I observed that nearly a tenth of the large revenues of one of our missionary societies was derived from the converts it had made — from New Zealanders, and Tahitians, and Hottentots, and Bechuanas; and other societies were aided from similar sources in a similar proportion! These simple facts are worth a thousand platform speeches. Let our Deistical " magicians" do the like by *their* enchantments. No, they can talk, and write (as Harrington says) " book-revelations against book-revelation," and dream their many-coloured, ever-impracticable dreams of human regeneration, and that is all. Till Deism does something more, Christianity has not much to fear from it.

And now, Reader, a hearty farewell. May it be long before we meet again; never, I trust, in connection with any personal controversy. May we meet at last, and Mr. Newman with us, on those peaceful shores on which these storms never beat; where the " tented field " as well of hostile polemics as of hostile armies is unknown; where the weapons of " spiritual " as well as physical " warfare " shall be beaten into implements of peace, — to gather in the eternal harvest of wisdom and joy and love.

And now let me make one little request. I have

been, as I think, rather injuriously assailed; and what is more, that which millions as well as myself deem most sacred, has also been most injuriously assailed. If in the heat of a necessarily hasty* composition, I have written anything which seems unworthy of the cause of Him whose claims I seek, however feebly, to advocate, then all I ask of you is, — BE JUST; lay the blame on *me*, and blame *me* as much as you will; but be *just* to *Him* who cannot be answerable for the offences of his disciples, since if they obeyed his precepts and imitated his example, they never could thus offend. And, at all events, believe this — for it is the simple truth — that if the thought of Him has not done all it ought, it has done something; I have suppressed many, as I think, most deserved sarcasms, which sprang into my mind in the ardour of composition, and have struck out many more which had flowed from my pen; and I have done both mainly from the recollection of HIM.

* The second edition of the "Phases" appeared in August last.

APPENDIX.

EXTRACTS FROM MR. NEWMAN'S CHAPTER ON THE
"MORAL PERFECTION OF CHRIST."

I.

" I HAVE been asserting, that he who believes Jesus to be a
mere man, ought at once to believe his moral excellence
finite and comparable to that of other men; and, that our
judgment to this effect cannot be reasonably overborne by
the 'universal consent' of Christendom. Thus far we are
dealing *à priori*, which here fully satisfies me: in such an
argument I need no *à posteriori* evidence to arrive at my
own conclusion. Nevertheless, I am met by taunts and
clamour, which are not meant to be indecent, but which to
my feeling are such. My critics point triumphantly to the
four gospels, and demand that I will make a personal attack
on a character which they revere, even when they know
that I cannot do so without giving great offence. *Now, if
any one were to call my old schoolmaster, or my old parish-
priest, a perfect and universal Model, and were to claim
that I would entitle him Lord, and think of him as the only
true revelation of God; should I not be at liberty to say,
without disrespect, that 'I most emphatically deprecate such
extravagant claims for him?'* Would this justify an out-
cry, that I will publicly avow what I judge to be his defects
of character, and will prove to all his admirers that he was
a sinner like other men?* Such a demand would be thought,
I believe, highly unbecoming and extremely unreasonable.
May not my modesty, or my regard for his memory, or my
unwillingness to pain his family, be accepted as sufficient

* The original *not* in italics.

reasons for silence? or would any one scoffingly attribute
my reluctance to attack him, to my conscious inability to
make good my case against his being 'God manifest in the
flesh?' Now what, if one of his admirers had written
panegyrical memorials of him; and his character, therein
described, was so faultless, that a stranger to him was not
able to descry any moral defect whatever in it? Is such a
stranger bound to believe him to be the Divine Standard of
morals, unless he can put his finger on certain passages of
the book which imply weaknesses and faults? And is it
insulting a man, to refuse to worship him? I utterly protest against every such pretence. As I have an infinitely
stronger conviction that Shakespeare was not in *intellect*
divinely and unapproachably perfect, than that I can certainly point out in him some definite intellectual defect; as,
moreover, I am vastly more sure that Socrates was *morally*
imperfect, than that I am able to censure him rightly; so
also, a disputant who concedes to me that Jesus is a mere
man, has no right to claim that I will point out some moral
flaw in him, or else acknowledge him to be a Unique Un-
paralleled Divine Soul. It is true, I do see defects, and very
serious ones, in the character of Jesus, as drawn by his disciples; but I cannot admit that my right to disown the pretensions made for him turns on my ability to define his
frailties. As long as (in common with my friend) I regard
Jesus as a man, so long I hold with *dogmatic* and *intense
conviction* the inference that he was morally imperfect, and
ought not to be held up as unapproachable in goodness; but
I have, in comparison, only *a modest* belief that I am able
to show his points of weakness." (Pp. 146-8.)

II.

" THE argument of Jesus concerning the tribute to Cæsar is
so dramatic, as to strike the imagination and rest on the
memory; and I know no reason for doubting that it has
been correctly reported. The book of Deuteronomy (xvii.
15.) distinctly forbids Israel to set over himself as king any
who is not a native Israelite; which appeared to be a reli-

gious condemnation of submission to Cæsar. Accordingly, since Jesus assumed the tone of unlimited wisdom, some of Herod's party asked him whether it was lawful to pay tribute to Cæsar. Jesus replied, 'Why tempt ye me, hypocrites? Show me the tribute money.' When one of the coins was handed to him, he asked, 'Whose image and superscription is this?' When they replied, 'Cæsar's,' he gave his authoritative decision, 'Render *therefore* to Cæsar the things that are Cæsar's.'

" In this reply not only the poor and uneducated, but many likewise of the rich and educated, recognise 'majesty and sanctity:' yet I find it hard to think that my strong-minded friend will defend the justness, wisdom, and honesty of it. To imagine that because a coin bears Cæsar's head, *therefore* it is Cæsar's property, and that he may demand to have as many of such coins as he chooses paid over to him, is puerile, and notoriously false. The circulation of foreign coin of every kind was as common in the Mediterranean then as now; and everybody knew that the coin was the property of the *holder*, not of him whose head it bore. Thus the reply of Jesus, which pretended to be a moral decision, was unsound and absurd ; yet it is uttered in a tone of dictatorial wisdom, and ushered in by a grave rebuke, 'Why tempt ye me, hypocrites ?' He is generally understood to mean, 'Why do you try to implicate me in a political charge?' and it is supposed that he prudently *evaded* the question. I have indeed heard this interpretation from high Trinitarians; which indicates to me how dead is their moral sense in everything which concerns the conduct of Jesus. No reason appears why he should not have replied, that Moses forbad Israel *voluntarily* to place himself under a foreign king, but did not inculcate fanatical and useless rebellion against overwhelming power. But such a reply, which would have satisfied a more commonplace mind, has in it nothing brilliant and striking. I cannot but think that Jesus shows a vain conceit in the cleverness of his answer : I do not think it so likely to have been a conscious evasion. But neither does his rebuke of the questioners at all commend itself to me. How can any man assume to be an authoritative teacher, and then claim that men shall not put his wisdom to the proof? Was it not their *duty* to do so? And when, in result, the trial has proved the defect of his wisdom, did they not perform a useful public service? In truth, I cannot see the Model Man in his rebuke.—Let not my friend say that the error was merely intellectual; blundering self-sufficiency is a moral weakness." (Pp. 151-3.)

III.

" I MIGHT go into detail concerning other discourses, where error and arrogance appear to me combined. But, not to be tedious, in general I must complain that Jesus purposely adopted an enigmatical and pretentious style of teaching, un-intelligible to his hearers, and needing explanation in private. That this was his systematic procedure, I believe, because, in spite of the great contrast of the fourth gospel to the others, it has this peculiarity in common with them. Christian divines are used to tell us that this mode was *peculiarly instructive* to the vulgar of Judæa; and they insist on the great wisdom displayed in his choice of the lucid parabolical style. But in Matt. xiii. 10—15., Jesus is made confidentially to avow precisely the opposite reason, viz. that he desires the vulgar *not* to understand him, but only the select few to whom he gives private explanations. I confess I believe the Evangelist rather than the modern Divine. I cannot conceive how so strange a notion could ever have possessed the companions of Jesus, if it had not been true. If really this parabolical method had been peculiarly intelligible, what could make them imagine the contrary? Unless they found it very obscure themselves, whence came the idea that it was obscure to the multitude? As a fact, it *is* very obscure, to this day. There is much that I most imperfectly understand, owing to unexplained metaphor; as, 'Agree with thine adversary quickly,' &c. &c. 'Whoso calls his brother *

---

* " I am acquainted with the interpretation, that the word Môrè is not here Geeek, *i.e., fool*, but is Hebrew, and means *rebel*, which is stronger than Raca, *silly fellow*. This gives partial, but only partial relief."

a fool, is in danger of hell fire.' 'Every one must be salted
with fire, and every sacrifice salted with salt. Have salt in
yourselves, and be at peace with one another.' Now every
man of original and singular genius has his own forms of
thought; in so far as they are natural, we must not complain, if to us they are obscure. But the moment *affectation*
comes in, thèy no longer are reconcilable with the perfect
character: they indicate vanity, and incipient sacerdotalism.
The distinct notice that Jesus avoided to expound his
parables to the multitude, and made this a boon to the privi-
leged few; and that without a parable he spake not to the
multitude; and the pious explanation, that this was a fulfil-
ment of Prophecy, 'I will open my mouth in parables, I will
utter dark sayings on the harp,' persuade me that the impression of the disciples was a deep reality. And it is in
entire keeping with the general narrative, which shows in
him so much of mystical assumption.

" Strip the parables of the imagery, and you find that sometimes one thought has been dished up four or five times, and
generally, that an idea is dressed into sacred grandeur. This
mystical method made a little wisdom go a great way with
the multitude ; and to such a mode of economising resources
the instinct of the uneducated man betakes itself, when he is
claiming to act a part for which he is imperfectly prepared."
(Pp. 153, 154.)

IV.

" It is common with orthodox Christians to take for granted
that unbelief of Jesus was a sin, and belief a merit, at a
time when no rational grounds of belief were as yet public.
Certainly, whoever asks questions with a view to *prove*
Jesus, is spoken of vituperatingly in the gospels; and it
does appear to me that the prevalent Christian belief is a
true echo of Jesus's own feeling. He disliked being put to
the proof. Instead of rejoicing in it, as a true and upright
man ought —instead of blaming those who accept his pretensions on too slight grounds — instead of encouraging full
inquiry and giving frank explanations, he resents doubt,

P

shuns everything that will test him, is very obscure as to his
own pretensions (so as to need probing and positive questions, whether he *does* or *does not* profess to be Messiah),
and yet is delighted at all easy belief.   When asked for
miracles, he sighs and groans at the unreasonableness of it;
yet does not honestly and plainly renounce pretension to
miracle, as Mr. Martineau would, but leaves room for
credit to himself for as many miracles as the credulous are
willing to impute to him.   It is possible that here the
narrative is unjust to his memory.   So far from being the
picture of perfection, it sometimes seems to me the picture
of a conscious and wilful impostor.   His general character
is too high for *this;* and I therefore make deductions from
the account.   Still, I do not see how the present narrative
could have grown up if he had been *really simple and
straightforward,* and not perverted by his essentially false
position.   *Enigma and mist seem to be his element; and
when I find his high satisfaction at all personal recognition
and bowing before his individuality, I almost doubt whether,
if one wished to draw the character of a vain and vacillating
pretender, it would be possible to draw anything more to the
purpose than this.** His general rule (before a certain date)
is, to be cautious in public, but bold in private, to the favoured few.   I cannot think that such a character, appearing
now, would seem to my friend a perfect Model of a Man."
(Pp. 154, 155.)

V.

" No precept bears on its face clearer marks of coming from
the genuine Jesus, than that of *selling all and following him.*
This was his original call to his disciples.   It was enun-
ciated authoritatively on various occasions.   It is incorpo-
rated with precepts of perpetual obligation, in such a way,
that we cannot without the greatest violence pretend that he
did not intend it as a precept to *all* his disciples.   In Luke,
xii. 22—40., he addresses the disciples collectively against

* Italics *not* in the original.

Avarice; and a part of the discourse is, 'Fear not, little flock; for it is your Father's good pleasure to give you the kingdom. *Sell that ye have, and give alms:* provide yourselves bags that wax not old; a treasure in the heavens that faileth not, &c. . . . . Let your loins be girded about, and your lights burning,' &c. To say that he was not intending to teach a universal morality, is to admit that his precepts are a trap; for they then mix up and confound mere contingent duties with universal sacred obligations, enunciating all in the same breath, and with the same solemnity. I cannot think that Jesus intended any separation. In fact, when a rich young man asked of him what he should do, that he might inherit eternal life, and pleaded that he had kept the ten commandments, but felt that to be insufficient, Jesus said unto him, '*If thou wilt be perfect,* go and sell that thou hast, and give to the poor, and thou shalt have treasure in heaven:' so that the duty was not contingent upon the peculiarity of a man possessing apostolic gifts, but was with Jesus the normal path for all who desired perfection. When the young man went away sorrowing, Jesus moralised on it, saying, 'How hardly shall a rich man enter into the kingdom of heaven:' which again shows that an abrupt renunciation of wealth was to be the general and ordinary method of entering the kingdom. Hereupon, when the disciples asked, 'Lo! we *have* forsaken all, and followed thee: what shall we have *therefore?*' Jesus, instead of rebuking their self-righteousness, promised them as a reward, that they should sit upon twelve thrones, judging the twelve tribes of Israel. A precept thus systematically enforced, is illustrated by the practice, not only of the twelve, but apparently of the seventy; and what is stronger still, by the practice of the five thousand disciples after the celebrated days of the first Pentecost. There was no longer a Jesus on earth to itinerate with, yet the disciples, in the fervour of first love, obeyed his precept: the rich sold their possessions, and laid the price at the apostles' feet.

" The mischiefs inherent in such a precept rapidly showed themselves, and good sense corrected the error. But this very fact proves most emphatically that the precept was pre-apostolic, and came from the genuine Jesus; otherwise it could never have found its way into the gospels. It is un-deniable, that the first disciples, by whose tradition alone we have any record of what Jesus taught, understood him to deliver this precept to *all* who desired to enter into the kingdom of heaven — all who desired to be perfect: why then are we to refuse belief, and remould the precepts of Jesus till they please our own morality? This is not the way to learn historical fact.

" That to inculcate religious beggary as the *only* form and mode of spiritual perfection, is fanatical and mischievous, even the Church of Rome will admit. Protestants uni-versally reject it as a deplorable absurdity ;—not merely wealthy bishops, squires, and merchants, but the poorest curates also. A man could not preach such doctrine in a Protestant pulpit without incurring deep reprobation and contempt; but when preached by Jesus, it is extolled as divine wisdom, — and disobeyed.

" Now I cannot look on this as a pure intellectual error, consistent with moral perfection. A deep mistake as to the nature of such perfection seems to me inherent in the precept itself; a mistake which indicates a moral unsoundness. The conduct of Jesus to the rich young man appears to me a melancholy exhibition of perverse doctrine, under an osten-tation of superior wisdom. The young man asked for bread, and Jesus gave him a stone. Justly he went away sorrow-ful at receiving a reply which his conscience rejected as false and foolish. But this is not all. Jesus was necessarily on trial, when any one, however sincere, came to ask ques-tions so deeply probing the quality of his wisdom as this : 'How may I be perfect?' and to be 'on trial was always disagreeable to him. He first gave the reply, 'Keep the commandments ;' and if the young man had been satisfied, and had gone away, it appears that Jesus would have been glad to be rid of him : for his tone is magisterial, decisive, and final. This, I confess, suggests to me, that the aim of Jesus was not so much to *enlighten* the young man, as to

stop his mouth, and keep up his own ostentation of om-
niscience. Had he desired to enlighten him, surely no mere
dry dogmatic command was needed, but an intelligent guidance of a willing and trusting soul. I do not pretend to
certain knowledge in these matters. Even when we hear
the tones of voice and watch the features, we often mistake.
We have no such means here of checking the narrative.
But the best general result which I can draw from the imperfect materials, is what I have said." (Pp. 155-7.)

VI.

" THE time arrived at last when Jesus felt that he must
publicly assert Messiahship ; and this was certain to bring
things to an issue. I suppose him to have hoped that he
was Messiah, until hope and the encouragement given him
by Peter and others grew into a persuasion strong enough
to act upon, but not always strong enough to still misgivings.
I say, I suppose this ; but I build nothing on my supposition.
I however see, that when he had resolved to claim Messiahship publicly, one of two results was inevitable, *if* that
claim was ill-founded : — viz., *either he must have become
an impostor, in order to screen his weakness ; or, he must
have retracted his pretensions amid much humiliation, and
have retired into privacy to learn sober wisdom.** From
these alternatives *there was escape only by death,* and upon
death Jesus purposely rushed.

" All Christendom has always believed that the death of
Jesus was *voluntarily* incurred ; and unless no man ever
became a wilful martyr, I cannot conceive why we are to
doubt the fact concerning Jesus. When he resolved to go
up to Jerusalem, he was warned by his disciples of the
danger ; but so far was he from being blind to it, that he
distinctly announced to them that he knew he should suffer
in Jerusalem the shameful death of a malefactor. On his
arrival in the suburbs, his first act was, ostentatiously to

---

* The original *not* in italics.

ride into the city on an ass's colt in the midst of the accla-
mations of the multitude, in order to exhibit himself as
having a just right to the throne of David.   Thus he gave
a handle to imputations of intended treason. — He next
entered the temple courts, where doves and lambs were sold
for sacrifice, and — (I must say it to my friend's amusement,
and in defiance of his kind but keen ridicule,) committed a
breach of the peace by flogging with a whip those who
trafficked in the area.   By such conduct he undoubtedly
made himself liable to legal punishment, and probably might
have been publicly scourged for it, had the rulers chosen to
moderate their vengeance.   But he 'meant to be prosecuted
for treason, not for felony,' to use the words of a modern
offender.   He therefore commenced the most exasperating
attacks on all the powerful, calling them hypocrites and
whited sepulchres and vipers' brood ; and denouncing upon
them the 'condemnation of hell.'   He was successful.   He
had both enraged the rulers up to the point of thirsting for
his life, and given colour to the charge of political rebellion.
He resolved to die; and he died.   Had his enemies contemptuously let him live, he would have been forced to act
the part of Jewish Messiah, or renounce Messiahship.

"If any one holds Jesus to be not amenable to the laws of
human morality, I am not now reasoning with such a one.
But if any one claims for him a human perfection, then I
say that his conduct on this occasion was neither laudable
nor justifiable; far otherwise.   There are cases in which
life may be thrown away for a great cause; as when a leader
in battle rushes upon certain death, in order to animate his
own men ; but the case before us has no similarity to that.
If our accounts are not wholly false, Jesus knowingly and
purposely exasperated the rulers into a great crime, — the
crime of taking his life from personal resentment. . . . If
Jesus had been aiming in a good cause to excite rebellion,
the mode of address which he assumed seems highly appropriate ; and in such a calamitous necessity, to risk exciting
murderous enmity would be the act of a hero : but as the
account stands, it seems to me the deed of a fanatic.   And

it is to me manifest that he overdid his attack, and failed to commend it to the conscience of his hearers. For up to this point the multitude was in his favour. He was notoriously so acceptable to the many, as to alarm the rulers; indeed the belief of his popularity had shielded him from prosecution. But after this fierce address he has no more popular support. At his public trial the vast majority judge him to deserve punishment, and prefer to ask free forgiveness for Barabbas, a bandit who was in prison for murder. We moderns, nursed in an arbitrary belief concerning these events, drink in with our first milk the assumption that Jesus alone was guiltless, and all the other actors in this sad affair inexcusably guilty. Let no one imagine that I defend for a moment the cruel punishment which raw resentment inflicted on him. But though the rulers felt the rage of Vengeance, the people who had suffered no personal wrong were moved only by ill-measured Indignation. The multitude love to hear the powerful exposed and reproached up to a certain limit; but if reproach go clearly beyond all that they feel to be deserved, a violent sentiment reacts on the head of the reviler: and though popular indignation (even when free from the element of selfishness) ill fixes the due *measure* of Punishment, I have a strong belief that it is righteous, when it pronounces the verdict Guilty.

"Does my friend deny that the death of Jesus was wilfully incurred? The 'orthodox' not merely admit, but maintain it. Their creed justifies it by the doctrine, that his death was a 'sacrifice' so pleasing to God, as to expiate the sins of the world. This honestly meets the objections to self-destruction; for how better could life be used, than by laying it down for such a prize? But besides all other difficulties in the very idea of atonement, the orthodox creed startles us by the incredible conception, that a voluntary sacrifice of life should be unacceptable to God, unless offered by ferocious and impious hands. If Jesus had 'authority from the Father to lay down his life,' was he unable to stab himself in the desert, or on the sacred altar of the Temple, without involving guilt to any human being? Did He, who is at once 'High Priest' and Victim, when 'offering up himself' and 'presenting his own blood unto God,' need any justification for using the sacrificial knife? The orthodox view *more clearly and unshrinkingly avows*, that Jesus deliberately goaded the wicked rulers into the deeper wickedness of murdering him; but on my friend's view, that Jesus was *no* sacrifice, but only a Model man, his death is an unrelieved calamity. Nothing but a long and complete life could possibly test the fact of his perfection; and the longer he lived, the better for the world." (Pp. 158-62.)

VII.

" I HAVE given more than enough indications of points in which the conduct of Jesus does not seem to me to have been that of a perfect man : how any one can think him a Universal Model, is to me still less intelligible. I might say much more on this subject. But I will merely add, that when my friend gives the weight of his noble testimony to the Perfection of Jesus, I think it is due to himself and to us that he should make clear what he means by this word 'Jesus.' He ought to publish — (I say it in deep seriousness, not sarcastically)—an expurgated gospel; for in truth I do not know how much of what I have now adduced from the gospel as *fact*, he will admit to be fact. I neglect, he tells me, 'a higher moral criticism,' which, if I rightly understand, would explode, as evidently unworthy of Jesus, many of the representations pervading the gospels : as, that Jesus claimed to be an oracular teacher, and attached spiritual life or death to belief or disbelief in this claim. My friend says, it is beyond all serious question *what* Jesus *was :* but his disbelief of the narrative seems to be so much wider than mine, as to leave me more uncertain than ever about it. If he will strike out of the gospels all that he disbelieves, and so enable me to understand *what* is the Jesus whom he reveres, I have so deep a sense of his moral and critical powers, that I am fully prepared to expect that he may remove many of my prejudices and relieve my objections :

but I cannot honestly say that I see the least probability of his altering my conviction, that in *consistency* of goodness Jesus fell far below vast numbers of his unhonoured disciples." (Pp. 164, 165.)

VIII.

(Referred to at Note, p. 180.)

IT is well said by Hume, that "no priestly dogmas ever shocked common sense so much as the infinite divisibility of matter with its consequences." He gives other examples of the similar insurmountable difficulties which beset us in every path of speculation.

The true mode of dealing with *objections*, merely, to any conclusion, is well expressed by the sagacious Locke, the careful study of whose great work would guard many a young intellect from the chief dangers of the present day. "The way to find truth, as far as we are able to reach it in this our dark and short-sighted state, is to pursue the hypothesis that seems to us to carry with it the most light and consistency, as far as we can, without raising objections, or striking at those that come in our way, till we have carried our present principle as far as it will go, and given what light and strength we can to all the parts of it. And when that is done, then to take into our consideration any objections that lie against it. . . . . . . Such is the weakness of our understandings, that, unless where we have clear demonstration, we can scarce make out to ourselves any truth which will not be liable to some exception beyond our power wholly to clear it from ; and therefore, if upon that ground we are presently bound to give up our former opinion, we shall be in perpetual fluctuation, every day changing our minds, and passing from one side to another ; we shall lose all stability of thought, and at last give up all probable truths as if there were no such thing, or, which is not much better, think it indifferent which side we take. . . . . The comparison of the evidence on both sides is the fairest way to search after truth, and the surest not to mistake on which side she is. There is scarce any controversy which is not a full instance of this, and if a man will embrace no opinion but what he can clear from all difficulties, and remove all objections, I fear he will have but very narrow thoughts, and find very little that he shall assent to. What, then, will you say, shall he embrace that for truth which has improbabilities in it that he cannot master? This has a clear answer. In contradicting opinions, one must be true, that he cannot doubt; which then shall he take? That which is accompanied with the greatest light and evidence, that which is freest from the grosser absurdities, though our narrow capacities cannot penetrate it on every side."—*Lord King's Life of Locke*, 4to. p. 315.

On several of the important subjects touched in the present little volume the reader will find much valuable matter in the Course of "Bampton Lectures" for the year 1852, by J. E. Riddle, M. A.

THE END.

LONDON:
SPOTTISWOODES and SHAW,
New-street-Square.